I'm Glad You're Dead

BOOK 1 OF THE PRETERNATURAL CHRONICLES

A Literary Eulogy for my Best Friend

H ello there, Reader, and welcome to my world.

If you are reading this, you probably came across the description somewhere and thought, "Meh, nothing else to read," and purchased my book. Little did you know the true story behind this . . . well . . . story.

It begins with two best friends who grew up together, shaping each other's personalities into the assholes they are today. Well, at least one of them, but I'll get to that momentarily. These two boys, let's call them Hunter and John, were all but inseparable. John excelled at music and being the funniest asshole for miles around, while Hunter dabbled, poorly I might add, in his humble writings. John respected Hunter's writings as much as I, I mean Hunter, respected John's musical prowess.

One fine day, after reading one of Hunter's horrifically detailed short stories about a serial killer, John asked him to write a story about him.

"Hell yeah, dude! What do you want to be?" Hunter asked, brimming with honor.

"A vampire," John responded with a gleam in his eye. "But not one of those sparkly ones. A true badass!"

"Done!" Hunter said with a smile and an accompanying high five.

"No, dude, promise. Promise you'll write and finish a book about me. You are the most prolific writer of our generation, and I would be proud to live on for eternity with your words as my life's blood," he said — or something like that. I might be paraphrasing a little bit, but you get the gist of it.

Hunter agreed, never to realize the weight of that promise until one Sunday morning when his mother called, crying. John had died, leaving Hunter without his best friend and doppelgänger.

Hunter still thinks about that moment to this day. How the morning light crept through the bedroom window while Hunter stared at the ceiling, noticing how the popcorn created jagged shadows, then how everything started to blur as his chest was crushed beneath the weight of what he was hearing, each word stacking heavily upon the other until not even sound could escape his throat. Only tears existed, and the horrific realization that Hunter had to make some of the hardest phone calls of his life to the circle of friends of which John had been the center of.

John had not only left Hunter, but Valenta as well. There were also Nathanial and Depweg, who were stricken with the loss of such a beloved character, and when all three found out that Hunter was keeping his promise to John and writing a book about him, they each wanted to be a part of that journey. Hunter asked them all what part they would like to play in this urban fantasy eulogy, and each immediately knew what they wanted to be.

So please, as you read the following pages, feel free to laugh. Laugh at the situations John is placed in and at his dickish dialogue with those around him, because John is 100% present in this story, without alteration (albeit he is a vampire). Laugh and let his memory live on inside the theater of your mind.

Thank you, sincerely, from the bottom of my beating heart, for giving John the chance to live again.

P.S.- Do people still say P.S.? Anyway, the Beard and Beanie logo throughout the series is actually based off a real picture of John Cook that he had sent to me when he had stolen my gray beanie. He wore it for the remainder of his life as his favorite, in his own words, "cranial accessory." That's saying something because he used to rock a baseball cap that said "Meatloaf" on it, which was a great conversation starter. So when he sent the text claiming he had procured my beanie, I didn't mind because it *was* just a beanie. Plus he looked like a gawt-dayum lumberjack in it, ready to chop down trees using only his epic beard.

It's funny, isn't it? How something as simple as a piece of cloth could have such an indescribable meaning to someone. And now you, too, get to share in that with me.

But enough of the cutting of onions! Let's get to the story readers have dubbed "Deadpool as a vampire!" Huzzah!

Dedications

Firstly, I'd have to dedicate this entire series to my unalive bromego who promised if he ever died, that he would haunt me by humming the theme to Mario for the rest of my life. Here's to you, John Cook. I made you a promise, and Lilith damn it, I kept it.

Second, to my beautiful wife, Amanda, who I'm glad has terrible vision. If not for those eyes of yours, you might have realized you are waaaaay too hot for me!

Then again, as the old saying goes: If you make them laugh, their eyes will be closed and unable to see how much better they could do.

Thirdly, to Valenta, Depweg, and Nathanial for wanting to be in the series and have the chance to still be a part of our dear friend's existence. As of this dedication writing, I am on book 3 and have included so many more of our friends in the series at their request. I would say it makes it easier to give depth to characters; but the truth is I had to tone most of you bastards WAY down. If I wrote you exactly like we all are in real life, no one would believe the story! I'm looking at you Valenta and Depweg, you crazy fools.

And finally, I am dedicating this book and series to anyone who has lost someone who was a substantial part of them. You are not alone. Rise up and live for them.

Contents

Epigraph

"I intend to live forever, or die trying."

-Groucho Marx

"My name will live on throughout History."

-Anonymous

Chapter 1

PRESENT DAY

I stood on the edge of a rusting warehouse in an industrial park in Houston, Texas. The targets were in the building across the alley, which was illuminated by a flickering floodlight.

Wind blew against my face, making my ancient black leather trench coat billow behind me—that might have been on purpose. The trench coat had been with me for several decades, and it showed its character with several patch-up jobs of whatever leather my tailor had had access to at the time. It reminded me of a quilt made by a granny who also happened to be in a biker gang.

Long, dark hair spilled over and down my neck, stopping at the top of my shoulders. Wind tugged at the exposed strands while a weathered gray beanie kept the majority secured.

The only missing component from my ominous, crime-fighting look was a bolt of lightning shooting through the night sky behind me.

From my vantage point, I could see inside the building through the second-story window. There was a group of shrouded figures painting a circle on the ground. They were using the limbs from some poor bastard as paintbrushes. And for the paint, you ask? Well, they weren't using Behr, that's for damn sure.

After the crimson circle was finished, they started making the lines to form a pentagram. I had planned my entrance, and the time to act was now.

As I stepped off the warehouse ledge, I whispered in my best Kevin Conroy voice, "I am the night," and dropped to the ground below. The wind was cut off by the buildings around me, causing the trench coat flaps to land over my face. I jerkily corrected the mishap then casually pivoted on one foot to look all around me. No one had seen. Good. *Still cool,* I thought to myself as I turned toward the steel doors I was about to burst through.

On the inside, the men had finished their pentagram and were setting up the candles, skulls, and other sundry items that were probably not from Hot Topic. They were all slightly startled after hearing a thunderous *BOOM* from the other end of the warehouse, followed closely by a thump and a muffled cry of, "Lilith damn it!" Glances were exchanged in tandem with shrugs that said, "Dude, I have no idea."

There was a pitter-patter of footsteps on the roof, and then an explosion of glass from above as a sexy figure (spoiler alert, it was me) landed with a shower of sparkling shards in the middle of the circle in a classic Batman move.

With both knuckles on the ground and one leg perched in front of me, I lifted my head and said, "Pardon me, but do you have any gre—" I was cut off when someone pulled a gun and shot me right in the face.

I fell back and lay still, also a classic Batman move. As if on cue, the one who had shot me approached slowly, kneeled down beside me, and felt for a heartbeat.

"He's dead," he said as he turned to the rest of the gang, relieved and still somewhat perplexed.

That's when the group got to try on a brand-new, fresh-off-the-shelf look of terror. The gunman looked at them, confused, until he felt breath on the back of his neck. Panic made him give shallow gasps, and before he could move, I reached around and grabbed the front of his throat, pulling him against me while he tried to fight against the unwavering grip to no avail.

While looking at his cult friends, my normally light-purple eyes turned dark crimson, and I pulled my lips back to reveal elongated canines with surgically sharp points.

"Technically, you aren't wrong," I whispered in the gunman's ear.

In a blur of motion, I sank my teeth into his carotid and yanked back, tearing it apart. Red life spurted in an arc several feet into the air and coated one of the goons. The few drops that had gotten into my mouth were making me euphoric.

With bulging, dismayed eyes, the soon-to-be-dead goon—let's call him Goon 1, or G1 for short—tried in vain to cover the hole with trembling hands. The blood that was still gushing out slowed, stopped, and then quivered in midair. With a quick focus of the mind, it congealed and morphed into the shape of flying snakes, complete with adorable little bloodwings. I sent them flying toward the remaining men as G1 slumped to the floor, eyes now glazed over. It was a bit theatrical, but had the desired effect on his comrades; they scattered in all directions.

I leaped through the air, coat billowing so hard it sounded like a bike with playing cards in the spokes going at light speed, and landed on the back of G2, who was closest to the exit. My feet went into his lower back and my hands grasped together under his chin as I pulled, ripping his head off with a yummy tearing sound. His spine came with, from neck to posterior.

G3 and G4, who had been just behind G2, skidded to a halt. I turned, smiled maniacally, and tossed the head at G3. I forced my own blood to snake out from my palms and form ropes several feet long. I whipped them back and forth like a lion tamer, the bloodwhips making piercing cracks. G3 caught then quickly dropped G2's head, turning to run. G4 stood frozen with his mouth agape. I whipped both bloodropes around their necks and concentrated on razor blades forming down the lengths. Both men gasped in shock and reached for the razor wire, shredding their own hands in the process. I commanded the goons' blood to flow from their grievous wounds, up my whips, and into my body. It had been a while since I had fed, and the infusion of their blood with my own ironically felt like the warm sun piercing a cold morning.

After they had been drained, I forcefully tugged at the ropes, cleanly cutting all the way through their necks, and leaving their heads precariously perched atop their shoulders. Half a second later, both men collapsed to the ground, heads rolling away from their bodies. The ropes slithered as they retracted back into my outstretched hands.

The next blood donor, G5, was a little braver and stood his ground while holding a ceremonial knife. His face displayed a controlled fear that I immediately respected. I ran straight at him at a slower speed so he could see me coming. Just before reaching arm's length, I preternaturally darted to his side. He thrust his knife straight at where he thought my neck would be. With a smooth karate chop to the pit of his elbow and a grab of his wrist, I guided his own knife into his forehead, killing him instantly. He deserved a warrior's swift death for his bravery.

After prying open dead fingers and grabbing the handle, I attempted to pull it out like a warm knife through butter; turns out, it was more like pulling a cold spoon through ice cream. "You lied, Rick Grimes!" I yelled and yanked the blade free with a tad more effort.

Turning to one of the few remaining bad guys, I threw the blade at center mass. Ridley Scott must have been in town because it pierced his back and burst through his chest. His arms didn't go up. His face didn't clench in agony. He didn't make awesome, "Ugh, oh no! I was only two days away from retirement!" noises. He just went rag doll and collapsed to the ground.

"*Et tu*, Arnold?" I mock cried (it wasn't mock). Was everything I saw on TV a lie?

Only two left, and they were both running in different directions. G6 was reaching for the gun the first Snuggie enthusiast still had, so I went for G7, who was already halfway up a ladder to the roof. A quick leap and a scary pose through the air later and I was at his back. His body went rigid as he yelped in surprise.

"Don't let go," I whispered in his ear just before I pierced his artery with my fangs. Blood flowed like a broken dam from his panicked state and exerting muscles. His frantic heart pumped fiercely.

The feeling of drinking blood is intoxicating. The strongest mortal drug is a sip of the weakest beer in comparison. I've been asked how I've been able to survive for centuries and not go insane from the repetition and boredom. The answer? I live for the next fix. It's like having your lover lightly drag their fingernails down your skin, but everywhere at once. Colors shine brighter. Smells are sweeter. I feel stronger after each mouthful, and that strength accumulates over the years, providing power to be used at my command. If the donor is a bad guy, well, that makes it all the better.

After a few gulps, I drained several pints of his life essence and his grip gave way. We fell toward the ground, with me still getting the last few drops. Just before we hit, I rolled off and landed on my feet as G7 smashed headfirst into the ground, doing his best impression of a turtle as his head retreated back into his neck.

"Neat," I said as I admired the aftermath.

There were several deafening cracks as an entire magazine was hastily emptied in my direction. Only one bullet hit its target—my gray beanie was ripped off my head and thrown to the floor in front of me.

My shoulder-length black hair spilled out around my head in sharp contrast to the neatly trimmed dark-red beard.

I looked at the beanie, reached down, and picked it up, probing the hole that had been created.

"That was my favorite beanie," I said coldly as I turned and strode over to where G6 stood pissing his pants.

"Wha-what are you?" he stammered.

"Someone who wants answers," I started. Slapping on my best *Kindergarten Cop* voice, I said, "Now I'm going to ask you some questions, and I want to have them answered immediately." I willed my words into his brain, asking his synapses to cooperate.

His tense posture loosened and he became relaxed; his eyes turned glassy. "Of course..." he whispered obediently.

A toothy smile spread across my face.

Chapter 2

IRELAND, 1480

They are almost upon us!" my mother exclaimed, losing the battle against her panic as we scrambled to collect our belongings.

"Fiona, what'd ye see?" my father asked as my mother's wide eyes stared out the window.

"The McPhersons' lands are ablaze!" she shrieked. "I see banners approaching our land! What do we do, Gerald?"

"Take John an' hide. These are me lands, and I will face them head on," he said. His eyes held an empty look about them.

"Ge-Gerald..." she stammered.

My father grabbed my mother's arms and whirled her around, bringing her to him. He kissed her like it was the last time.

"Hide *now* fer Christ's sake!" He pointed at the cellar door. "John, protect yer ma!"

Bewildered, we did as we were told, and just as he was about to shut the door, he said, "I love ye both. Ye're me flesh, and I will protect ye. Now hush now, nay matter what happens!"

The cellar door shut, and he slid the rug over the door.

From outside, an authoritative British voice called, "Gerald Cook, come out and face your charges."

Whispering, he said in our direction, "N'matter what, son!"

He then stood and faced the front of the house. From between the floorboards, I saw him say to the men standing outside, "This inquisition is as much fer take'n property from the conversos as fer defending the faith. 'Tis the *goods* that are the heretics," my father said accusingly.

"Come out now, or we will burn your farm to ashes," the man said, annoyed he had had to repeat himself.

My father stood in silence looking sternly out the window, seemingly deep in thought. "Burn it."

My father quickly followed with, "I'm comin' out!"

"Very well. Do so quickly," the voice instructed.

My father stepped to the door, grabbed the handle, and then turned and looked toward where my mother and I were hiding. I saw the despair in his eyes, but there was strength there too. He took a deep breath, pulled the door open, and stepped into the light of dawn. He closed his eyes and outstretched his arms, feeling the morning air and the welcoming warmth of the cresting sun.

"Stop right there," said the man. "Where is the rest of your flock?" Papers rustled before he continued, "Wife, Fiona, and son, John."

Without missing a beat, my father lied, "They are visit'n their aunt 'cross the river and through the mountain pass."

"And why are they there?" the man inquired dubiously, expecting to catch him in a lie.

"John, he be sick. My brother-in-law learned medicine. I could show ye the letters if ye would prefer," he said, pointing behind him at the house.

I whispered in my mother's ear, "Stay here," and pulled away from her grip. I slowly inched my way to the edge of the cellar where there was a small gap in the stones, careful not to rustle up any dust or move any pebbles.

The man seemed to ponder for a moment, studying my father. He then nodded, seemingly to himself, and without turning his gaze from my father, uttered the words that began the destruction of everything I knew.

"Burn it down."

"*No!*" my father screamed as he lunged for the advancing soldier. They wrestled for control over the flame, with my father having the upper hand due to his will to protect us.

A dagger flew from the commander's hand and slid into my father's thigh, embedding itself with a thump; metal crushing bone. Gerald Cook fell to the ground, as if his leg had been rendered completely useless, and reached for the blade with shaking hands. Through clenched teeth, he screamed as he tried to pull the weapon free. I knew my father was adept with a knife, and for a moment there was the briefest sliver of hope in my chest that the man I had always looked up to and aspired to be like could fight off these men intruding on our lands.

As the knife slowly withdrew a fraction of an inch at a time, there was a sound that reminded me of porridge being mixed in a bowl. Blood began to pour out like an open wine cask, staining his pants and dribbling to the dirt.

The commander stepped off his horse, smiling, and walked to where my father lay struggling. He put his foot on the hilt of the blade and started to push it slowly back into its new sheath. My father put more muscle into his efforts, the cords on his neck standing out.

After a few moments of toying with him, the commander's smile faded as he slammed his foot down, until even the hilt had started sinking in. It took my father a moment to gasp in more air than he had ever breathed in his entire life before he released it in a scream of pure agony.

"Oh..." the commander cooed, "Can't let you bleed out before your trial, can we?"

My father swayed and then passed out. With a motion of the commander, soldiers dragged my father to a cart, where they threw him in.

"*No!*" I screamed before I could cover my mouth.

With a snap of his eyes, the commander's gaze locked with mine through the stone gap.

"Just as I thought," he said with pleasure. "Find the door, look under every rug and table, and bring them to me." The man turned and returned to his horse, content that his task was complete. They had the farm.

My mother collapsed and started sobbing uncontrollably. The anger in my throat sunk down to my chest and created a black hole of dread in my guts. I had just given them my mom.

I heard the rug being yanked away. Dust and light flowed through the cracks and into my eyes. The door was almost pulled off its hinges as several men peered in and reached down. Greedy hands grasped my mother's limbs as I rushed to her, trying to fight them off. Several viselike grips dug painfully into my skin and muscles as I felt myself being hoisted through the cellar door. My eyes burned from the dirt in them. I heard my mother scream, and squinted to see her being struck in the head.

Everything went into pinpoint focus. My feet found purchase as they cleared the cellar, and I shoved with all my might, throwing my captors off balance. I felt their hands releasing me as they tried to catch themselves. I pivoted as I fell and used my momentum to bring my fists down like hammers on the closest soldier. His mouth had been open in surprise, and as I rained my anger and rage on his chin, it snapped, meeting his own throat and caving it inward. The panic was immediate, akin to a stuck pig. Helpless hands grasped at his crushed throat. A crimson cloud escaped the snakelike jaws as he tried to inhale precious air. The sound dampened and then cut off completely as his throat swelled shut. His eyes searched around desperately for help, but after a handful of heartbeats, they went unfocused, leaving only the steady gurgling of his last breath squeezing out. Red bubbles boiled out of his mouth and nose, then ceased.

I started to pick myself up to attack the next one when there was a flash of blinding light accompanied by a crack of thunder, and my head snapped forward. I was distantly aware of my teeth clattering as my chin hit my chest. The stars in my vision faded to black, and I felt myself falling into nothingness.

Chapter 3

PRESENT DAY

E uphoric with blood, I was practically dancing as I approached Father Thomes Philseep's church to report on the resounding success of my mission.

What's that, you say? Vampires can't enter churches...and...and crucifixes and what not?

Balderdash, I say to you. Another myth to make humans feel safe. Vampires aren't inherently evil, as movies and books would have you believe, or emotional crybabies, like those sparkly twats.

We choose what to do with our dark gift. Though the "dark" part doesn't make it sound like all halos and harps, admittedly. I didn't name it, but it's better than "the fuchsia gift."

Humans make their choice to be good or not so good. It is the same with most supernatural beings. Otherwise, the news would bukkake the public with stories and videos of mountains made from mangled human bodies. So, much like a man who has murdered his neighbor can enter a church, so can I.

The decaying cathedral was seemingly ancient and in a #WhitePeopleLockingCarDoors part of town. A century's worth of grime coated the stained-glass windows. The once gray stone was now a deliciously creepy shade of dirty black. Even the noble statues that had once guarded the grounds seemed to have transformed into eerie, shapeless figures. One even had a face that looked like a black skull peering down at you.

Around the property, the iron fence was rusting, the gravestones were indiscernible, and the trees and grass were all dead. I absolutely loved it. It was like it had been made just for little ol' me.

I ascended the crumbling stone steps to the door with a bounce in my step, where I knocked my secret after-hours knock: the theme to *Terminator*.

After a few moments, I heard rustling behind the weathered wooden door. I could tell by the creaking that someone had stopped at the threshold—which was another myth for human's peace of mind, by the way. I could cross them just fine, even without an invitation. If I wasn't mistaken, it was only the Fae, ghosts, and demons that had to abide by the rules of Sacred Hospitality.

"What's the secret phrase?" a confident, calm voice asked through the thick wooden door.

I responded in my best Arnold impression, "I nheed yourh cloothes, yourh boohts, and yourh motorcycle."

There was a grinding metallic groan as locks were freed and the ancient door creaked open.

Father Thomes appeared in the doorway wearing, and I kid you not, a blue and white striped pj's set complete with a matching cap and slippers.

"*What* are you wearing?" I asked, giving him a once over.

"Traditional old-man nightwear," he responded with a smile. "Come inside, my son."

"Thanks, Dad," I said. Did I mention I was witty? "You know I was kidding about the passphrase after hours, right? I mean, who else would come knocking on this decadently eerie place at night? Ha! I rhymed."

"I know you were *undying* to try out your impression," he returned with a smirk while putting a fist to his mouth, trying to stifle the laughter from his dad joke.

"Touché, Father T," I said with mock annoyance. Secretly, I notated the "undying" pun for later use.

Once again summoning my inner Arnold, I informed the father, "the tarhgets have been turhmenated."

"Blessed be the Father!" he exclaimed. "That is the third attempted summoning this month alone. They are increasing in regularity, it would seem. I fear the balance is shifting out of our favor. I just got word that a lesser demon has broken through."

We walked into the room with all the pews, and Father Thomes eased himself down. I sat across the middle aisle from him.

"Yeah, I heard from one of the goons that they are really trying to make this shit happen; recruiting and whatnot. What's odd is that no one knows the name of the person they are working for, only the steps needed for an actual summoning. Not a single Ouija board between them. I don't know who their boss is, but he knows what he's doing."

"Though what you say is interesting, we still need to send the demon back," Father Thomes said, still focusing on the immediate problem at hand.

"Tomorrow night, Papa T," I responded. "It's too near dawn, and I'm already clocked out for the night. Plus, my manager said no OT or he'd write me up. Besides, the demon will have to lay low during the day. So, I'm going to have a drink and then hit the coffin. Care to join me for half of my nightly agenda?"

Accepting my point, he said while stifling another dad joke chuckle, "No, thank you, John. I'm not fond of coffins."

"Dang! Is that what I'm like? No wonder I can't get a date!" I joked while rubbing my temples and shaking my head in faux exasperation.

"Thank you for the drink offer, John, but I am ready to return to my chambers," he said, standing and walking back toward his room.

"Father, I'm not going to be able to stop them all. Sooner or later, they'll wise up. Might even set a trap for yours truly," I told him grimly.

Father Thomes stopped and turned to face me. "Perhaps it is time to seek help, my son."

I replied with my best Christian Bale voice, "I work alone. You know that."

"This is important, John. Is there no one who will answer your call?" he asked.

I continued, "Harvey Dent, can we trust him?"

Turning back around, he continued to his room and said casually, "Be back here tomorrow night. Lock the door behind you, and if you take the hearse, return it filled up, won't you? That's a good lad." His voice trailed off toward the end as he rounded a corner down the hall.

I stared after him for a while, taking a deep breath and feeling a prod of worry entering my mind. Something was off, and I could feel it. Maybe he was right. Maybe I needed some help. Even with my sharp wit, platinum tongue, and sexy body, I hadn't made as many friends as you would think over the years. I didn't really have a Facebook or LinkedIn account.

I took in a deep breath and shifted my gaze up to the man on the cross. Thinking about my next steps, I exhaled and said, "Jesus, I need a drink."

Chapter 4

IRELAND, 1480

T he sound of wood being thrown together stirred me, and I blinked awake after some effort. I was terrified to only have muddy darkness enter my vision. I could make out a stone structure with what I thought to be chains hanging from the walls, and a small window on one of the walls let in the dimmest of pale light. It took me a moment to realize that it must have been night now, which meant I had been unconscious for the entire day.

Assessing the room, I was struck by a surge of stabbing fire as I turned my head. With every vein in my head pulsing in a painful rhythm, I let my chin drop back to my bruised chest. My numb arms must have been shackled above my head because they hadn't responded to the instinct of covering my throbbing skull at the point of impact. I could feel them pressing on either side of my head, useless.

Outside, the wind had started to howl. Rising and falling, like the wailing of an apparition.

I attempted to stand, only to find my legs had been confined to the wall. I was in a sitting position, with my backside resting on my calves. Out of nowhere, I recalled a story my father had told me, and I was relieved that they hadn't hung me from my ankles with metal shackles. He had told me of men whose feet had eventually been pulled off from being hung upside down, like a chicken leg at dinner.

The brief thought of my father filled me with anger. I gathered my strength and tried to pull the restraints off, in vain. I felt like a fish on a hook being pulled from the safety of the water. My breaths were ragged as snot and spittle shot from my nose and gritted teeth.

They had taken him, and my mother. Tears brimmed in my eyes from the frustration and helplessness.

From the darkness came an eerie chuckle.

"So, you are John," the calm voice of a cultured British man said with mild amusement. "If you stay here, they might string you up by your feet yet."

I froze in pure terror. "Wh-who's there?" I pathetically stammered.

He spoke with dramatic pauses and emphasis, "Worry not, John..."

"Where's me Da? Whe...where's me Ma?" The brimming tears fell from my eyes. I could taste the salt as they ran past the corners of my mouth.

"Ah-ah-*aah*, John. Let us not be rude. There will be time for your questions, but first, I would enjoy a game. Will you play it?"

"Game? What game, ye bodach? Why the shite am I here!" Rage started to build from deep within my core. "Me fam did nuthin' wrong!"

Still calm, and with his words slithering smoothly into my ears like a snake, he retorted with, "A game where, if you win, you will live and harness the power of the gods; the power to send all those who have wronged you into oblivion. But if you lose, your agony will be eternal, as will be the knowledge that you could have been free. As for your family's wrongdoings, you are sheep who are guilty of possessing what a wolf desires."

His words froze me. My heart beat furiously, and I forgot how to breathe as his words sunk in. Only the howls of the wind drifted in the air.

"They only wanted our land?" I asked in disbelief.

"Precisely. Now, what is your answer, John?" he almost purred with anticipation.

"Ye will free me and help me stop the men from hurtin' me family?" I said to myself. "Then I will walk tru' the fires of Hell if that's what I must do!"

In the darkness, a throaty chuckle started, which rapidly cascaded into full-bodied laughter. I even heard foot stomps on the ground, as if a child had just been given back their long-lost favorite toy.

"How delightful!" he exclaimed, with his voice pitching higher as the words came out.

There was the sound of two firm stomps and clothes rustling as the man stood in the darkness. A pause, and then a step. Another pause and a closer step. He was coming from directly in front of me. More steps. At some point, I should have been able to see something moving in the darkness, but my eyes only revealed unmoving shapes in the infinite blackness. The steps stopped no more than a foot in front of where I was chained. I squinted my eyes, struggling to see.

The smell of molding clothes and dirt wafted into my nostrils as a whisper came from behind me. Startled, I tried to turn my head when cold, stonelike hands grasped either side of my face and forced my gaze into two beautifully colored orbs that had opened in the blackness in front of me. They were indescribable, as if painted using the colors of a sunset. Purples, blues, and reds circled the irises in a captivating and elegant dance. I was mesmerized, and nothing else in the universe mattered except those eyes.

More sternly, without the pauses or emphasis, he asked, "Are you a man of honor?"

I didn't remember telling my mouth to speak or my mind to formulate an answer, but the word, "Aye," dreamily slipped out.

He continued, "If I were to aid in the revenge of you and yours, would you feel indebted to me?"

"Aye," I drawled. The inside of my head felt like being in a warm bed on a winter's morning.

"Wonderful!" he said as his grip fell from my face. My head cleared as his eyes melted into a single shade of purple.

His speech slid back into the theatrics. "My name is Ulric, and I need someone of this age to be my companion and guide. You see, I have been asleep for some time and would appreciate a current view on the modern world. Our time together will be filled with travel, riches, power, and revenge." At this last word, he smiled a wide grin, exposing his teeth. There were two that were particularly noticeable, as they were longer and ended in sharp points, akin to those of wolves.

"Rodents, actually," he stated as if I had spoken my thoughts aloud. "Wolves' jaws are made for holding their prey in place and tearing flesh. Rodents, bats specifically, have piercing fangs that puncture their prey without tearing so that blood flows most efficiently."

Confused, I asked, "A'ye claiming t'be a rat?"

He threw his head back and gave a throaty and dramatic laugh. After he recovered, he said, "No, no, my dear boy. You would say that a fox and a cat are different creatures, would you not?"

"Aye, a'course."

"Yet they both share the same feeding style. The jaws grab the throat of their prey and squeeze until the air stops. And *voila*! The animal can no longer draw breath and expires. I share similarities with that of the bat."

"Ye survive on blood?! Are ye a demon?!" I felt panic starting to rise in my core, tightening my chest.

He smiled. "Perhaps," he pondered. There was a pause as he considered. The wind had died down outside, leaving only the sound of a roaring fire somewhere close by. "Perhaps not. I do not really know, to be honest. What I do know is this: after centuries of walking this world, I am the last. Until now, that is."

With a waving gesture from his hand, the torches in the dungeon blazed to life, bathing everything in an orange haze. The light scorched my unprepared eyes, making my head ache and my stomach lurch, and I had to squeeze them shut with discernible effort. After a few moments, I was able to blink them open and focus on the dirt-encrusted man in front of me. His clothing was rotting away, as if he were a street urchin. The red coat he wore was now a dirty dark brown with rusted buttons that once could have been brass or some other distinguished metal. There were frills coming out of the sleeves, which were matted and in tatters, and his pantaloons were riddled with holes. The silk shirt underneath his coat was mostly intact, and the leather shoes he wore were also in good condition, albeit coated in dirt.

The man looked like he had been caught in a mudslide and survived. He had short dark hair—covered with earth—that slightly receded on either side of a widow's peak; a clean jaw stood proportional to the rest of his face; crow's feet had only just begun at the corners of his eyes, and frown lines jutted between his eyebrows. Pearly teeth were overexposed from the widest grin I had ever seen. It unnerved me. Sailors described man-eating fish that shared the same smile. I had thought them the tales of drunkards, but here they were, gleaming in the dark.

He pointed his fisted hand toward me, then long fingers opened dramatically and my chains crumbled to dust around my wrists. My numb arms dropped in front of me and pulled the rest of my body down with them. The stone floor covered in dirt and blood rushed up to meet my face. Familiar stars danced just behind my eyelids, and my stomach threatened to expel the bile it contained.

"It would appear that the strike to the back of your skull was more severe than I first thought. No matter. All will be well in a moment. But first, I want you to enjoy your death." He let the last syllable linger, tasting the weight of the word.

Getting my elbows underneath me and looking up at the strange man, my throat tried to escape to the pit of my stomach. The pain throughout my body was dulled by my brain pulling all resources to focus on what he had just said.

Swallowing what felt like razor blades down my barren throat, I croaked, "Me...me death?"

My breathing became shallow, and fear blossomed with every pounding heartbeat, trying to convince my numb limbs to flee as he walked over. The man effortlessly picked me up by my shoulders and pulled my face close to his.

"Yes, child. For you to accept my gift, you must first die. Only after will you have the means to seek revenge on those who killed your father...and your mother." The last words were purposeful and drawn out.

The blood drained from my face and I started to get light-headed. Only this monster in man's clothing holding me up kept my limp body from collapsing to the ground. I could barely hear my own voice, as if speaking through a dream, "Me...ma?" Tears threatened to leap to their death from the corners of my eyes.

"Just now, I'm afraid," he said as he dragged me over to the small barred window. With ease, he turned me around in his hands and let me peer outside. There, indeed, was a roaring fire that I had vaguely been aware of. In the center of it stood a statue of a bull made from bronze. Soldiers stood around it, with the commander giving orders to douse the flames. It took several buckets from the stream close by to extinguish the blaze. A few more were thrown over the bull, the water sizzling into steam and sending a white cloud billowing through the night's air.

I could see there was a door in the middle of the bull. The realization of what I was seeing began to tickle the front of my brain as a soldier reached over and grabbed the handle. With a yelp, he pulled back and dropped to his knees, grasping the wrist of the hand that was now blistering.

The commander scolded him further, "Use a gauntlet or deerskin, you fool."

The soldier looked at him with pain-filled eyes and a gaping mouth. "Y-yes ma'lord," he stammered.

He reached into his satchel, pulled out a piece of deerskin, and tentatively grabbed the handle with it. With a twist and a pull, the door fell open and steam rushed to escape, hitting the soldier. He took several steps back while waving his hands in front of his face, less he be consumed by the cloud. A light breeze brought the acrid smell of seared flesh.

I stood watching, not wanting to believe, as the vapor dissipated. Inside was a lump of scalded flesh in a fetal position. It had my mother's dress on.

My mouth tried to say the words, "The wind," but nothing came out. Tears brimmed and fell down my dirty cheeks, creating streaks through the blood and dirt. Snot bubbled out of my nose. My heart sank as what I was seeing took hold. I sobbed, painfully. My body jerked with every breath. The stranger wrapped his arm around my face, where my sobs of heartache were muffled by his sleeve at the crook of his arm. I was vaguely aware of the smell of dirt filling my nose, but that was a distant thought in my reeling mind.

"That was not the wind you heard," Ulric purred into my ear, his voice just above a whisper. "Those were her screams of anguish inside the bull. They roasted your mother alive, John."

Centuries later, in a decimated library in Nazi-occupied France, I found a book on what are now known as medieval tortures. I read through it with a knotted stomach, clenched jaw, and blurry eyes. A fire is built under the bull, causing the bronze to slowly heat. Flesh bubbles and splits. Meat separates from bone. It takes several minutes for the person to go into shock.

Several mortal lifetimes later, the pain feels as fresh as a gaping wound that refuses to heal.

With Ulric still holding me, my vision sharpened, and all I could focus on was the commander who had killed my family. I felt my teeth clench, and my breaths came in ragged shudders.

"I'm...going...to...kill...ye," I said between furious, heart-wrenching sobs.

"So you accept my proposal, then?" Ulric asked with a smile in his voice.

"Aye, aye, a thousand times aye!" I growled. "I will laugh into tha' fiends face as he dies. Then he can burn in Hell."

"Then let us begin."

Still looking out the window, I felt his breath on my neck.

"Now, this might hurt a little," he purred, and then an explosion of fire pierced my neck. The burning spread down my side and up my head. I stayed focused on my nemesis as my vision blackened around the edges. My heart drummed erratically, trying to pump blood that was quickly diminishing. My breathing became shallow as darkness enveloped my sight. Everything went still as my heart stopped.

Chapter 5

PRESENT DAY

V alenta's Saloon was only a handful of blocks away from the church, and closer still to my resting place. Its convenience was only rivaled by the fact that the saloon was a hub that catered to the supernatural elements of Houston. It sat on a street nestled between dilapidated buildings that used to sell cars or give massages. A single flickering security bulb illuminated the weed-infested parking lot, which contained cars of varying cost and rarity. I was confident that most were unlocked, considering no one would dare touch a car in Valenta's parking lot. On the rare occasions it had happened, the patrons had found the thieves, though the police couldn't say the same.

As I pushed past the saloon-style doors, I surveyed the room. It was emptier than usual, with only a few supes occupying a table in the back corner. I couldn't see past their glamour, but I could smell that they were of the troll family. Trolls were notoriously difficult to kill because of their healing factor. Though not as fast or as efficient as my own, they could have a limb removed and, as long as they didn't lose it, could sew the pieces back together and heal within hours.

Normally I would keep my eye on their ilk, but Val's Saloon was neutral ground to all supes. Anyone who violated the agreement would be dealt with by any and all without consequence.

I walked past the threshold and made my way toward the bar.

The room was a big square, with Val's actual bar taking up one full side. There were tables spread throughout made from various woods of varying ages. Val would never admit to anything, but it was rumored that his bar had been taken straight from Valhalla itself, where the fallen would enjoy their drinks for free. Not a lot of profit to be made.

The chairs matched the wood of their respective tables. No one knew how old Valenta was. So, my theory was that he had been the proprietor of a saloon or some apropos variant over the centuries. As the business would grow, he would keep the old furniture and make new ones himself. I'd seen him whittling away behind the bar, and had taken notice of his efficiency with a blade.

When I first met Val, I was my usual witty, borderline-standoffish self and made a "your mom" joke. Without taking his eyes off me, he pulled up a raw piece of wood from a pile just under the bar and took his pocket knife to it with unparalleled craftsmanship. Within less than a minute, a nice, sharp stake was placed on the bar right in front of me. The message was clear. He motioned for me to pick it up, which I hesitantly did. My eyes were drawn to the carving of a man with strikingly similar characteristics to myself being impaled in the chest by the hooded personification of Death. I was quick to apologize and explain my particular sense of humor. We've been good ever since.

"Hey, Val, did your bar get bigger or are you serving clam chowder again?" I asked the man standing behind the counter as I approached, motioning to the empty seats.

"Fuck'n smartass," the man responded with a thick southern drawl. Valenta was a man of average height and thick muscle hidden underneath long, flannel sleeves that were slightly rolled up to just above the wrist. His hair was the same light brown color as his eyes, which hid a world of confidence, age, and wisdom behind them. Every time I saw him, I could swear he had a different facial hair style. This time, it was a handlebar moustache leading up to muttonchops.

"Summoning your inner Wyatt Earp?" I joked while stroking my own lavish face muscle known as a beard.

"Breaks up the monotony of existence, son," he responded without looking up from the glass he was cleaning. This was one of my favorite things about Val; he was OCD when it came to cleanliness. I had brought it up to him one time and his response had been, "Next to godliness."

Moving on, I inquired, "Seriously though, why's the place deader than *Fantastic Four*'s sequel?"

Looking up from his duties, he stared into my eyes with an impossibly *more* serious expression and said, "There's been chatter, John. One of them Hell zealots..."

"Hell-lots!" I interrupted excitedly, fisting the air at my pun.

Without missing a beat, Val picked up where he had left off, "...is going to be successful in open'n the doorway to the pits below. Somethen's commen, and supes are gettin' while the gettin's good."

To scare supernaturals was no easy feat. An image of Father Thomes flashed in my mind; he had mentioned the surplus of summonings as of late. They were on the precipice of getting out of hand. My blood ran cold...er.

"What do your little birdies say about this chatter?" I asked with feigned confidence, fearing that I already knew the answer.

"The prophecy, boy. The final showdown at the O.K. Corral between above and below," he said grimly, shaking his head. His attention had refocused on his glass, which was now clean. He picked up another and held it up to one of the dim lights, inspecting it for imperfections left by the industrial washer.

"Then where the fuck is everyone running to?!" I all but cried out in frustration. "Hoboken, New Jersey?"

"There are more planes than these three, boy," he matter-of-factly reminded me.

The pit dropped from my stomach. "You mean, they are freaking hiding in *those* planes because they think it's safer?! Val, what the hell is coming?"

"Exactly," he said. "I 'magen the Fae are have'n a heyday with the surplus of inventory. Now, what'll you have, son?"

After a moment of searching his eyes, I sighed and said, "Give me a Bloody Jack, and make it a double."

While Val mixed the enchanted Jack with a fresh bag of blood from the local clinic where he had connections, my mind drifted to the horrors Ulric had informed me of in regards to the other planes. He had made sure to implant a healthy respect bordering on fear of the Fae court in particular. They were a crafty lot, as beautiful as they were fierce. Their intelligence was rivaled only by their cunning.

Ulric had told me a story about a man lost in a forest during a particularly harsh winter storm, who had begged the gods for a fire to keep him warm. It hadn't been a god who had answered. The most beautiful woman the man had ever seen appeared beside him and asked, "If I give you warmth, will you return the favor?" To which the man had vivaciously nodded his head in agreement. With a wave of her hand on the kindling the man had stacked, she started a roaring fire that provided him with enough warmth to survive the night.

In the morning, it was said that she had skinned the man to make a coat to return the favor. Word was that, to this day, a member of Fae royalty still walked around with her man-coat. I vaguely wondered if PETA would have a problem with that.

There were lesser Fae, like the trolls in the corner, who were just straight up barbaric in their approach. I much preferred them over anyone in the courts.

Returning to my train of thought, I asked Val, "Any specifics about the prophecy I should know?"

Shaking his head, he replied, "I've told you 'bout as much as I know. 'Cept there was one thing. Legend has it that there are documents, scrolls of some sort, that share insight into what's comin'. Maybe even how to prevent it."

"Let me guess," I said, rolling my eyes, "no one knows where they are."

"Bingo," he said, sliding my drink across the bar. He poured a shot of home-brewed whiskey for himself, held his glass up, and toasted, "Salud."

"To the end of creation," I responded, clinking my glass with his before taking a delicious sip. Blood removed from a living body and kept cold wasn't the same as straight from the tap, but it did help sate the cravings, similar to putting aloe vera on a sunburn, or so I'd been told. I didn't get in the sun much.

As I enjoyed my drink and let myself relax, I said to Val, "This is a little above my paygrade, isn't it? Maybe I should let this one go and sit back."

"Th'only thing necessary for the triumph o' evil is fer good men t'do nothen," Val responded.

At that, the front door slammed open, followed by a gust of wind that swirled throughout the saloon, knocking over glasses and sending napkins flying into a vortex.

Val simply covered his drink with his palm while I rushed to shoot it down my throat, spilling enough of it to warrant another dry-cleaning bill. Luckily, I knew a guy.

In walked Captain Dickhead himself, followed by a small entourage of hired goons.

Nathanial Locke stood around 6'4" with long, sinewy limbs, and liked to shop at Hot Topic. I guess black was his color, as it was hard to be the head of the supes criminal organization while wearing pink. The dark suit he had on was probably from the Victorian era, complete with black frills spilling out from everywhere. Someone should tell him that it was a two-button world now. The black mask he wore was outlined in pure gold, going from his greasy hairline down to his upper lip, and then continuing down both sides of his mouth to his jawline. Only his lips and cleanly shaven chin showed.

Word around town was that he had sustained severe burns from his predecessor, leading him to plan his rise to power. No one knew for sure what had happened to his old boss, but what was known garnered him respect from even the most powerful of supes. Last I'd heard, his boss' soul was locked in a special place in Hell, just for him, that Locke could visit anytime. No one was sure how he had managed to do it, but the speculation was that Locke worked for the Devil himself.

Nathanial's piercing eyes quickly locked onto me as I tried to dab my drink from my lap.

"Jonathan," he drawled, letting the last syllable hang in the air a moment longer than necessary.

"It's just John. If I had a birth certificate, it would not have the added letters, Nathan Locke the wizard," I retorted while I kept my eyes on my drink.

"*I*," he paused for emphasis, "am a warlock, and you will address me as such."

At that, two goons started spilling in around him, their intentions clear. They were enormous caricatures that looked like they belonged in a *Looney Toons* episode, complete with ashen gray suits that barely fit over their bulging frames. The electronic lights from the outside world were blotted out of existence as the men stood shoulder to shoulder just behind their master.

Valenta spoke up with unquestioned authority, "Hold it right there, boys. Y'know the rules. An' know the consequences o' breaking them rules," he stared at them intently.

The goons balked at this and looked at their leader for guidance.

"A simple misunderstanding," Nathanial said, waving his hand dismissively.

His entourage visibly relaxed but maintained their posts. Their gazes returned to me.

Finally turning to look at him, I asked, "What do you want, Nathan?"

"Just as your certificate would have fewer letters, mine would contain more. But you already knew this," he calmly spoke while checking his nails for dirt. "But enough formalities. I am here to deliver a message."

"Please leave a message after the 'fuck off.'" I replied without hesitation, turning back to Val. He gave me a look that said, "Don't do nothin' stupid."

"Jonathan—"

"Fuck off."

"My employer wants you to stay out of what is coming," he started. It was clear he was waiting for me to come back with a witty retort. I just turned and stared at him in answer.

Nathanial continued, "He is willing to pay you quite well for your, let's say, neutrality."

"And what, exactly, is coming?" I asked, eyes squinting at Locke.

"What did I just say?" He turned to one of his henchmen and asked again, "Seriously, what did I just say?"

The henchman shifted uncomfortably and said in a gruff, cavernous voice, "You told him he will be paid to be dumb."

"Is that what you get paid to do, big boy?" He shoots, he scores. The furrow on the goon's ample brow turned into the Mariana trench. He bared his teeth and clenched his hamhocks.

Trying to press the issue, I swiveled in the chair to face him directly and smiled a toothy smile.

"John. Stop, now," Valenta commanded. "The rules apply t'all parties."

I put a little effort and asked the chair to continue slowly turning until I was facing the bar again, my smile now a comical frown. I rubbed at invisible tears with my fists. "My business is my own, Locke," I said while motioning for another drink. "But here's the ironic thing; now I'm definitely going to go all balls deep into whatever this is, just to piss you off. So, take care now. Bye, bye, then."

The air grew chilly, and a breath-stealing wall of subzero air barreled through the saloon. Patches of frost grew on the bar and walls like an accelerated bacteria growth. The lights dimmed then flickered out. The patrons in the corner stood, their chairs skittering across the floor, and retreated to the furthest wall. Frost started growing on the tip of my nose. I crossed my eyes to look at it.

A booming voice erupted, piercing the dimness and birthing light back into the saloon. "*Enough!*" Bulbs bloomed back into life and, for a moment, threatened to explode before receding to normality.

My eyes uncrossed to see Valenta's glowing white gaze intent on Locke, who had a look of astonishment on his face. He let his expression fall back into inscrutability.

"My employer will be very disappointed," Locke said coldly.

The cold air retreated, filling the air with comforting warmth, like stepping out of a cool, early-morning bedroom into a bathroom with a hot shower running. The accumulated frost melted. Water dripped off my nose, and I shifted my eyes to the mirror on the wall to see that the doorway was clear. The doors were swinging open and closed like a pendulum, until their diminishing movements ceased.

Valenta broke my focus and said, "Damnit, boy. One o' these days I'm not gonna be able to protect ya. Y'know what them muscles were, don't ya?"

"Ogres," I stated blankly. "How the Hades does Locke have Fae on his payroll?"

"Y'think only the three planes are interested in this war, John? The Fae have a stake in the outcome as well. It's clear t'me which side they are bet'n on, waltzing in here with the likes of Nathanial Locke. Y'just pissed off more than you can drink there, boy."

"Take it easy there, Bear Grylls. I (maybe) have some (kinda) friends I can (hopefully) count on (probably not). But first, ANOTHER!" I threw down the glass, and to my dismay, it didn't break. It simply bounced off the ground and rolled to a stop under a table.

My look of confusion prompted Valenta to say, "Upgraded 'em since the last time. More expensive but damn near unbreakable. Your sense of humor's shared by only you. However," he chuckled before continuing, "your face is pretty damn funny right now, boy." He poured me a drink in a new glass as I looked at him in appreciation.

Chapter 6

IRELAND, 1480

I couldn't see, couldn't hear, couldn't feel. There was an overwhelming sense of nonexistence, floating in the starless abyss that was my black universe. Panic and serenity fought for dominance. In my sensory deprivation, time seemed to stand still, or to not exist at all. After a lifetime in an indeterminate reality, I felt myself beginning to lose grip on my sanity. Was this what waited for us when we died? An unending expanse of nothingness?

In the distance, a brilliant speck appeared and began to grow, beckoning me to it. The closer I drifted, the more I yearned for the light. It spread over me, promising happiness and well-being. I closed my eyes as the light that warmed my skin became blinding.

A dull pain, like an insect bite, began to grow on my neck. My hand instinctively swatted at the bug that didn't exist, rubbing the spot feverishly as the sharp ache descended into my neck.

I felt something press on my chest, and I stopped floating toward eternity. My eyes squinted open as a shadowed, winged figure partially blocked the piercing light, its outstretched, armored arm planting a firm hand on me. I noted absently that the armor was white with an outline of gold.

A deep, powerful commanding voice reverberated *inside* my head, *"Heaven is not for you, abomination."*

The light was abruptly squelched out of existence, and the blackness regained its dominant hold. The figure was gone, and I was alone in the nothing, the nowhere. I jerked my head in all directions, trying to spot something, *anything*. I waved my hands and feet, trying to pivot in place. I couldn't tell if I was making any headway.

The throb in my neck grew to a sharp, flaming pain. It quickly became the center of my universe, the only thing that mattered. I grasped fruitlessly at the spreading inferno as it enveloped my entire body, bringing with it a torture I could never have even dreamed about. My soul spasmed and twitched relentlessly, contorting my incorporeal body without quarter. I managed to condense myself into a ball and tried to ride out the storm—and wherever it was taking me.

Curled into a fetal position with my eyes squeezed shut, I saw red and purple lines of ghostly fire snake across my vision, branding my essence. Forcing my eyes open, I saw my hands growing black where the ghost flames had touched. I couldn't scream; the piercing agony had stolen my breath and caused my body to seize uncontrollably once more, forcing me out of my fetal position.

After what felt like hours, I was aware of my feet, and finally toes, being scalded. As quickly as it had begun, the pain receded, and I was left floating in the nothingness with a raw, charred body. The electrified agony let its clutch over my existence wane and fade, leaving behind a case of the worst pins and needles in the history of me.

Numbness spread and then withdrew, leaving behind a tingle of pure energy. I looked at my hands, which were normal again, but they felt...different. I couldn't describe what had happened, but I was aware of a fundamental change.

Something tugged me backward, like a hooked fish being reeled in. I was aware of being pulled at unfathomable speeds through the void. Dots of light started popping into existence, forming the stars I was accustomed to seeing at night when I lay in the fields staring into the vast ocean in the sky. I turned in midair and saw a blue, green, and brown sphere rushing toward me. Each color was assigned to its own domain, with interlapping sections coalescing into a unified partnership. Green slowly turned lighter to meet brown that slowly turned darker, combining and warring for eternity on who would control the area. Here and there, blue wantonly interjected itself right in the middle, defiant of the other colors' claims. A beautiful swirl of white was mixed in sporadically, passing over the other colors at its leisure, careless of the fight for control below, and content to just watch.

The world was expanding, filling all that I could see, and I started to panic. A wall of white clouds came into view, and I sliced through them like an arrow through fog. Once through, I began to scream as I free-fell toward the green fields and solid ground that were becoming vaguely familiar. In the distance, I could see the unmistakable outline of my farm, my home. It was ablaze, with the fires having already consumed most of the structure. The pens where we kept the livestock were all open and empty, presumably taken by the heretics.

An amalgamation of anger and sorrow filled my veins as my home retreated from my vision and an encampment rushed to welcome me back to my grim reality. My eyes locked onto the bronze bull, which now stood alone with its belly closed. I tried to glance inside with the hopeless thought that maybe my mother would crawl out, once again whole, and tell me everything was fine; that everything had been just a dream, and I should go back to bed before I woke my father up. Then I was launched through a wall into darkness.

As I flew through the stone blocks of my prison, I slammed into my body with enough force that if Ulric hadn't still been holding me, I would have been thrown back. As my soul reattached itself to my once mortal flesh, there was a sense of completion that was indescribable. As if my body had been dying without its soul.

There was a warm, metallic taste in my mouth, and I weakly looked up to see Ulric had been holding his palm up to my mouth.

He let go of me, and I collapsed to the ground.

"Oh dear. Not strong enough yet, I see," Ulric said. With the same teeth that had taken my life, he had given a new one. Still grinning, he dramatically bit into the freshly closed veins on his palm and let the blood well. The wound was deep, causing a spillover that he directed into my gaping, eager mouth. Ulric focused, preventing the wound from closing.

Electricity shot through my entire being as his pure life force hit my tongue and slid down my throat. Warmth grew from my throat and stomach, rapidly expanding like a wildfire. Elation overtook everything I knew. There was no pain in those moments; even my parents were a distant, nagging memory I couldn't quite pinpoint. I pulled his palm to my mouth and wrapped my lips around the wound. My body convulsed in the purest pleasure. Every cell grew stronger with the powerful life energy. My vision cleared, as if I had been blind my entire life and only now saw the world for its beauty. I became dizzy with ecstasy. Ulric pulled away, cutting me off from the fountain of eternal life and happiness. The bliss remained, and I had to fight my swimming, carefree thoughts to focus back on reality.

"Was he there?" Ulric asked, letting his focus drop and his palm close. His voice was a lighthouse in the distance, and I used it for guidance. I needed more.

Climbing to my hands and knees, I reached for his arm. He took a casual step back and swatted my hands as if I were a child who was reaching for another dessert.

I looked up with a frown, grasping at the words he had spoken, and muttered with crimson teeth, "Wh-who?"

"The Gatekeeper. Hard to miss."

Fragments of memory staggered back into place, and I could recall the winged man with the armor. "Yes," I managed. "Who is he?" My voice caught the periphery of my attention. It was far away, but there.

"Let me guess, 'abomination' was his selected term?" Ulric asked, bemused.

"Y-yes...why'd he refer to me as that?" The weight of the meaning was attempting to sink in. The gatekeeper to Heaven had called me an abomination. Pretty sure that wasn't good.

"Because that's what we are in their eyes. We will discuss this, and more, in time. Now it is time to feed."

Chapter 7

PRESENT DAY

B oy, you got 'bout twenty minutes till dawn. Best be on your way," Val informed me, prompting a panicked glance at my bare wrist. Damn it, I needed a watch.

"*Merde*!" I exclaimed finding the mocking clock hanging smugly on the wall. "Guess I was lost in my own brain. Easy to do with all the empty space up there."

I slammed the rest of my drink and made my way to the parking lot. With the sun only minutes away from cresting the horizon, the sky was already blinding to my preternatural eyes. I wasted no time and bounded down the street, twenty feet at a time, to the cemetery where my coffin awaited. Strategically, it was only a few blocks away from my favorite relaxation spot, and I made it with plenty of time to spare.

Walking up to a large, gauche mausoleum, I placed my hands on the cold stone slab and pushed. The rock groaned as it moved, and I shifted my hands to push it to one side. Once inside, I closed the chic sliding door behind me and lowered a titanium beam in place to secure it, which had not been cheap to come by— so I had stolen it. Using my preternatural eyes, I located the false stone on the wall behind the raised coffin platform and pressed it in. There was a click, then the platform lifted and slid to one side, revealing a darkened staircase carved from the hard rock and earth beneath.

Along its length, I had placed spooky torches that I could ignite with the force of my will. All it took was for me to excite the molecules within the wicks. There was no other reason to do this than that it looked really, really cool. Plus, I had paid for them. They had been cheaper than the titanium beam and less suspicious, so damn right I was going to use them. I pressed another stone, and the platform slid back into place with a resounding thud.

The stone stairs descended forty feet into the earth. I had done this so some gravedigger wouldn't accidentally break through my ceiling, especially considering only soft earth lay between my hidey-hole and the surface. There usually wasn't any underground piping running beneath cemeteries, which had made it fairly easy to dig but had cost me in structural integrity. The hard part had been digging a hole by myself that was big enough to fit the large freight containers I had procured, place them, and then cover the hole—all before dawn and without anyone noticing. Not to mention dispersing the several hundred square feet of excess dirt across the entire cemetery to avoid suspicion from the employees. I had then tapped into the electricity supply of the groundskeeper's building and put in a ventilation system hidden in the trunk of a hollowed-out tree a few yards from the hidden entrance. I'd even built a rainwater filtration system so I could shower. God, I fucking loved YouTube and Pintere— Ahem, push-ups. I meant push-ups, not that other thing you thought I was about to say.

After a couple hours of hanging drywall, installing laminate flooring, cabinets, and all the other DIY accoutrements, my home had been ready.

"Da, I'm home!" I proclaimed to the Fortress of Solitaire.

A man's cultured British accent responded, "About bloody time. I was about to list all your worldly possessions on Craigslist."

"You better not even *think* about touching my *Battlefield Earth* cups. They're collectibles!" I said as I rushed to my locked cabinet, where I opened the doors to reveal a stunning collection. Picking up my favorite glass, I ran my finger over John Travolta's disfigured face longingly. "Oh, Rocky Dennis. You showed them all, didn't you?"

"I can never tell when you're serious," Da said.

"*Un-dead* serious," I clutched my fist and shook it in a gesture of accomplishment for using the pun so soon. Da just stared at me, unblinking.

Da has been my companion for countless decades. He found me at a time when I really needed someone, and since then has tried to guide me down the path of light by playing Devil's Advocate—hence the nickname Da.

Da is a faerie that hates faeries and simply *refuses* to even acknowledge his predicament. He insists, vehemently, that he is an angel—with no wings or flaming sword. Normally he stands at about 5 inches tall, and he likes to pal around on my shoulder proffering sage advice. Plus, he has the wisdom of the Fae, so he is pretty indispensable, though I'd never admit that to him.

As he floated into the living room, I noted his handmade silk pj's, reminiscent of one Hugh Hefner.

"What took you so long, John? I thought you were only supposed to scare a group of 'probably teenagers' from 'pretending to summon the devil,' or so you put." He added air quotes to mock me.

"I think this one was the real deal, Da. They had like, robes and candles and...other items. Plus, there was a, uh, flagrant, uh, energy in the air."

He stopped in midair and raised an eyebrow.

"Sorry, it is on my daily word calendar," I said.

"Do you even bother to read the definition below the word?" he asked like a teacher who knew the child didn't even have a dog.

Moving up my sleeve with my middle finger, I said, "Boy, would you look at the time. Would love to stay and be talked down to by a faer— I mean...five-inch angel, but the sun is almost up. So, I bid you ahfuckyou." That last part had a French twist to it akin to their farewell.

As I strode past him and into the bedroom, my preter-ears heard him mutter, "I'll show you five inches."

"Very angelic of you, Da," I called over my shoulder.

The bedroom had a king-size mattress and frame that provided the real cover for my 100% iron coffin, which was hidden underneath. The iron prevented divination or ranged attacks, such as curses. What can I say? I haven't lived for more than five hundred years by not having redundancies in place.

I lifted the foot of the mattress, which was on hydraulics, and revealed my safe space. Bullies would never be able to hurt me here! Inside were a few books by Jim Butcher, Stephen King, Kevin Hearne, and Richard Kadrey that I hadn't finished yet. There was also a laptop (no, I don't get Wi-Fi forty feet underground...yet) and LED lighting surrounding the frame.

At the foot of my hidden bed I had even managed to install a compact industrial fridge to keep my secret stash of "store-packed" red blood cells. They could last me anywhere from six weeks to twelve months depending on the temperature; but the older the blood, the less it quenched. An unsatiated thirst could be excruciating, like a south Texas marathon runner who hadn't adequately rationed his water bottle. It could consume your every thought and eventually drive you insane. Men had drunk seawater, knowing full well that it would spell their doom, because they hadn't been able to take it anymore. There was no cost too great in order to get even a semblance of water to pass over their tongues and slide down their throats.

If a vampire was not hibernating, they could lose their mind in a matter of months of sobriety. So, should I ever become trapped, I had enough blood to sustain me for several weeks, or even months, somewhat comfortably. Or at least enough so I didn't lose my precious mind. After that, it would be up to Future Me to figure out a plan of escape. Present Me was satisfied knowing I at least had a BOB, otherwise known as a Blood-Out-Bag.

I lay inside and pulled the strap attached to my coffin lid, closing it, and flipped the switch that turned off all the lights in the bedroom. Next to it was another switch that turned on the LEDs. I flipped it and grabbed the latest book in the current series I was enjoying. Technically, I could ingest entire pages worth of content with just a glance due to my photographic memory; but for the books I read for fun, I preferred the old-fashioned way. Word by word. Had taken me months to read *IT* by Stephen King. The man creeped me out sometimes.

As I started to read about a wizard being hired by Bigfoot, my mind started to lose focus and replay the events of the night. My brain just couldn't fathom how cataclysmic whatever was coming was that other supes were forced to hide in *those* planes. One of which was presided by the Fae, who were twisted little fucks that could spend centuries torturing anyone who crossed into their territory. Plus, in their world, the Fae were as strong to supes as supes were to humans on this plane. Made my gonads want to retreat into my pelvic cavity every time I tried to comprehend the predatory shift of the food chain.

I placed the Darth Vader bookmark back between the pages and set it aside. Turning off the LEDs, I stared into the darkness and let scenarios of what might lay ahead run through my mind. Then the dawn was upon me and unconsciousness took hold.

Chapter 8

IRELAND, 1480

I stood up, feeling as if I weighed nothing at all, and Ulric placed a hand firmly on my shoulder, steadying me.

"Careful, John. You could have jumped through the top of this enclosure simply by standing. It will take you time to become accustomed to the new power coursing through your veins," Ulric informed me like a proud father.

My eyes shot down to my hands, with the rest of my head following suit. They were normal at first glance, no markings or lines. I flexed them curiously, first stretching them out in a fan as much as I could, then making a fist.

Ulric strode to the nearest wall and, with a smile in my direction, hammered a fist into the stone wall, exploding out a section.

Voices could be heard from outside, shouting with urgency. Their commander didn't appreciate failure, and the men rightfully feared him.

Ulric picked up a piece of stone that had tumbled to the ground and walked over to where I stood dumfounded. He held it out with an expectant look, and I took the rock from his hand.

"Crush it," he said. There was no curiosity in his voice, only a direct command that he fully expected would be followed.

"With what?" I asked meekly.

"With your hand," he said without sarcasm or reproach.

"That's impossible," I said, my brow deeply furrowed with bewilderment at the in-conceivable task laid at my feet. Or more appropriately, my hands.

"For a mortal, yes, but you are no longer human. Now do as I command." His gaze sharpened, daring me to protest further.

I squeezed as hard as I could, but the rock stayed whole.

"John, stop believing in your limitations. Close your eyes," he said.

"Why?" I asked.

An unseen hand swiped the side of my head, stinging a little.

"What was that for?" I asked dumbly.

"You will learn to obey me, John. It is for your own good. But first, you must learn. If you are willing to be my protégé, I will hone your powers, and you, John, you will avenge your family."

"Family," I whispered to myself, allowing the flood of emotion that had been placed behind the dam of my rebirth to break free.

My hands clenched into fists and the rock exploded into sand, falling through my fingers like water.

"Very good, John. It is time to forget the limitations of your past and embrace the strength of an Eternal," Ulric said. "Have you noticed your speech has adapted?"

That brought me out of my focused hate.

"Ye-yes," I said, unbelieving. "How?"

With a smile, Ulric said, "The gift affects us all in subtle, various ways, but there are several consistencies. You probably view your accent now as the proper way of speaking. Because of your subconscious wish, your preternaturally enhanced brain made it so. You can slide in and out of any dialect you wish. New languages will become clear to you, like the brightest moon piercing the thinnest of clouds. Information will flow from the pages of every scroll you gaze upon. It will be as if the ink is replicated onto your mind. One of your lessons will be to create a library in your headspace. Otherwise, you might go insane, as your thoughts will be uncontrollable with so much raw information floating around."

I processed what Ulric had said. My mouth salivated with the fantasy of learning every language and knowing everything. It felt like I had just become a man again, realizing that the hay bale I could only drag as a child was now within my power to lift and throw around at my will.

"The men who took your family are on the other side of that wall," he said, interrupting my thoughts and pointing to where he had hammered out a new window.

Footsteps were surrounding the structure on all sides, looking for the cause of the noise. I was able to hone in on a set of footsteps walking past the wall in front of us.

Everything went still. My eyes could perceive a distorted red silhouette through the stone.

"You see him, yes?" asked Ulric.

I nodded slowly in affirmation. An unknown part of me was taking control, and I could feel my posture changing, becoming more predatory. My shoulders squared and followed the red shadow on the wall. I bent slightly at the knees and leaned forward, my elbows tucking into my sides with my hands outstretched, ready to grab. There was a movement inside my eyes that I had never felt before, and the world around me sharpened. My upper jaw on either side of my lips flexed, and my tongue felt preposterously sharp, foreign teeth. But this was just a tickle of a thought as I followed my prey. Everything else took a back seat to feeding. I felt myself become a spectator in my own body. The muscles and thoughts were no longer mine to control. Only the red blur existed, and my overwhelming desire, no, *need* to consume.

"Eventually, you'll be able to see him as if he were right in front of you, not just an outline," he said. "Now grab him, and drink."

The thought of blood motivated me. I didn't hesitate this time. Slamming both my fists through the wall, I grabbed the guard by the shoulders and pulled him through, collapsing the wall. The falling stones and force of yanking him had damaged his body. Both his shoulders were dislocated, and his eyes were foggy. His neck had been broken by the whiplash. Bricks had crushed his nose and knocked out his front teeth. Blood had started to pool in his mouth. A torrent of saliva flooded my mouth, threatening to spill over my lips as the metallic smell invaded my nostrils. The hairs on my skin stood upright, and my nipples hardened.

"Quickly," Ulric said, breaking my wave of elation. "Before he passes. Drain his blood."

Instinct took control and I pulled him close to me. As he went unconscious, his head tilted to one side. His heart was audibly struggling to beat. My teeth slid into his neck with ease, piercing the artery with an almost practiced precision. Blood spread over my tongue and down my throat, sending shivers through my entire body. My mouth opened in ecstasy, and Ulric had to gently push my mouth back to his neck.

"Keep drinking, John. Don't just let it pour freely. Control it," he said.

It was as if he were a thousand miles away, but I could register what he was saying. Anything to make this feeling continue, I would do without hesitation.

Warmth grew from my stomach like a wildfire, spreading throughout my entire body. With the flames came untold, indescribable pleasures that no mortal man had ever been capable of putting into words. The awakening was like making love for the first time; before the climax, it was only self-gratification that you *knew* could never get any better. After, and especially during coital release, you realized how naïve you had been.

All the raging waters of worry and pain subsided into a pristine glass-top lake as the stolen energy encapsulated my entire being.

This blood was stronger, substantially more fulfilling than what had come from Ulric, as if the life energy was pure and unfiltered; straight from the well of life.

Once he was dry, Ulric had to pry me away from the corpse. I reached for it like an infant reaching for its mother's breast. Irritation was plastered all over my face.

"He is drained, John," Ulric said curtly. "There are more fresh soldiers to take."

At that, I perked up like a dog seeing his master picking up a stick. I *needed* that feeling again, and now. It's all that mattered.

More footsteps were approaching from the commotion that had been created.

"Follow me. And remember, be faster than you know you are," he said. With that, he dashed through the hole to the bushes ten yards away.

I took a deep breath, grabbed the edges of the hole for leverage, then leaped with all my might, hitting the ground sprinting. I weaved between trees and over a creek, barely able to keep up with how fast the forest was rushing to meet me; dodging and weaving. My predatory self was still in control and was able to gracefully evade the rushing foliage.

After a few moments, a vise grabbed the back of my neck and stopped me cold in my tracks. My legs flew out in front of me with the momentum, where they waved in the air for a moment. It felt like my shoes were about to fly off.

"Very good," Ulric purred in my ear. "You are overcoming the limitations of your mind quite well. But it will take time to learn and hone your new abilities. Now then, let us go exact the revenge you seek," he said with a knowing smile. I felt completely out of my depth, but was willing to learn.

While consciously taking a degree of control back from my predatory self but still sharing the workload, we turned and I ran at a more controlled pace back toward the compound. I focused on controlling my movements, willing my legs to move with supernatural speed while my PS focused on the peripheral dangers. I dodged rogue limbs that reached out greedily, my feet always finding purchase. There was a slight nuisance, however, with bugs.

Ulric and I ran through the pitch-black woods, but we were able to see as if it were the brightest day. As the encampment came into view, we stopped at the edge of the bushes.

Ulric brushed at his face with his sleeve and I did the same, not knowing what I was expecting. A few crushed insects smeared on my shirt.

"Disgusting," I said.

"Quiet," Ulric whispered, pointing to the prison I had just escaped.

The rest of the men had gathered at the hole and found the severely mangled ghost-white guard. They were on alert, but had their backs to us.

I looked at Ulric, and he nodded. I leaped forward and slammed the heads of two soldiers against the wall, crushing them under their helmets and squeezing out mashed brains, a torrent of blood, and chunks of flesh.

"Don't waste the precious blood if you can help it, John," Ulric said from right behind me. "Like this."

The guards stood completely motionless with their mouths agape and eyes wide, frozen in confusion. Their brains were unable to comprehend what had just happened, as there was nothing logical that could explain what I had just done.

Ulric walked to the closest paralyzed guard and, with a fluid motion, swiped his hand across the guard's neck. After a heartbeat, blood spurted out from a clean line, causing the soldier to drop his weapon and reach for his neck. Ulric quickly grabbed his arms and pulled, ripping both limbs completely off. He lifted his hand, and the blood erupting from the three holes started to stream and then change direction toward Ulric while in midair. He moved his hand closer to his mouth, and the three streams joined into one and started sliding down his throat. Ulric closed his eyes in obvious pleasure as the blood defied the laws of nature. Everyone stood there stunned, watching. Including me. I was awestruck.

After a few moments, the blood stopped, and the man collapsed to the ground, white as marble. I heard footsteps slowly shuffling backward. Turning, my PS saw the prey retreating and instinct took over. I reached out and leaped on the closest man to me, taking us both to the ground. My teeth bit in and then pulled, sending blood flowing from the wound and onto the ground. I could *feel* the blood, but I couldn't control it.

"In time, my eager pupil," Ulric said. "For now, drink. The more you take unto yourself, the stronger you will become." He finished his statement with a show of what was to come. Pressing his palms together, he twisted his left hand and proceeded to pull a crimson dagger out of his right palm.

The few remaining men lay on the ground, trembling in pain and shock after having had all their limbs broken at the joints. Ulric had immobilized them while I'd been lost in my blood wonderland. With a fluid arc of his left hand, Ulric threw the dagger into the right side of one of the men's abdomen; at the blood-soaked liver. Attached to the hilt was a rope made of the same blood that extended all the way to Ulric's palm. Blood seeped from the wound and ran up the manifestation, flowing into Ulric's hand. His eyes closed in delight, and his mouth hung slightly open.

I stood in awe, watching the master who had spent untold centuries honing his craft. This must have been what it was like to watch as the Pied Piper lured his prey away, some two hundred years before this very day. A grim story my father had told me. But the way he'd played the lute with such grace and magnificence echoed through my mind as I watched Ulric guide the soldier's life essence unto himself. Blood marched up and around the rope, like an army of liquid ants. With a wheeze, the soldier stopped breathing. Ulric whipped the rope, and the blade shot back into his palm. Ulric shivered for a moment as the last drop became a part of him, surrendering its sacred energy to its new master.

As Ulric recomposed himself, a muffled sobbing stole my attention. I turned, and my gaze fell upon my next trip to paradise. The last soldier lay on the ground, a small—*pathetic*—pool of tears growing around where his face lay on the ground.

Pathetic? The thought had come from me, but it hadn't been *me*.

"Free him from his misery, John," Ulric said, eyes gleaming. He was creating a monster with minimal resistance, and it pleased him.

I shook the conflicting thoughts from my head and focused on the feeling that I was about to be submerged in. I bent down and bit into his neck, cleanly. The soldier inhaled sharply but didn't scream. I drank deeply, allowing the new life to enter every cell in my body. I was vaguely aware that I was moaning, or perhaps it was the soldier. I couldn't be sure.

After the last drop was taken, I jumped up and threw my hands out. I took in a deep breath and half screamed, half laughed into the night's air in ecstasy. The wind swept over my skin, bringing a cool breeze to my now hot flesh. But I still wasn't sated. It reminded me of tending to the farm on a glaring summer day and running out of water while the day's work wasn't over yet.

"I need more!" I shouted "I need to be there again!" My fists pumped the air and I pounded my chest.

"The camp is clear, I'm afraid," Ulric said.

Disappointment set in, then panic struck. "What about the commander?!" I asked concerned.

"He left after your mother was declared deceased. Probably to attend other camps in the land. I've followed them with some interest."

"We must follow him!" I shouted with a sense of urgency. My supernatural voice boomed with unrestrained power, causing the stone wall to reverberate, and leaves to fall from their trees in a mass suicide.

"Then we will," Ulric said patiently. "But first, it is time to sleep."

"*No!*" I shouted at him. "*Now!*" A chunk of the wall crumbled away from the hole and tumbled on the ground, attempting to escape my wrath.

Ulric didn't even flinch at my verbal onslaught, even as dust rose from his clothing like a beaten rug. He just stared at me with understanding in his eyes. Behind that was annoyance at the spoiled brat who wanted his way or he'd throw a tantrum.

He took in a long, contemplative breath and said, "Dawn approaches," then pointed to the distance. A scowl creasing my face, I followed his hand and had my frustration melt into awe as flames drifted up from the horizon to a quarter of the way into the early morning sky. The flaming tendrils wavered erratically in a beautiful and horrifying dance. They crisscrossed in front of each other, competing for dominance on who would be the biggest and the brightest. The longer I looked, the higher the flames reached into the sky, threatening to envelope the heavens like some sort of tentacled world-eating monster. I had to squint after a minute of taking in the fearsome beauty, as the light began to burn my eyes. I noticed my skin was growing uncomfortably warmer as well, like waking in the middle of a hot summer's night and throwing the blanket off before you cooked to death.

Birds woke up and flew from their branches into the growing inferno of the morning sky. Winged black dots were swallowed by the brightness that only Ulric and I were privy to. Our own private sun-pocalypse.

"That's long enough, John. Time to find a place to sleep. Oblivion will always return to humbly remind us of our place in the universe," Ulric said as he started walking into the woods at a swift pace.

After a few minutes, when the flames were blazing across half of the sky and I had to squint to see, we stopped at a clearing. Ulric said, "This will suffice." He put his hand out in front of him, palm outstretched, and a string of blood left his body. It snaked in the air then divided into two ropes which divided yet again and pierced the ground at four different points. The ropes—bloodropes I guess you would call them— started moving in a rectangle pattern, leaving lines in the earth. After the shape was complete, the blood congealed into one wide line and shoved into the bottom of the rectangle like a shovel, then moved forward, lifting the dirt. The blood raised a large section of earth ten feet into the air, creating a large hole that was three or four feet deep. Ulric stepped in, lay down comfortably, and said, "You better get started." The earth started slowly descending on him. "Otherwise, the sun will burn your immortal essence away." Just as he finished, the dirt was upon him, sealing him off with only a slight mound to indicate his presence.

I stood looking at the mound and repeated out loud what he had said, "Burn your immortal essence." At that, the sun crested the horizon, and I could feel its power stinging my skin. The direct light was still in the sky, not even touching the treetops yet, but the fierce power threatened to ignite every cell in my body.

Dropping to my knees, I started frantically digging into the earth beside Ulric. I was growing weaker as the seconds ticked by. My eyes were growing heavy, and my arms were filling with sand, becoming less agile and ignoring my direct commands. I got about halfway through when I saw the light hit the top of the trees next to where I was.

Staring at them, I could see with my new eyes that the air was wavering with heat where the light touched. Panic could be an amazing motivator, but the closer the light came, the harder it was to move my muscles. At some point, I lifted my head in exhaustion, the light slamming into the back of my skull. A white sheet of pain spread down my head and through my body, stunning me. I fell forward, incapacitated. My slack-jawed face lay on the ground, staring as the light approached, inch by inch.

I weakly pulled my limp body as far as I could into the incredibly small hole I had made. Grabbing a mound of dirt with my clawed, numb hands, I pulled as much earth over my head, neck, and upper back as I could. As I reached up again to try and shovel more dirt, the sun struck my hands and incinerated them. I could tell by the sound that they had fallen to the ground, useless.

The burning was immeasurable and impossible to describe with words. I could only sob in agony as the light moved up my arms and down the rest of my uncovered back. I could feel the skin start to bubble and liquid ooze down my sides. I inhaled a mouthful of dirt and tried to scream, but nothing came out except a squeak. The dirt underneath my face soaked with a flood of tears.

I could feel my body contort as the muscles dried out and shrunk, threatening to pull my head free. I flexed my neck and abdomen to the point of snapping to try and keep my head submerged. My back muscles withered and crumbled to ash. The sun violated my internal organs next, causing blood to bubble up and seep through my mouth. I had to focus on the fact that I wasn't choking because I didn't need to breathe anymore.

I couldn't feel my legs any longer, and the skin on my stomach was starting to smolder. I gritted my teeth and felt a tooth shatter.

After minutes of immense suffering, my nerve endings finally shriveled and became worthless. Once the pain subsided and the damage was done, I plummeted into unconsciousness and my first preternatural dreams.

Chapter 9

PRESENT DAY

Dreams for a vampire were in a league of their own. The preternatural mind could weave such vivid horrors that even H.R. Giger would curl into a fetal position and weep in terror. It could also construct the purest, most blissful dreams that made you never want to wake up. This night's was particularly terrifying.

Winged men sheathed in blindingly reflective golden armor and wielding gladius swords coated in fierce white-blue flames battled grotesque monstrosities adorned with black armor and brandishing crude weapons—both made from obsidian originating from the immense lava pits in Hell.

Scattered over the seared ground were beautiful cadavers intermixed with deformed beasts, all of which had varying degrees of mutilation and carnage. An extinguished gladius lay nearby with a coat of black, viscous demon blood. Not far was a severed hellion's hand with a sheet of pristine flesh pierced on its claws. On closer inspection, it was a face sagging in a perpetual frown, like the Tragedy mask associated with the theater. My eyes continued to take in the disastrous scene.

The skyline appeared to be a decimated downtown Houston, as if a meteor had hit a bull's-eye on the city's center. Skyscrapers had crumbled. Everything in sight was bathed in flames. The sky swirled angrily with black clouds and crimson linings. Balls of fire dropped from the heavens and course corrected to the heat of the battle, crashing in an explosion of white flames. Savage angels rose stoically from the points of impact and joined the fray.

Colossal craters spouting red-and-green hellfire littered the ground as far as the eye could see. Clawed, nightmarish limbs grasped the dead earth and hauled truly horrifying behemoths onto this plane. Thunderous bellows shook the ground, sending shock waves that would liquify a mortal's organs.

I stood in the middle of the chaos. The pure dread and terror of what I knew was happening froze me in place, paralyzed by what I had done. This was my fault...*I* had done this. The entire plane would be engulfed in heavenflame and hellfire and burned to a cinder. The forces would battle until the last man stood. With the gates to both above and below open, mortal souls would be collateral damage. All the humans to have ever existed throughout history would pay for my mistakes. Demons would destroy the souls of the righteous in Heaven out of envious anger, while the angels would extinguish the souls of sinners in Hell.

The clashing of weapons against armor ceased all at once, creating a deafening silence where only fire cracked and the wind whispered its ghostly lullaby through blackened ribcages.

My eyes widened at the realization that both the angels and demons were staring directly at me. I peed a little. The biggest of the hellion monsters lumbered toward me, both factions moving out of the way to allow this house-sized beast better access to my tender, succulent body.

He stood at least twenty feet tall and was just as wide, with bulging arms running the length of his body and knuckles dragging the ground. Black scales ran over his entire frame, with curving red bone spikes emerging at his joints and along his spine. His eyes were made of hatred and fire, like looking into a black hole with a crimson event horizon, and seemed further back in his head than they should have been. Stopping once he reached my trembling self, the monster house opened his enormous jaws to reveal a salivating mouth encrusted with row after row of serrated shark's teeth. Black fumes escaped his throat and billowed up either side of his face.

Looking down at me, he smiled. Row after row of flesh shredders lined together like a morbid puzzle. I peed a lot. There was a blur of teeth that clamped around my entire body, and I screamed like a girl.

Chapter 10

IRELAND, 1480

I drifted in a familiar ocean of absolute nothingness for what felt like days, and then weeks. The expectation of seeing either of the dots appear at polar opposites of existence became my every thought. It hadn't taken this long last time, and I was positive that I was *more* dead on this go-around. I'd felt my entire body smolder into John ash. There was a distant thought among my growing panic; what had happened to my bones? Had they burned up and turned to dust? Or had they just bleached in the sun?

There was no need for sleep here, which meant I couldn't. There was only the constant hope for either doorway to eternity to open. Anything was better than this. Hell was a more desirable eternity than this...nothingness. A lake of fire forever seemed like a warm, relaxing bath right now. Wait, what if Hell was custom-made per its denizen's worst fears, and this was mine? Was this Hell?

Madness started to creep into my mind, until something grabbed my heart and pulled me through the vast expanse of oblivion.

With a hand on my exposed ribcage, Ulric held me down as my soul slammed into my ashen body.

Pain welcomed me as Ulric leaned over me with an exposed, bleeding palm dripping precious blood into my mouth. The blood brought vigorous, supernaturally powered healing properties that gave life back to my barren body. As the nerves cultivated and grew, so too did the agony.

It started down my spine and expanded down my boney legs. My instinct was to gasp as the brand-new exposed nerves came alive, but I didn't have any lungs to suck in the air.

My head rocked back and forth as I flirted with unconsciousness, black dots swirling in my vision like a swarm. Ulric grabbed my mud-caked forehead with his other hand and forcefully held it in place, allowing the blood to reach its target.

Once the length of my body had been reached, the nerves multiplied like lightning bolts forking over my ribcage. The black dots in my vision grew until there was a single blackness where I no longer felt the pain.

My head was knocked to the side with a deafening thud. The swarm diminished, and I saw Ulric as he reared back again and slapped me, hard. I could hear him speaking to me, but I might as well have had cotton balls in my ears. Another head smack and my ears opened up. I caught the end of what he was saying, "...learn a lesson."

My eyes focused and I raised my neck—which I was vaguely surprised I could even do—and saw that my entire body was comprised of raw, unprotected meat. Patches of skin started growing sporadically and connected over the exposed muscles, organs, and bones.

Ulric licked his palm and let the wound close. He stood and watched as my skin grew. I noticed his skin was pale and his eyes were sunken.

"How clever you are, John, to have covered your head," Ulric said weakly.

"What...what happened?" I managed to ask as my body finished the repair process by growing hair. I instinctively reached down and felt my Little John. I closed my eyes and sighed in relief.

"You learned a lesson, by dying," Ulric stated flatly. "The sun burns our essence," he said while looking me up and down, admiring his handiwork. "Luckily, you were not too far gone and were able to return to this life."

"You said we were immortal!" I exclaimed, realizing I was now naked.

"I did, indeed. However, there are rules and limitations that one must adhere to in order to survive the centuries. Rule one, find a resting place before the sun rises. The ground is the most viable, but deep caves also work; and I do mean deep. You would not enjoy getting caught in a shallow cave where the light bounces off the walls and burns you from every direction."

"What about houses?" I asked.

"Think about your home. Is there anywhere, even in the cellar, where light cannot find?" he asked.

Looking down, I remembered how I had watched the commander attack my father through a crack in the stone. I shook my head once.

"I thought not. We are vulnerable in the light. Day saps us of our strength and reduces us to helpless sheep," Ulric said with a touch of disgust.

I lifted myself up on my elbows and examined my body. After a moment, I looked up at him and asked, "What happened to me? It felt like I was burned alive."

"You were, in a manner of speaking," Ulric said. "The sun cleanses the world of most magic, which is now infused within you. You only survived because you protected what cannot be replaced."

"My...head?" I asked.

"You are more than your head, John. It is what is inside that makes you who you are. If only your head had been burned and I brought you back, you wouldn't be you anymore. You'd be a newborn child in a dangerous body."

"So, I'd be dead?" I asked.

"Well, undead, actually," Ulric informed, glancing at his fingernails and cleaning out the dirt underneath one by one. "But yes, who you are now would no longer exist. Now then," he continued, "it's time for both of us to feed. If I remember correctly, and I always do, there is a small farm nearby." He started walking due north.

"A farm? What are we going to feed on?" I asked, fearing the answer.

"Oh, John," he said, stopping to turn and look at me. "You cannot afford to be so naïve. The sooner you leave your mortality behind, the easier things will become."

"But they are innocent!" I protested getting to my feet.

"They are food. Plus, you are naked," Ulric said flatly.

I looked in his eyes for any semblance of weakness in his resolve. There wasn't any that I could see, and it frightened me. I threw out exactly what I was feeling in hopes that he would relent.

Breathing heavily, I tilted my head downward while my eyes remained locked on his and said, "My family was innocent, Ulric. I will not harm the weak."

"You will do as I command, boy!" Ulric strode over to me, voice booming and eyes blazing. His eyes were a shade of purple that was shifting to a crimson red. It was mesmerizing.

With no leverage, I threw out the first thing that came to mind. "You want a companion, right? Someone to share your time with that understands how today's world works?" I reached.

At this, the intensity in his eyes diminished a tad. Though he didn't respond, his demeanor suggested his willingness to listen.

"Let's make a deal. I'll do whatever you ask and be your companion. All I ask in return is that we feed on those who have earned our attention," I pleaded.

His eyes slowly returned to their original color as he pondered.

I continued, feeling more confident. "You have nothing to lose with this, and everything to gain."

His gaze shifted to the scenery around us, and he put one hand on his chin in deep contemplation.

"I am not used to opposition, John. But your bargain is acceptable. You will do whatever I ask and be by my side, teaching me as I teach you. In return, we will feed on...*bad* men." He took a breath between the last words and put emphasis on bad.

He continued before I could ask him why. "Now then, let us find something around the camp indicating other locales." With that, he strode back in the opposite direction of the farm.

I took a deep breath and exhaled, relieved to have saved an innocent family from a fate they didn't deserve. I ran to catch up to him, praying we would find any information—and pants. I was hungry, and naked.

Chapter 11

PRESENT DAY

I screamed and jerked my body awake, slamming headfirst into the top of my coffin. The darkness of my sleeping chamber was then illuminated by floating stars from the impact. I felt like a Looney Toons character.

"Lilith damn it!" I exclaimed as I rubbed my forehead. With my free hand, I flipped the switch to open the coffin and turn on the lights. I was aware of a warm liquid dripping down my face. It had apparently already reached my crotch and soaked through.

Still holding my forehead, I pulled my hand away to see that I indeed would be adding my sheets and shirt to the dry-cleaning bill. Looking down I saw that there was no red on my pants.

Asking no one, I said in my best Keanu impression, "If you pee in the matrix, do you pee here?"

Da floated into the room and asked in alarm, "What is all the screaming about?! Why are you bloody bleeding?"

"I told you to knock, Mom! I could have been...you know...watching *My Little Pony* or something."

"I'm sure. However, the question still warrants an answer. Why were you screaming, and why are you bleeding?" he asked with narrowing eyes.

"I had a daymare and slammed my noggin on the feckin' iron lid," I explained, wincing in pain. An Irish expletive snuck into my phrasing as I temporarily lost focus on my accent.

"That won't heal for some time, then. That is the double-edged sword you swing when creating a sleeping chamber made from a material that cancels all magic. I'll get the superglue," he said as he floated off to wherever we kept the glue, duct tape, and spare batteries.

After a few moments, he returned with some paper towels, Elmer's Glue, and a smile.

My eyes kept switching between the glue and him; I made sure to convey my annoyance visually.

"It was the only adhesive we had, John," he explained as if telling a child why he had to wear the pink Band-Aid.

"Why do we even have Elmer's Glue? Did you make me a popsicle stick house for my birthday?" I mocked.

"One of us purchased the item in question. Would you like to guess as to whom that was? A five-inch ang—"

"Faerie," I interrupted.

He continued, "Or a mostly average-looking blood bag able to walk among humans without causing a commotion." He looked at me with eyes that accused as much as any finger could have.

After some dabbing of the excess blood and pinching my forehead together, he was able to get the glue to keep the wound closed.

I stood and walked to the bathroom, flipped on the light, and stared into the mirror. The hardening white glue was lying horizontally across my forehead and dripping down a little.

"I look like Ben Stiller just said, 'There's something about John.'"

"Your power of illustration never ceases to amaze me," he sarcastically replied.

"I read at a fourth-grade level," I said.

"Quite. Now, if you'll excuse me, I have business elsewhere. Do return the items to the utility drawer, if you would," he said before winking out of this plane before I could retort.

I strode over to where the paper towel roll and children's glue lay, picked them up, thought about squeezing the cow's face until it exploded, decided the cleanup wouldn't be worth it, and walked into the kitchen where the drawer was. I pulled the knob, sliding the drawer open and revealing batteries, scissors, paper clips, and a tub of clear superglue. The cow's gooey insides exploded through my clenched fists.

Chapter 12

IRELAND, 1480

After rummaging through the soldiers' sleeping quarters, I came across a chest filled with clothes that mostly fit me. After I slipped on the boots, I stood up and walked outside to where my mother was still in her bronze prison.

I stood in front of the bull positioned over the smoldering ashes. My arms became heavy as I told them to reach for the latch on the side. All I could do was stare.

Ulric walked up beside me, grasping the situation. "Leave her, John. She's gone, and there's nothing you can do."

"She deserves a proper burial." Tears stung my eyes. "As does my father."

Ulric seemed puzzled at the impracticality, but understood he hadn't experienced the loss of a family member in several lifetimes. It was all a distant memory from when he had been mortal. But he did recognize a man who was determined, and decided it was best to help in order to continue on with the mission.

I willed my hands to undo the latch that kept my mother imprisoned in her tomb. The door swung open, and the smell of charred flesh and hair wafted heavily into my face, adding insult to injury.

"They must have closed the latch whenever they heard us," Ulric said contemplatively. He was still weak from giving me most of his life essence.

There she was, lying on her side, her dress plastered onto her body and one clawed hand reaching up the neck of the bull. All her nails had been broken off as she had desperately scratched at the metal. Dried blood streaked all along the inside in four-line patterns.

The heat had completely dried out her skin, etching a look of horror and anguish on her face as the flesh shrunk, revealing bare teeth and bulging red eyes. Dried blood ran down her cheeks where capillaries had burst in her sockets. The cords in her neck were prominently displayed through paper-thin skin.

I reached in and cradled my mother, who was stiff from lack of moisture in the body. I walked her over to a spot in the grass and laid her down. My hands moved to her eyelids and tried to close them. The now brittle flesh remained shrunk into her sockets. Her once beautiful, loving eyes remained staring, wide and horrified. I ripped a piece of my shirt off at the bottom and laid it across her eyes.

After a quick search, we located my father in a locked room. As I effortlessly burst through the lock, a gasp stole my voice at the sight of him strapped to the table with his intestines strung up above him through a hole in his stomach. The significance of seeing my father's unmoving body grew exponentially in my chest. I kept expecting him to turn his head and tell me he was fine, and that he had tricked his captors into thinking he had died an excruciating death.

But my father, who had always been the example of the man I wanted to be, didn't move. His head remained motionless. There was no rise and fall of his chest. Life had left his body long ago, leaving behind an empty, mortal shell.

Ulric placed his hand on my shoulder, not apologizing for my loss, but not rushing me either. The gesture brought me back to the now. I shook my head to clear the daze and stepped to the table.

After unwinding his innards, I pushed them back into his cavity the best I could before picking him up with one arm under his shoulders and the other supporting the back of his knees. Ulric moved to help.

"No. I need to do this," I told him. Ulric nodded his head, not saying anything.

I laid my father on the cool, evening grass next to my mother. I stood upright and looked at them both.

"They didn't deserve this," I said, mostly to myself.

"You will avenge them, John," Ulric comforted.

I dropped to my knees next to my mother and father, and started digging in the earth. Ulric stood over, watching in placation.

After several minutes, I buried both of my parents. I stood over their mounds, closed my eyes, and said an old Irish prayer under my breath. My father had taught it to me as a child, and it seemed fitting.

Once the prayer was complete and a few moments had passed, Ulric said, "John, it is time. We must feed this night."

I nodded slowly in agreement, not only because I was feeling the pull of the thirst, but because I wanted to make every single one of those cowards pay. If they swore loyalty to the commander, they were mine.

A quick search revealed a map used by messengers to deliver orders between camps. Ulric picked it up, glanced at it for a fraction of a second, and then let it drop to the ground.

"Quickly now," he said. "I am famished."

"Wait!" I exclaimed, picking up the map. "Don't you need this?"

He stopped in his tracks and took a deep breath in frustration. He turned, not accustomed to having to explain himself, and said, "Look at the paper, John."

I did as he commanded.

"Now take it in. Open your mind and etch it like a chisel on stone," he said.

I stared at the paper, squinting.

"Not like that," Ulric said. "Don't force it. Let it into your mind."

"How?" I asked frustrated, letting my hands drop to my sides.

He walked to me, grabbed my wrists, and lifted my hands so the paper was in front of me again.

"Don't *try* to etch it into your memory. Just *let* it," he said. His lips were cracked.

I closed my eyes, took a deep breath, and held it. After a few moments, I exhaled and opened my eyes, not staring at any specific spot. The ink jumped off the paper, and I could feel a pressure behind my eyes, as if a storm were on the horizon. After an instance, it was gone.

I dropped the paper and rubbed my eyes, "What was that?" I asked.

"It will feel a little unusual at first. You will grow used to it," Ulric replied. "Can you tell me where the nearest camp is?"

With my eyes still closed, I focused in finding the map floating in my memory. It was easy to become lost, as my capacity for storage had been a house before I met Ulric and now was an entire village, with houses, shops, and even castles.

I located the map, and could read it as if it were in my hands.

"Due west. A little over a two-day walk," I said as if in a trance.

"Night, not day," Ulric corrected before he clapped his hands in excitement and said, "Excellent. She chose wisely indeed."

I found the exit in my brain and returned to the reins of my mind. Opening my eyes, I asked, "Who?"

"Not for you to know, yet. Now, let's go if we are to make it to the next camp before midnight."

"Before midnight? But it's a two-*night* walk!" I protested, changing my vernacular accordingly.

Now it was Ulric's turn to rub his eyes, "Must you question my every command, John?"

"Yes," I said. "How else am I to learn?"

"Trust in your teacher. Follow," he said, turning and walking out the door.

Outside he said, "Orient on the camp using the stars."

"That will be easy. My father taught me..." I trailed off then whispered, "My father..." My hands curled into fists and my jaw clenched. Something was happening to my eyes. The trees around me grew sharper, becoming their own separate beings rather than one wooded landscape. Insects flying around the camp became visible. The smell of decaying bodies was picked up by my nose, and the smell of burnt flesh.

"Control it, John," Ulric said, "or the bloodlust will control you."

I felt like I was standing on the edge of a steep cliff, and if I missed a step, I wouldn't be able to control my descent. I took in a deep breath and closed my eyes. I focused on my emotions and forced myself to calm down. In my mind, I was lying in a field on a cool spring night, staring into the stars. They passed overhead as thick as clouds and promised all sorts of secrets.

When I opened my eyes, everything was back to normal. The woods became one again, and the smell diminished to an afterthought.

I started walking in the direction of the next camp.

"Make haste!" Ulric said.

I started jogging, and then running. Soon I was at a full sprint. At the precipice between mortal and supernatural speed, I willed my legs to move even quicker. Before I realized how fast I was going, we were through the clearing and at the tree line. Refusing to break speed, I weaved between the trees and undergrowth in the direction of my next meal.

A couple branches caught my clothing and face, but I held fast, letting my resolve guide me. I gave up part of the reins to my PS, who helped keep me on track.

We were through another clearing when I checked my mental map again. I shifted course slightly and continued. I was amazed that I wasn't tiring.

I could hear Ulric running alongside me, letting me guide the way.

"Now that we are through the trees," Ulric said, "I want you to leap through the clearing. Watch me."

With that, he started taking small jumps that built into complete bounds that propelled him farther than even I could run. I followed suit. After a few shorter jumps, I started leaping greater distances. After a few moments I even passed Ulric, who was smiling. My head turned to watch him, impressed that I had overtaken him, and was greeted by a giant tree that obviously needed a hug.

My momentum was abruptly brought to a halt, and I felt my ribs crack.

Damn it, PS, I thought to my other self. I was met with a mental shrug.

Ulric stopped just before where I was now a part of the tree and started laughing maniacally.

"Oh, Lilith! Always be aware of your surroundings, John," he managed between heaves of laughter.

I murmured something under my breath about where I'd like to stick this tree on Ulric's person, then tried to pull myself free.

I inhaled sharply when I moved as white sheets of pain shot outward from my ribs. I cried out in pain, which caused another bolt of lightning to explode from my jaw. Confused, I tried to bite down and was not-so-pleasantly surprised to discover my upper and lower teeth no longer aligned.

Ulric fell onto his backside, laughing up a storm. I delicately pushed myself back using my arms and fell to the ground, where a squeak of pain escaped my lips.

Ulric couldn't take it anymore and went fully on his back, kicking and punching the air while tears streamed down his face from uncontrollable laughter.

"I've..." Ulric said between heaves of mirth, "I've seen plays held for kings and queens with the most decorated thespians across the lands, and *nothing* was as amusing as you! Oh, I clearly made the right decision with you, John."

My ribs started to repair themselves with audible cracks. I forced my tender jaw back into place until the tendons healed themselves. Once able, I said, "Glad I could entertain you, sire. Might I wear a jester's hat during my next performance?" I stood up and bowed.

He clapped in excitement, "Oh, Lilith! Yes, please!" he said, delighted.

"Shall we continue, ma'lord?" I asked, then added, "And who's Lilith?"

Ulric sighed, disappointed the laughing session was over, and waved his hand, dismissing my last question. Wiping a tear from his eye, he replied, "You are right, of course. You lead." He stifled a laugh at the end.

We ran for a few more hours without incident. A little past midnight, we made it to the camp.

Chapter 13

PRESENT DAY

I ron cut closed, it was time to head to the only person who would probably help me: Depweg. He was my werewolf friend, and was basically my complete opposite in every respect: lived aboveground, could discern good from evil without a second thought, didn't make it a habit to piss everyone off with his Oscar-winning wit, didn't have a beard, and had friends who weren't faeries that didn't believe in faeries.

Deppyweg, as I enjoyed calling him, lived several miles outside of town, on the country road going toward the one K-Mart town of Lufkin. Given the distance, I chose to drive rather than sprint the entire way and get covered with dead bugs. Ulric had told me of ancient vampires who had had the ability to fly wherever they wanted. I'd tried on several occasions, but the energy needed damn near caused a blackout after only a few seconds. So, the Kia would do.

Before you say anything, my Kia has been good to me. It even has a turbo, which means it goes fast with less gas, I think. I don't really know, but it sounds cool. *Turbo.*

I walked to the nearby storage facility where I kept my pearl-white Optima and hopped in. As I pushed the start button, I was met with the beautiful sounds of Mastodon's latest album. I threw "Mortis" into drive and pulled out of my storage box. A quick focus of mind and the big metal door shut behind me. No need to lock it, as my steed was the only thing I kept in there. I pulled out onto the road and started my journey while belting out lyrics enthusiastically.

Along the way, I was met with drones who got off work late or families who had just eaten, all of whom were too tired or full to push on the gas pedal. I cursed under my breath as these zombies went under the speed limit on a two-way, two-lane road. I would catch myself about to ask the rubber on their tires to just kind of stop being so darn dense and let the problem take care of itself. But each time I even started to think about it, I pictured Papa T with his arms crossed and a disapproving scowl creasing his forehead. So instead, I said through gritted teeth my relaxation chant, "Three, two, one, one, two, three, what the heck is bothering me?"

"What *is* bothering you, Jonathan?" A silky woman's voice purred next to me.

I swerved hard into oncoming traffic and overcorrected back into my lane and then onto the shoulder, where I drifted in a full circle. Baffled faces briefly lit up and passed into view from the other cars that had been in the cavalcade behind me due to the slow drivers. We finished the spin and faced forward again, with half the car on the shoulder and the other half in the dirt and grass. Honks and high-beam headlights angrily passed by, making sure I knew I was, in fact, a complete idiot.

Relaxing my death grip on the wheel and putting Mortis in park, I slowly turned my head to face Lily. She was one of the Fae High Court patrons, and a not-so-secret admirer of yours truly. More like a demanding admirer. Women, am I right?

"It's just John!" I spit out, nerves dancing under my skin and hairs on end.

She sat in the passenger seat with her curly blonde hair that touched the middle of her back. Tonight's attire consisted of yoga pants—which she *knew* were one of my weaknesses, like Superman's green rock—and a tight athletic top complete with small straps that revealed toned arms and firm breasts. I audibly gulped.

Light blue eyes that were almost white were gazing into mine, and her smell wafted up my nose like a cartoon hand beckoning me to completely zone out of the rest of the world. It was just us sitting in the middle of nowhere, with her scent and eyes holding me captive. My pants became uncomfortably tight.

"Maybe later, John," she purred as she glanced at my super manly and impressive monster of a bulge. "The little guy can wait." Zing!

Clearing my throat, I shifted in my seat and, as casually as possible, pulled on the fabric of my jeans to make things a tad more comfortable.

"Lily, what a pleasant surprise! What can I do you for?" I asked playfully.

"Well, Jo—"

"'Cause I only have like five bucks," I mocked as I pulled some ones out of my front pocket.

The money burst into little flames which grew into tiny devils that started dancing on my palm. Suggestively, I might add. Once they started performing R-rated acts on one another, I shifted my eyes to Lily and closed my hand. Tiny screams escaped as my fingers tightened.

"Nice touch," I said. "Can I return the favor?"

"Touching comes later, maybe. But first, to business, Jonathan," she purred.

"Who's this clearly attractive and buff Jonathan fellow? I keep getting mistaken for him," I said, rolling my eyes. She smirked, saying nothing. "Look, I'm on my way to a friend, so can we hurry this up, please?"

"You sure are far from home, John. Why so far?" she asked cutely.

"I need help building my new IKEA bedroom set," I said sarcastically. "The picture shows a frowny face if you only have one person."

Her smell let go of my mind, and her eyes shifted to a darker, ocean blue. "You are going to need more help than what your dog can provide," she said with impatience seeping into her voice.

I sat stunned. A dark lump formed in the pit of my gut. "Help? It's...just IKEA," I said lamely.

"How are your dreams lately, lover? Anything unusual?" Her voice returned to normal, and she began putting on shiny clear lip gloss using the visor mirror.

"H-How...?" I stammered, like an idiot. I felt as exposed as a teenage boy whose mom walked in and asked about all the tissues on the ground.

"Lucky guess," she cooed while capping her lip gloss and turning to me. "You need my help."

"I don't want the help of the Fae. I know the strings that shit comes with. You could make the Eiffel Tower with those," I said while pantomiming making shapes with invisible strings between my fingers and open hands. "What do you even care? Your plane wouldn't be affected."

"I like it here, John. Plus, I have vested interests that pay dividends, giving me an advantage where needed." She had manifested a small file and was giving her perfect nails a good once over, checking them in the visor light. "I ask nothing in return, as this would be mutually beneficial," she placed her hand on my inner thigh, "for both of us."

I coughed into my hand, "Bullshit! Oh dear, excuse me. Must be the pine, from the trees." I looked through the windshield and squinted into the darkness at the trees lining both sides of the road barely visible in the sporadic yellow streetlights.

"Bless you. And no, there is nothing that comes attached with my help. We want the same things here, and it would behoove us to work in unison." Her hand slid further up, a fraction of an inch away from where mini-me lay ready for action. Concentrating, I willed the blood out of my member, letting him noticeably draw back to safety.

She pursed her lips and furrowed her brow in faux disappointment and said, "Oh, boo. You're no fun." She smiled, changing her eye color back to seduction and releasing her pheromones, rendering me completely in her power. Part of me was standing straight up as I sat in the driver's seat, rushing to her hand like a puppy running to meet its owner at the door. As soon as I reached her fingers, she thumped me *hard* and laughed. I gasped in jolted pain. With laughter lingering in the air, she vanished into a singularity that caused a deafening sonic boom, blowing out my windows and cracking the windshield into a massive spiderweb.

Covered in broken glass and holding my throbbing wiener dog, all I could do was mutter, "I *hate* blue balls."

With my left hand holding my crotch, I threw the gears into drive with my right and grabbed the steering wheel, pulling from the shoulder and back onto the main road.

Still using my right hand, because I had priorities, I let go of the wheel and let my knee do the steering. I reached for my phone and Yelped a glass repair place in the vicinity. Last thing I needed was to get pulled over and have to answer stupid questions that were being recorded and uploaded to a central police station.

After a few minutes, I found Ed's Auto Repair and Tanning Salon. I followed the directions and arrived just after 8:00 p.m. to a worn parking lot where the painted parking spots had long since vanished. After looking at the sign for a few moments in disbelief and mouthing the words "tanning salon," I parked and went inside to talk to an orange man with a toothpick between his teeth named, you guessed it.

"Ed, I'm ecstatic that you escaped Wonka." Handing the still smiling man my keys, I finished with, "Replace all the glass by dawn and I'll double your fee."

He looked at my forehead for a moment, moved the toothpick around in his mouth, and asked, "Boy, the hell is on your forehead? You one of them queers from the rest stop up the way?"

I played along and added a lisp, "Oh yes, sweetie. We decided to fool the cops and started meeting at 8:00 p.m. for our wild sex orgies rather than 3:00 a.m. Keeps them Honey Buns on their toes."

Still smiling, he grabbed the keys and said, "A funny guy, huh? Welp, dawn's gonna take more than a normal fee. Might I suggest..."

After our business was done, I walked outside and stopped when I reached the edge of the dilapidated parking lot.

Looking down at the ground with a wrinkled brow, I asked no one in particular, "The fuck am I supposed to do with five years of prepaid *premium* tanning?"

I was just lucky that the tanning part of his entrepreneurship kept him open past the usual five or six of most repair places I'd found on my phone.

Night was fully upon us now, and the road was mostly empty, everyone having already returned home from their nine-to-five jobs. I chuckled to myself at the palpable irony of there being no traffic after I dropped my car off. With a deep breath and squinted eyes, I turned and started bounding down the highway toward Depweg's.

It only took a few leaps before a giant, juicy bug exploded in my face as I ran at a pace that made the few cars on the road seem like they were parked. Blinded by guts of the gargantuan insect, I missed my footing and tumbled to the ground, bouncing off a tractor trailer and rebounding into the trees, breaking several in a line before having an ancient motherfucker break my warp-speed tumble. An upside-down, me-sized imprint had been created on the beast, which I was currently stuck in.

"Could this night get any worse?" I tried to ask of the universe. My face was now a part of the wood. In response to the question, my legs started peeling away from the tree, like one of those sticky hands children play with for five minutes before they get coated in dirt.

As I started to reach the point of no return, I just said to myself what Bill Cosby said to his dates, "Just let it happen, Jell-O," and fell to the ground, which was considerably farther than I'd thought.

Landing with an "oomph" and with my face in the dirt, I mumbled, "Anything else?" At that, the tree started to crack where I had violated its virgin bark. That prompted me to quickly get to my feet and back away, yelling into the sky, "I *get it!* Lilith, I *hate* trees!"

With a sparkle of hope, I said out loud, "Can this night get any better?" The tree snapped at the impact site and started falling in my direction.

"That...is...it..." I jumped at the descending goliath and screamed, "*Hadoken*" and punched it with all my rage, causing an explosion of toothpicks to rain from above.

For good measure, I landed on the ground next to the remaining tree stump, which still had a considerable amount of tree left on it extending up twenty feet or so, and swiped my hand right through it like a white-hot spoon through ice cream. The tree started falling over, and as it did, I whispered, "Now you might feel some pressure, so take a deep breath," before shoving my fist up the stump. "Now cough."

With my arm up the ass of the insolent tree, I forced energy from my hand, through the center, and up its length in a small circle a few inches in diameter. With a snap of my focus, the tree exploded around the energy, leaving only a sliver of smooth wood in the shape of a staff about five feet in length.

I admired my revenge/handiwork as I twirled the staff around me, kung fu style. After holding one of my supersexy poses, I noticed I was covered in tree guts in the form of toothpicks. Stabbing the staff into the ground, I started raking my hands up and down my sleeves, torso, head, and legs. Pulling the staff out of the ground, I used it to wipe at my back where I couldn't reach. After inspecting that I was good to go, I spit in the tree's general direction and then oriented myself back toward the road by using the path I had created.

Back on the road, I ignored the pulled over semi whose driver was examining the damage from some unknown animal. Before he had the chance to turn around and see me emerging from the woods, I started sprinting through the night air again—*this time* spinning the staff in front of me like a propeller. It didn't take long before I started to feel and hear the smashing of bugs. I smiled—and was immediately rewarded with a bukkake of bug limbs. I kept smiling my grim smile.

Within a short period, I closed the rest of the distance to the dirt road turnoff that led to Depweg's cabin in the woods. He owned a large lot that he had purchased long ago, at least two hundred acres, that he kept stocked with all kinds of wildlife, especially deer. At the front of his dirt road was a sign that read *Canine Haven* hanging over the iron gate. Depweg ran a shelter for hopeless dogs that were unadoptable due to a various number of reasons. It was a great tax write-off as well as a big help for his fellow canines. Though I really thought a loup-garou—or "werwolf," the German term that Depweg preferred—was as distant from canines as humans were from primates.

Leaping the iron fence, I started my quiet descent into the thickening woods toward his cabin, leaving the staff at the gate to await my return. No dogs had smelled or noticed me yet, which meant the game was on.

His cabin had been handmade by him using the wood he had cleared as well as moss, mud, and other all-natural items to insulate. He'd even built his own solar panels and attached them to a battery system he had rigged. Off to the side was a rainwater collection and filtration system that he "used for the dogs," according to his tax records. His carbon footprint was in the resounding negative when it came to treating nature with respect.

I landed on his brick chimney and stuck my ear close to the hole, trying to hear inside. It sounded like he was in the kitchen using utensils in preparation for a meal. I couldn't wait to see his face when I snuck up on him.

I silently slid down to the ground level, careful not to disturb the sleeping dogs in their endless row of kennels just a handful of yards away from his back door. I could hear a few of them having dreams that leaked into reality as they whimpered and half barked between closed jaws. One of the closest kennels held a pit bull terrier that woke itself up from a dream and looked around, startled. I shrunk back into the darkness provided by the roofline and stayed still as it turned its head right at me. I couldn't see its eyes from the distance, but I knew he was looking at me. He yawned with gleaming white fangs shining in the darkness, and laid his head down on his front paws. After a moment, his breathing became snores. I sighed in relief.

Tiptoeing, I made my way to the open window of the kitchen, where I ever so slowly peeked in with one eye. I could smell he was close.

If only I could have seen my face as a wooden chopstick was driven into my exposed eyeball with enough inertia to throw me on my ass with a loud, "Oomph," grasping at the utensil. Every dog on the property immediately started to bark and howl at the intruder.

I pulled at the chopstick but stopped when I felt my orb start to slide precariously out of its socket. I relented and asked, "How? I was so quiet this time!"

"The wind gave you away as you moved preternaturally down my driveway. To my ears, you might as well have had bells and whistles on while operatically singing *Carmen*," he said casually as he wiped my blood from his hands before continuing his meal prep. "And what's on your forehead? Did Ben Stil—"

"Stiller, yeah, yeah. I already made that joke," I said.

Standing up, I dusted my pants off and sauntered to the window. I climbed in and walked to the microwave, where I could see that the chopstick was a bull's-eye on my pupil. As I looked back and forth, the stick moved with my gaze. Up, down, left, and right. "Neat," I said before placing one hand over my eye with the accessory sticking out between my middle and ring finger. With my free hand, I grabbed and pulled quickly, the hand over my eye keeping it in the socket.

Before you ask, vampires do have a reflection with modern mirrors. The only reason why this is considered canon is due to the fact that mirrors used to be made with silver, which, like iron, cancels supernatural properties.

I placed my head on Depweg's left shoulder to see what he was making, and as he turned his head, my right hand went over his right shoulder and dropped the chopstick over his ingredients. Without missing a beat, he caught it and tried to stab my other eye, but I was too quick for him and my head was already on his other shoulder. He stabbed air and sighed as I gave him a quick peck on the neck. He turned his head back to the right and I was already sitting in his chair rubbing my eye, which was knitting itself back together.

"So, what's for dinner? Kibbles and bits of people?" I jested.

"Fresh venison. Blue rare," he responded while turning his attention back to his prep station. He had homegrown veggies on a wok above a wood stove that filled the air with spices. "Why are you here, John?" he asked directly.

"What? I can't come by for a friendly visit with my best friend Deppyweg?" I asked in mock surprise.

"Only friend," he corrected. "You never just come by without an agenda, so spit it out."

"Okay, Dad." I took in a deep breath, held it, and said while releasing, "There might be an apocalypse coming that will destroy this plane along with Heaven and/or Hell, and

I'm just trying to get a few extra superspecial people together to prevent the end of days, like Arnold in...*End of Days*." I dramatically sucked in another lungful of air and finished with, "So you in?"

The question lingered in the air as Depweg added his meat to the wok.

After he flipped the meat, searing it on both sides before sliding it onto a plate, he asked with his back still to me, "What have you done?"

"*Moi*? Done something?" My voice went higher in pitch at the end of the question.

He turned, holding his plate of ultra rare meat, and walked over to his homemade leather recliner. "With this nose comes the ability to smell bullshit," he said while cutting into his tender deer.

"Alright, alright. You know how I've been helping Father Philseep, right? Taking out cults trying to summon demons, stopping certain unsavory characters from coming into power, rescuing kittens from trees...I mean dogs. Cute little puppers."

"The point, please," he casually urged while taking another bite.

"I..." I began, but was interrupted by a tugging at my pant leg. I looked down at my favorite of Depweg's rejects. Tiny Tim was a miniature short-haired shepherd with gimp rear legs. Depweg had manufactured a makeshift wheelchair to support his lower body, allowing his front legs to pull him around. For this reason, Depweg kept him in the house so he wouldn't have to traverse the lush grass.

Immediately, I picked him up and placed him on my lap, asking in the typical this-is-the-cutest-dog-in-the-whole-wide-world voice, "Oh my goodness, who's a good boy? Who's a good boy? It's you! Yes, it is!"

Timmy responded by wagging his tail as hard as he could and scrambling with his front paws to move up to my face. I helped pull him up and was met with a barrage of puppy kisses.

"Make sure he gets your teeth," said Depweg.

Turning my head slowly toward where he sat, I produced my most creepy, toothy smile, full of dead bug parts. "Do you have a toothpick by chance?" I asked, still showing the graveyard.

After picking the last remnants of what had to be an entire generation of insects, I explained the situation in detail. Tim rested in my lap, and I stroked his head and back absently. After a few hours, all was laid out. At the end, I asked Depweg directly, "Look, no bullshit, this is big, and there's no one else I trust to have my back. Can I count on you or what, man?"

He had finished eating and had set the plate on the coffee table in front of us. He slid forward on the edge of his chair, looked me right in the eyes, and said with full sincerity, "You know I've always had your back, John. Even if it wasn't to stop the apocalypse, I'd still have your six. You are just too proud to ask."

"Thanks, man," I whispered while staring at the place where Tiny Tim was asleep on my lap, too embarrassed to look up at him.

We spent the better part of the night coming up with a game plan, utilizing his military expertise. He even gave me a Glock .45 ACP with a spare magazine filled with hollow points that had a resin shot with silver and iron pellets at their core. This would create problems for any supe that was hit. The bullet would impact and mushroom, sending the pellets into the body to ricochet around. The wounds would not heal, and they would more than likely bleed to death. A heart or head shot meant insta-death for most supes.

Depweg also gave me a ballistic vest infused with iron to help shield from magical attacks, both physical and energy based. I gulped at the magnitude of the situation as it started weighing on my guts. Like Martin Lawrence said in *Bad Boys*, "Shit just got real."

"The irony of a werewolf having silver bullets is palpable, you realize?" I asked.

"No more than a mortal owning, well, *any* gun," he responded matter-of-factly.

"Point, match, Depweg."

"Well, it is time to feed the dogs. Might I suggest..." Depweg started.

"Yeah, yeah. I'll leave before you release the hounds. I know how they love supes like me." I set Tim down on the ground and then squatted next to where my buddy was whining, "Except Tiny Tim here. He's my bestest friend, yes he is!" My hand was attacked with puppy kisses and little nips here and there. "Okay, boy, I gotta go now. Be a good puppers for me, okay?" He yipped in agreement. I scratched him behind the ears and leaned down to kiss his head one last time before standing up.

"Welp, time to make like a tree and get the fuck outta here," I said.

"Was good seeing you, John," Depweg bid farewell.

After slinging the backpack Depweg had given me with the armor and Glock, I made my way out the front door and back to the gate where my bug propeller awaited. Picking it up, my hand was met with bug parts that had become one with the wood. I dropped it on the ground and rolled it in the damp early morning grass before picking it back up and starting my way back to my car.

Chapter 14

IRELAND, 1480

The camp was fortified with a wall and sentry posts complete with guards wielding bows. The grounds were adequately lit with torches spread out along the perimeter.

I started moving out of the tree line and down a hill to the camp when Ulric placed a hand on my shoulder, stopping me.

"How many do you see, John?" Ulric asked.

"I can't tell," I said. "Only a few in the sentry posts."

"Use your sight," he said.

"How?" I asked.

"Do you think your father cried out in his final moments?" Ulric asked, looking down to casually adjust his clothing.

The disrespect of his comment and nonchalant attitude with which he had asked made me freeze with rage. PS grabbed both reins. My eyes focused and ears became attuned to the sounds around me. I could smell the oil from the torches and the sweat on their skins.

Ulric beamed at me. "Good, John. That is how it is done. You harness your emotion and use it as a weapon. Now," he pointed, "tell me how many you see down there."

With sheer will, I forced my gaze off him and looked down the hill. I could see the red, blurry outlines of men in their tents. In the stone buildings, I could only make out a small patch of warmth about two feet off the ground, then another three feet above that. I pointed at them and asked, "What are..."

Ulric interrupted, knowing what I was going to ask, "Men sleeping in their bunks close to the wall. I noticed this at the other camp. You will grow to become observant of such details."

"Can you see the others in the building?" I asked, intrigued.

"Unfortunately, no," he sighed, as if he had asked the same question when he was but a fledgling vampire. "However," he continued, "when near, I rely on my other senses. Come." He started down the hill, silent as an apparition. I followed.

He stopped at the bottom of one of the sentry posts and looked up, his eyes changing to predator red.

He climbed up the wood without a sound and hopped over the edge, where there was a gasp of surprise. I could hear the guard's heartbeat speed up in panic, then falter, and finally, stop.

Ulric jumped down and landed in a crouch, then stood up and wiped his mouth with a handkerchief he had removed from his inner coat pocket. His skin had plumped back up, and the rings around his eyes had diminished significantly. He must have drained the poor bastard completely before his heart had even thought about quitting.

"Now your turn," Ulric said as he pointed at the next corner of the compound. There was a renewed vigor in his words.

I ran along the wall just outside of the immediate light of the torches, and stopped at the bottom. I squinted up but couldn't see the outline. Ulric approached.

"This one must be empty," I said, and started walking to the next one.

"Wait," Ulric whispered. "Look again."

I stopped and looked up.

Ulric asked, "Why was your mother executed, I wonder? Seemed unnecessary."

My teeth clenched and then relaxed as I realized more and more what he was doing. I grabbed one rein and PS grabbed the other.

The red outline of a man sitting with his head propped on his knees came into view through the wooden planks. I could hear his snoring from below.

Ulric motioned for me to go.

I scaled the building easily and jumped over the ledge, catching my foot and falling on my face with an, "*Oomph!*"

The man quickly woke up, like a person who knew they weren't supposed to be sleeping on the job and their chief walked by. His eyes locked on mine, and he shot up to his feet and pulled out a sword, swinging it with both hands.

I was still recovering from my fall when the blade hit. All I could do was close my eyes and wait. There was a thud on my shoulder, followed by a yelp. I opened my eyes and looked up to see the blade had bounced off my shoulder and rebounded into the man's neck and chest.

"Take the blood before it goes to waste," Ulric whispered loudly from below.

I stood up and grabbed the sword, pulling it free. A torrent of blood erupted and streamed down his new chest cavity like a wild river. I put my hand on his chin and pushed it in the opposite direction of the cut in his neck, opening the wound more. I crouched down and let the blood flow into my mouth.

It was delectable. Energy flowed through my limbs, making my hairs stand on end. The man managed a sob before taking his last breath.

The blood continued to flow, though not as forcefully. I frowned in disappointment as the elation and power I felt faded to a whimper as the blood dripped from the dead man's corpse.

I let him drop to the ground and then hopped over the ledge, landing next to Ulric.

"Why—"

"Once the soul leaves the body, the blood is not as effective," Ulric said, again anticipating my question.

"Wait, are you saying we *eat* their souls?" I asked, mortified.

"I am not entirely sure, if I am to be honest. What I do know is we can feed and not kill, and the mortal appears fine after a few nights. There are even those who gladly provide us sustenance at our leisure," Ulric said.

"So, we don't have to kill anyone? Those men last night..."

"Do not attempt to go down that righteous path with me, fledgling," Ulric commanded firmly. "Even if you had not needed to feed on those soldiers, you would still have ended their existence with glee. Do you blame the fox for eating the chicken?"

"I—"

"No, you do not. Why is that? Because it is the way of things. We are vampires. They," he said, pointing to the camp, "are food."

"If there are those who willingly provide us with sustenance, what do they get in return?" I asked, intrigued.

Ulric calmed at the question and said, "Some do it for wealth. Others, protection. Still others want to be one of us, so a bargain is made. My taste was for those who wanted a rival to be killed. If their reason was greed and not something like vengeance, I would drink them dry instead. It was amusing." Ulric smiled as his eyes focused on nothing, reliving numerous memories inside the theater of his own mind.

I stood in silence looking at my mentor, assessing him. It felt as if I had been given a riddle to solve; but with each word in a different language or missing entirely.

"I grow tired of this cloak-and-daggers game." Ulric looked at me, smiled, and said, "For my next trick..." and clapped his hands together. Every torch in the complex violently blew out one by one down the line. There was a shout of confusion somewhere in the camp as it was enveloped in darkness.

He jumped over the wall in one effortless leap and started casually walking through the camp. I followed. There was a stone structure with rows of tents just beyond. It was clear that this spot was chosen because of —what I hoped was—the abandoned building. It made me shudder to think a family might have been forced out, or worse.

We approached a wall with a red blur, and Ulric punched through the stone, pulling out a very dazed young man. His torso was the only thing exposed; his lower half remained inside the building. Ulric drained him quickly and then swiped his hand parallel to the wall, bisecting the man just above the waist.

"You cut here, John, because it allows the entrails to fall out." He threw the body up and over the roof; it landed in the center of the tent line. Organs came tumbling out with a sickening slosh.

Ulric raised one hand to his ear, closed his eyes, and waited. After a moment, we heard a tent rustling, followed by a gasp and then a scream of terror.

"There it is," Ulric purred, a smile creasing his face. He burst through the wall like it was made of sticks, and grabbed the cowering soldier on the top bunk by the neck as the bed fell to the ground. These men had to be barely of fighting age. Ulric turned with the boy clutching at his hands, desperate for air, and held him out for me.

"He," I started, "he's so young."

Ulric, on the verge of losing his patience, said to me flatly, "How many innocents has this boy murdered?"

"By command of their superior," I retorted.

"What do his victims think of his orders? They can't think, can they, John? They're *dead*," he said while stepping forward. The boy was turning purple. The capillaries in his eyes were bursting one at a time. "End his pain, John. Be his salvation and redemption."

The boy looked at me with crimson eyes and mouthed, "Please..." before falling unconscious. Ulric didn't let up on his grip.

I stood horrified looking at the boy with the purple face. My eyes moved past him and saw the anger growing on Ulric's face. He closed his fist completely, with the boy's neck still in his hand. The sound reminded me of a head of lettuce being struck with a mallet. Blood started pouring out of the child soldier's nose, eyes, and ears. His heart beat one last frantic beat, then stopped.

"Wasteful insolent fledgling!" Ulric screamed before throwing the boy through the opposite wall with a thunderous boom. The body rolled like a rag doll into the nearest tent. Stone tumbled with him.

Ulric looked at me and said forcefully, "If you do not obey, your parents will never know vengeance. Now, decide!"

He strode out into the center of the compound and started ripping soldiers apart as they approached, weapons drawn. All I could do was watch, frozen with indecision.

Ulric manifested two bloodswords from a time long since passed and began cutting and stabbing those who rushed him. With each thrust, I saw the soldiers' blood pass from their bodies to his. Ulric was laughing maniacally.

At one point, Ulric stopped mauling and laughing as he turned and looked at me. The soldiers continued to attack, swords bouncing off his impervious flesh.

I moved forward, letting my predatory self take control. Rather, I just gave up and let go of the reins, which PS grabbed with enthusiasm.

It was a beautiful dance. The soldiers played their part, chaotic and frantic, while Ulric and myself performed with grace and finesse. Blood splattered the ground like paint on a canvas. My hands were my brush, swiping through leather and armor like a scythe through wheat. My teeth pierced flesh as if taking a bite of warm cheese.

The cool air carried the steam from the mutilated corpses off the ground. Our bellies were full. My skin tingled with warmth and elation. A shudder rippled through my body as I exhaled, sending a plume of steam through the air.

Ulric looked at me approvingly. With the prey downed, my predatory self contently sauntered aside, letting me reluctantly take control again.

I fell to my knees, cupping my face with my hands.

"Oh, do not start now, John. You did so well!" Ulric said, pleading. "You are no longer a puppet to your human emotions. Realize this and cut the strings tying you to mortality. *Embrace* the freedom of eternity."

I let my hands drop to my lap and looked at him. Ultimately, he was right. The longer I fought, the harder it would be. These men were a means to an end. Once the commander was dead at my feet, I would be able to best decide about my future with Ulric—damn any promises. This man...this *monster* would not corrupt my soul. At least, not fully.

We searched the camp and found only tidbits of information that could potentially lead us to the commander. Our only recourse was to travel to the next site and hope we found something more substantial.

"Anything?" Ulric asked as I rifled through papers on a desk.

"Nothing," I said, defeated.

"Then on to the next camp," Ulric said triumphantly, and we were on our way.

Chapter 15

PRESENT DAY

I knocked on the door of the house behind the tanning salon/repair shop. After a few minutes, a porch light came on and Ed sleepily opened the door wearing a sweat-stained wifebeater and old blue and white striped boxers. He already had my keys in his hand, and held them out without saying a word.

"Gracias, senior," I said, severely mispronouncing the words. "Would you happen to know the time?"

He mumbled with half-open eyes, "It's late. Or early. I'm going back to bed." With that, he shut the door and turned off the porch light.

I made my way around his shop to where my car sat with brand-new glass. I would have to get them tinted later. Opening the door, I noticed the broken glass was still everywhere inside. "Guess I didn't ask him to clean it, did I? But shouldn't that be a standard?" I asked the wind.

After I swept most of the glass onto the parking lot (his problem now), I opened the trunk and placed Depweg's goodie bag inside and climbed into the driver's seat, pushing the engine start button.

Taking my eyes off the road for a second, I checked the clock to see that dawn was about thirty minutes away. I snorted angrily and cursed at my lack of time management. There was no time; I was going to have to find a place to sleep for the day, and quick.

When something like this happens, there are a few alternatives:

1) I can dig a hole in the earth and sleep there. This is a messy option because not only do I have to wash my clothes with a garden hose in the backyard, but I will find dirt in crevices for weeks.

2) I could pull into a Walmart or another 24-hour establishment and hide in the trunk. With this, getting towed or broken into could be a real problem, especially if they open the trunk, exposing me to sunlight and effectively ending the last of the vampires. Can't do that option. There's already too much pressure on my shoulders being the last without the fear of dying and wiping an entire supernatural species off the map in a Walmart parking lot.

I used to do option one fairly often before Valenta once suggested a hotel after I had dropped ear dirt into my drink and just stared at it, debating if I should continue to drink it or not. After he had made his suggestion, I'd lifted my head slowly with fierce eyes and a clenched jaw and said, "Well, if you wanna take the *easy* way out, I guess." I was mentally punching myself for never even considering that.

My time management hasn't improved over the centuries, so at this point I am a Hilton Diamond member.

I pulled into my closest Home2 Suites by Hilton and checked in right as the beginning rays of dawn were piercing the morning sky. Sun tendrils were already dancing in the sky.

I was sweating bullets (or would have if I could actually sweat) and had to squint my eyes to see while speaking to the front desk attendant who, thankfully, was approvingly efficient at her job and got me my key card within a few minutes. Though she did keep glancing at my forehead where the glue was surely peeling off by now.

After she handed me my key, I touched my forehead and said, "Cut myself shaving," before making my way to the elevators and up to my room.

As I walked in, the sun's rays were already hitting the top of the room and moving down the walls quickly. I ran over to the window to close the drapes right as the sun snuck through a gap in the tree line, and I was hit in the face with the magic-canceling light of morning.

Movies would have you believe vampires hissed when hurt or threatened. That was total bullshit. A massive, super manly, and not at all like a little girl's scream escaped my throat as I slammed the thick window treatments closed and collapsed to the ground, holding my burnt face.

After a minute of (not) crying on the floor, the phone started to ring. I opened my eyes to see nothing but black. "SIT!" I cursed with a new speech impediment. "I'n hucking 'lind!" My fingers explored the sockets to find that my orbs had indeed been melted in the split second they had been exposed.

What remained of my eyes was gooey sludge. My trembling hands explored the rest of the damage; skin and hair had been incinerated into dust, leaving behind aching muscles and tendons. Even my upper lip was gone, leaving behind only my pearly whites. "Lilith damn it," I said.

The phone continued to ring, so I felt my way over, using the bed as a guide, to where the nightstand was. I grabbed the receiver, took in a deep breath to control the pain, brought it up to where my ear used to be, and said through lipless teeth, "Hello? Yeth. Oh, thorry a'out tat. 'it eye ton. Huh? I. Dit. Eye. Tong. Yeth. Eye eye."

I placed the phone down, foolishly searching for the receiver. I turned toward one of the two queen beds and let myself fall facedown with a sigh of relief. The ground met me instead of nice, soft pillows and a thick blanket. Did I get the single king room instead of the two queens? Yes. Yes, I did.

"Thuck it," I said and fell asleep right on the floor.

Chapter 16

EUROPE, 1483

Ulric and I went from camp to camp, gathering any information we could find that would lead me to the commander. They were never ending; across the land and seas; high up in the mountains, and down in the valleys; deep in the forests, and resting at the edge of the oceans. I lost track of time. It felt like the commander was always one step ahead of us.

"Why is there never any useful information?" I angrily asked Ulric.

"It would appear he is aware of our path and is not leaving behind any sufficient clues," Ulric thought out loud.

"How is it we don't even know his name by now?" The frustration was evident in my voice.

"Commander Godwin," Ulric said conversationally and without looking at me.

I paused, not able to quite articulate the unrest I felt at what Ulric had just said so casually.

"How long have you known?" I asked, narrowing my eyes.

"Saw it at the last camp, I think. Did I not tell you?" he asked, still blowing this mountain of a revelation off as if he had only forgotten to return a borrowed tool or some other menial everyday task.

"No. No, you did not, Ulric," I said, anger and annoyance evident in my voice.

"Well, you know now, do you not?" he responded while turning to meet my gaze. It was stern and unrelenting.

I decided it was best to let it go, convincing myself to be satisfied that I had at least learned the bastard's name. Godwin. I had never hated a name so much in my life, or *unlife* for that matter. Godwin. Even mouthing it to myself made my blood boil. I wanted to spit on the ground every time the syllables were wordlessly formed by my lips and tongue. On the body-half-full-of-blood way of looking at things, at least I had his name. It powered my resolve and became a beacon for my rage.

As the nights came and went, I continued to develop my abilities with Ulric as he taught me the ways of the preternatural. I grew stronger with each kill, siphoning the mortal's life energy into myself. My predatory side and my consciousness became accustomed to one another and worked out a symbiotic partnership, allowing me to remain in control while listening to its guidance. In return, it remained next to me, ready to grab a rein at any time rather than being in the carriage by himself. This made me an efficient killing machine, but with control enough to not hunt every person in the vicinity once I started feeding.

I had problems wrapping my head around some of what Ulric taught, such as there being multiple planes of existence where monsters resided. Monsters that could tear even vampires apart like leaves on a tree.

One of my lessons consisted of controlling the mind of a mortal. We left two soldiers alive after one of our nightly escapades and sat them by a fire.

Ulric explained that first, in order to control the mind, you had to learn the brain. This would allow for information harvesting as well as entertainment, at least for Ulric.

The soldier closest to Ulric was tied and gagged, sitting in the dirt back to back with another soldier. Tears had cleaned paths down his cheeks, and his mouth hung open in a perpetual sob, soaking the cloth in his mouth.

Ulric dramatically lifted his hand, fingers spread wide and palm open, toward the soldier. He yelped and tensed his body in surprise, as if stung by a painful insect, then relaxed, with eyes becoming unfocused.

"Look up," Ulric commanded.

The soldier did.

"Hold up your hands."

The soldier raised his bound hands into the air.

"Now, void your bowels," Ulric said with a smile.

With his hands still in the air, the soldier pushed, straining to the point where veins popped out in his forehead and neck. His face turned red, and his eyeballs seemed ready to explode. This went on for a full minute before Ulric intervened.

"What is wrong?" Ulric asked, still amused but curious.

The soldier spoke like he was deep in a dream, "I cannot right now. I was in the privy when everyone started screaming."

"Ah," Ulric said, accepting his answer.

"Let me try," I said eagerly.

"Wait!" Ulric exclaimed. But it was too late. I held up my hand and focused my will on the soldier who sat in front of me. I felt an extension of my essence stretch from my hand and envelope his head. He gasped like the first soldier, but didn't relax. Instead, tremors started in his hands and feet, followed by his arms and legs, until his core was convulsing. A little at first, but quickly grew to violent spasms. His eyes rolled into his head, and blood started to pour down the white orbs like an artist who had dumped his paint on top of a blank canvas. Little streams of crimson started falling out of his nose and ears, which quickly became raging rivers. The convulsions grew increasingly violent, and soon he was kicking up dirt and grass.

I dropped my hand and released my focus, feeling the essence retract back into me. The soldier stopped convulsing, and he reached his bound hands up to his face. He sucked in a long, deep breath, and produced a startling screech that sounded more like a dying animal than a human. His fingers grabbed at his forehead and pressed in. His knuckles went white from the pressure, and bright blood began to trickle down where his fingernails pierced his skin. He sucked in another breath and screamed again, this time while slowly clawing at his face. Strips of flesh came with his hands and peeled away like a banana. His bottom eyelids tore away like a ravaged bedsheet flapping in the wind. When he got to his nose, a fingernail caught and ripped a nostril away. His fingers went into his mouth and continued their downward journey, prying teeth from gums and tearing his bottom lip to shreds. Bright blood ran freely from his face onto his clothing, creating a growing pool of rubies that sparkled in the firelight.

I sat in awe and glanced at Ulric, who seemed to be intrigued. He had let his focus fade from his play toy, and the soldier was coming to, startled by the inhuman wails. He struggled to arch and turn his head, only to see the back of the other soldier. The look of confusion evaporated into terror as he realized his companion was pulling away hands painted in crimson and gore. He cried out and tried to squirm away, prompting Ulric to casually put his foot down on the rope that restrained the man's feet, all without taking his eyes off the self-mutilating soldier. My wide eyes went back to the decimation taking place before me.

Another breath and his hands went up for more, not satisfied with their progress. This time, his fingers found purchase and pulled the meat from his face; muscle, skin, everything. In its wake, a scarlet skeleton was being born. He pulled past the eyes, nose, and finally lips. The sound reminded me of slowly peeling an orange. What was left was a screaming skull complete with lidless eyes and exposed teeth coated in flowing blood.

The man stopped screaming and closed his jaw as he looked right at me; the muscles attaching his upper and lower jaws were the only meat remaining on his entire head. His perfectly round eyeballs, out of place amidst the bone, stared at me. Though it was impossible to see any expression, I knew what I saw was pure, unhinged madness.

He reached his hands up and stuck his thumb, index, and middle fingers around his exposed eyeballs. The madman pushed them back deeper into his skull, the blood making it easier to slide between the orbs and sockets, until all the knuckles of each finger were submerged completely. The fingers tightened, and he pulled. Tissue snapped under the stress, and his eyes came free of their sockets, with only meaty cords connecting them to his skull. He pulled them forward and two loud twangs pierced the night, like bowstrings being cut. The soldier held his hands out to me and opened them palms up, revealing his gifts. He started a throaty chuckle which grew in intensity until his naked jaw opened and closed with every laugh. It escalated into hysteria, with his head lifting to the sky.

"That's enough," Ulric said, holding his own hand up to the man, prompting...nothing. Nothing happened. The soldier continued to bark out high-pitched laughs that shook his entire body and stretched his jaw to the point that the muscles gave way and snapped apart, leaving a slack-jawed skull bellowing madness.

Annoyance entwined with anger as Ulric stood and grabbed the top of the man's head, pushing the laughing skull into the chest cavity with a wet slosh. The sound mixed with that of breaking bones, like dry foliage underfoot. Bound, red-coated hands, still holding onto their treasure, fell lifelessly to the soldier's lap; the eyes rolled into the dirt and grass. One stopped just at my feet, the iris looking right at me. I lifted my foot and squashed it, unnerved.

The final sound the man made was a gurgle of escaping air being forced out of his crushed lungs. Then, silence. Only the sound of the remaining soldier whimpering and the crackle of fire were left in the night's air. A breeze picked up the heavy smell of freshly spilled blood.

The other soldier started rocking back and forth.

Ulric beckoned for me to sit next to him. As I sat on the log, he said, "I want you to feel what I feel. Put your hand over mine." His hand stretched out to the soldier, who flinched back, and I put my hand on his. I let my essence flow over his hand and then piggyback as his own went into the soldier's mind.

Ulric went slow and controlled, first joining with the soldier's aura, then gently descending inside his mind.

"Close your eyes and open your mind," Ulric said to me. I did as he instructed and closed my eyes. I took in a breath, concentrated, and opened my mind. We were standing behind the scenes of the campfire. The wind blew through the trees at a fraction of its normal pace. Everything seemed darker. Looking down, I could see that Ulric, the soldier, and myself were all ghostly outlines, as if we were made of mist. My eyes followed the mist as it left our hands and swirled around the soldier's head. In it, tendrils snaked into his skull from all angles.

"Follow them, John," Ulric said through the dream.

I let myself soar over our hands and down the mist until I reached the first tendril. I willed myself into it and was taken to a scene of the soldier—his name was Adam—sitting in a tree with a young woman named Beth. As their lips touched, Adam knew that he loved her and knew they were destined to spend their lives together.

My perspective shifted, and I was no longer looking at Adam. Beth was standing in the doorway, holding her bulging stomach. She watched as I mounted the horse and made my way to my uncle's farm. We lived miles from anyone, and my uncle made sure to pay me more than I deserved to help with my growing family.

I remembered the feeling in my stomach as I'd made my way up the path at the end of the day and seen the blackened ruins of my home. I had leaped off the horse and burst through the weakened wood of the door to see my wife charred and crushed under the single beam that ran along the roofline. I had screamed so loud and for so long that my throat had never fully recovered. Now I just didn't speak.

I was standing in the church with her father yelling at me that I hadn't built our cabin right. I stared past him at the closed casket that held my entire world.

The water was cold, freezing even. From this height, if the fall didn't kill me, the temperature would. I was about to step off the ledge when a tall, gaunt man approached.

He offered meaning to my life. Structure. A sense of belonging. I took his hand and stepped safely off the ledge.

"Damned stew," I said as what must have been fire left my body. It had tasted good going in. I started to clean myself when I heard screams. My heart pounded and my breathing became labored. My hands shook uncontrollably as I reached for my pants. The screaming stopped and I opened the privy door. A hand grabbed my throat, and I had never been more terrified in my entire life. The last thought that flashed in my mind before blackness washed over me was: I don't want to die anymore.

My eyes fluttered open and I was sitting in the dirt next to a fire. A disheveled-looking man was sitting on a log in front of me. It looked like he had slept in a mound of dirt.

I rushed out of the soldier's head, back up the mist and into my own body. My eyes flew open and I shot to my feet. As I started pacing, I looked at Ulric and asked in a frantic voice, "*What was that?!*"

Ulric let his hand drop and looked at me, understanding in his eyes.

"It is imperative that you only see what you want to see. It will take time to control the path you follow. What you saw is a direct reflection of your own mind," Ulric informed me, patiently.

"I'm Adam! She was my wife! I..." I stammered, wide-eyed. Ulric stood and placed a hand on my shoulder, calming me.

"Who are we but a collection of memories," Ulric said. "You dove too deep."

"Dove too deep!" I shrieked, "I lived for weeks as Adam! I loved Beth! Oh God, my baby! It's all my fault!"

"It will wear off," Ulric said impatiently. "We are done for tonight."

After a few ragged breaths, I calmed my mind. It wasn't me. It wasn't me. I was John Cook. My parents were...my parents were dead. That did the trick—reality was back with a vengeance.

"What are we going to do with m— with him?" I asked with a steady voice, but scared of the answer.

"I already took care of the matter," Ulric said calmly.

I looked at Adam as he slumped forward, head dangling, and saw that his skin was pale. Two dots on his neck leaked a few droplets of blood. I stood there, staring at his body. My innards were a mingle of emotions. But somewhere in the mix, I was happy he was with Beth and his child again.

Chapter 17

PRESENT DAY

D ay waned and receded while the night slid into existence, taking its rightful place. It brought with it the freedom most supernatural beings needed, including yours truly, in order to thrive.

I awoke face down in a pool of my own drool. I could *see* the puddle on the ground. Reaching up, I probed my head under my gray beanie, starting with my thick, strong hair then down my smooth forehead to my nose and lips. Wait, smooth forehead. *Yes!* My jizz stain was gone; though it had been an excellent conversation starter. Everything was back to its original glory. Even my dense, reddish mustache had grown back to join with the rest of my beard.

After checking out, I returned to my car and drove the rest of the way home without incident. Leaving the radio off, only my thoughts kept me company.

Something didn't feel right. It was as if I was standing on the tracks as a train barreled at me from behind. I couldn't see it, but I knew it was there, and I knew what was going to happen if I didn't do something. I needed to move off the tracks.

I turned down the road leading to the storage unit where I kept Mortis. After dropping him off at the stables, I started walking down to Valenta's. As the saloon came into view, I noticed the parking lot was even emptier than in my last visit. Pushing through the doors, I stepped inside.

Valenta stood behind the bar, reading a brown-paged book that was old enough for the cover to have dissolved. I could smell the must from the ancient pages from where I stood.

"Welcome to the party, son," Valenta said without looking up from his book. He licked his finger and casually turned the page.

"Where—?"

"Gone," he interrupted. "Did'je hear 'bout the demon that was summoned earlier tonight? Wreaking havoc downtown. Lots dead, including supes."

"Just got back into town," I gulped. Father Thomes was going to be unhappy I hadn't come see him last night. "Papa T come by?" I asked.

"Nah, but I'm sure he'll have words with ya bein' out o' town. Surely, he knew'a one was a'commen." He looked up from his book and gave me a "you're gonna get it" look.

"Hey! Don't you give me that look, young man! *You* were the one who suggested I go make friends!" I said as I sat in my favorite stool.

"My name's Paul and that shit's 'tween ya'll," he said, returning his gaze to his book. "Bess be moven along, John. Got work t'do."

Message received. "I don't get paid enough for this shit," I said while getting up from the bar and heading to the door.

"Ya don't get paid at'all," he reminded me.

I stopped with my hand on the door, "Wait, supes dead? Why were they attacking it? And how big was this fucker?"

"Supes got a responsibility t'stop demons, boy. As for yer second question: big," Valenta said as he licked his finger, turning another page.

Taking my cue, I walked back to the storage place and opened my trunk, pulling out the bag Depweg had given me. I took off my shirt and strapped the iron-infused Kevlar over my torso. I put the Glock and its inner-waistband holster at the small of my back. I replaced my shirt, looked in the direction of downtown while closing the storage unit, and leaped into the air, on my way to face God only knew what.

Chapter 18

LONDON, 1666

U lric and I walked through filthy back alleys, where human excrement poured into the streets. Rats congregated in droves, chittering their defiance at the passersby.

We had just arrived in town, having exhausted any and all leads. The Inquisition continued to trudge forward, replacing camps as quickly as they were taken down by Ulric and myself. We had saved many families the pain I had endured at the hands of the commander, whose trail had grown cold many seasons ago. I wasn't sure how long it had been, but my patience was near snapping. Ulric always knew just what to say to string me along a little longer.

A crumpled newspaper tumbled down the alley, propelled by a rancid breeze. I leaned down and scooped it up as it passed, with my free hand holding onto my recently procured top hat that the man at the shop had said was a must for all gentlemen. I called it a top hat, but it was just a tall hat with a large brim and a moderate crown. It matched our dark coats, which only came to our ribcages and had sleeves that barely covered our elbows. It bothered me how impractical the garments were in this part of the world. Not to mention the fancy pantaloons.

I lifted the newspaper and uncrumpled it. As I held the paper up to the lone burning oil lamp which illuminated the alley, a scowl creased my face as I noticed the date at the top.

"Ulric," I said.

"Yes?" Ulric responded as he stopped and turned to face me.

"Does London use a different calendar than the rest of the world?" I asked, perplexed at the 1666 at the top of the paper.

Ulric looked at me and then down at the paper I held. A flash of shock passed over his face like a lightning bolt. As quickly as it appeared, it was gone. I took note of this.

"Ulric?"

Ulric sighed and looked me in the eyes. "No, John. They use the same system of time as everywhere else we have been."

I pointed at the date on the paper and turned it to show him.

"So, this date is accurate?!" I asked, straining to keep my voice calm. The feeling of self-control started to slip from my grasp. Even PS was agitated and confused. Ulric was at the center of the brewing storm, but I couldn't figure out how or why.

"Yes," Ulric said with a tone that suggested he had been waiting for this very moment for a long time, but was still dismayed that it had actually arrived.

"How's it been s'long, Ulric? Where's th' feck'n commander?" I screamed, barely able to speak coherently.

"Dead," Ulric said without pause. "His mortal existence was extinguished long ago, even if by natural causation."

My eyes grew wide in disbelief. I had put up with this animal for decades, no, *centuries*. Oh Lilith, centuries. My gaze shifted to the ground and everything went unfocused as I dug deep into the perfect recall of my memories. I entered the city of my mind and went to the theatre, where I rewatched the events of every search in an instant. Camp after camp. After all our travels. Not a single calendar could be seen in my mind's eye.

"Ulric," I started calmly but with a flat undertone, "why did not a single camp have a calendar? A dated scroll?" I looked at him after speaking, awaiting his response.

Ulric sighed and did something I wasn't expecting; he looked right at me with cold eyes and said in a tone of finality, "Because I removed them before you could figure out that the mortal commander was long since dead, you petulant child."

PS knocked me over and grabbed the reins, hard. In one instant, I stood paralyzed in disbelief. In the next, I was flying through the air at Ulric with a bloodlongsword in my hands. It was the mightiest weapon I could imagine in my fury. As I swung, Ulric moved with impossible speed, even for my eyes, and what must have been a cannonball was shot point-blank into my stomach. My momentum was canceled completely, and I hunched over Ulric's fist, utterly stunned.

Ulric removed his fist from my stomach and used his index finger to raise my chin high so that our eyes met. His were predatory red.

Still hunched over, I put all my strength into my legs and jumped off the ground with enough force to leap over tall buildings. As my feet left the ground, I tucked one knee up and went for Ulric's jaw.

As if I were moving in slow motion, he turned around and hooked his hands around the back of my bent knee. All I could manage was a grimace as the filthy cobblestones rushed up to meet my face. As I lay stunned, I noticed vermin had stopped to watch the show, twitching their noses in interest.

Regaining my senses, I rolled onto my back and whipped the sword around in an arc toward Ulric's knees. The sword went into the nearby brick wall and lodged itself. Ulric stood on top of the blade, pretending to check his nails for dirt with a smirk at the corners of his mouth.

While still on my back, I swung a leg around to try and trip up Ulric, who all but vanished in front of my own supernatural eyes. Lilith, he was fucking fast.

Eyes wide and searching, I got up, using my moment of reprieve to yank my sword off the wall. I pulled, hard, and wound up back on my ass as the sword came loose.

Ulric appeared behind me, emerging from the shadows, a chuckle escaping from between his lips.

Sighing, Ulric said, "I will miss your buffoonery, child." His words straightened my spine and stole my breath, like jumping into a frozen lake.

I shot up, holding my sword in my right hand and my left hand in a defensive position in front of my body.

One instant, Ulric was ten feet in front of me, his eyes intent on their prey. In another, we were standing nose to nose. I choked in surprise and started to fall backward.

Ulric grabbed my sword-wielding wrist with one hand and my elbow with his other. With barely a grunt of effort, my hand was ripped off and replaced with a white sheet of pain that sent a bolt of lightning through my entire body. I went to my knees, mouth agape and eyes glazing as I began to tumble from my vantage point behind my eyes and into the welcoming darkness. I fought to regain control and swam back to an unfocused world. A crimson river flowed from my jagged forearm. In the back of my mind, an image of my father hanging a freshly butchered pig flashed; its throat slashed and gushing as it thrashed, helpless to its fate.

I was unable to focus on the wound and close it due to not only the blinding pain, but the pure loss of life energy that left me empty.

With eyes that trembled in their sockets, I managed to focus on Ulric, who was standing a few paces away now, holding my hand and the sword that was still in it. The long, heavy blade was melting like an ice sculpture exposed to a roaring flame. Ulric smiled at me with his abnormally wide mouth, teeth on full display; but it wasn't a smile I had ever been on the receiving end of. In all of our travels, he had been tough with me, but it had all been for the sake of learning to be better than I was. This grin was reserved for the most defiant of his prey, knowing that the end was coming and the mortal wouldn't be able to stop him. I had only seen it a few times, and it had always unnerved me how malicious it was. Now I was its recipient.

The loss of energy stunned me for an uncomfortable period. This must be what it felt like to a soldier when he lost a limb on the battlefield; their brains unable to comprehend what was happening and refusing to step through the doorway of their new reality and accept the loss, as if in fighting it, the limb might reappear.

Though I couldn't dissect the thought, the overwhelming feeling of being powerless grew inside my mind. I might as well have been the hanging pig to Ulric.

"Do you feel that, John?" Ulric cooed in a silken, nefarious voice. His eyes narrowed at me as he started to casually pace around where I knelt. "It is your final lesson, one that I had been saving for just such an occasion. If we lose our blood manifestations, we are forever cut off from the power it took to create it. This sword," he gestured to the half-melted sword still in my hand, which was in *his* hand, "took a lot of uncontrolled energy to create. You precariously expended too much of yourself, child. Letting your emotions get the better of you has cost you dearly. I dared not counter the attack directly, as I was not willing to risk pouring that much of my own life into a weapon. I learned that long ago. Instead, I used my clear mind to, if you will forgive the expression, disarm you," he chuckled to himself toward the end. As he finished, the sword coalesced into a pool on the ground.

As Ulric was wrapping up his monologue, I reached out to PS in my mind. He was just as scared as I was. Ulric had always been the alpha, and PS knew this; respected it. Now he was placed in a position to bite the hand that feeds, or potentially die. Ulric's motives weren't clear to PS yet, but I knew what the words he spoke meant.

As if on cue, Ulric pulled out his own sword, a rapier. The choice of those in charge on the battlefield. I had witnessed him pulling out the same sword on those who were damned by the malicious shark's grin he had just pointed at me.

He's going to decapitate us! I urgently shouted at PS. His response was to lower his head and close his eyes tight, a show of submission. I was on my own.

My eyes flickered around, desperate for anything. Ulric was smiling as he ran a finger down his blade, dramatically testing its sharpness. The blade glinted in the light.

The lamp! I yelled at PS. He looked up at me and nodded, hope and desperation growing in his eyes.

Ulric paced back and forth in front of me, savoring every syllable of his monologue. When he turned his back to me, I reached out with my good hand and extended a whip to the lamp. It wrapped around the base, and I almost fainted from the use of energy.

With my remaining strength, I lunged forward and threw my weight into my arm, ripping the lamp from the wall.

Seemingly in slow motion, Ulric turned with a contorted, dumbfounded look on his face. The lamp struck home and exploded against his shoulder, spreading oil and flames all over the side of his body.

I remember his primal, piercing screams with crystal clarity. Walls shook. Rats scattered, trying to flee from the audible assault.

As he flailed, I cried out to him, "Ulric, what was the lesson on vampires and fire?"

Ulric turned to face me directly, teeth bared, as his face began to liquefy. He did something that would haunt my day-dreams forever and lunged for me, flaming arms outstretched. As he leaped, I fell on my back, startled, and pushed my legs out in front of me instinctively. My feet landed directly into his stomach as our momentum rolled me backward, and I sent him flying overhead, a flaming artillery shell. A claw raked my face and popped an eyeball as he flew past and into a pile of discarded wooden boxes that contained remnants of hay. They ignited in a blaze of hungry fire and choking smoke. Ulric continued to scream. I could hear his vocal cords bubbling from the flames. It sounded as if he was trying to swallow thick porridge while screaming.

The fire raged on, and all I could do was watch in morbid fascination.

A melted, glowing hand reached out from the flaming debris and hooked on the cobblestone. Bones, glowing red and black like embers, were pulled with shriveling muscles until lidless, glaring eyes were freed from the flames. They disintegrated while staring directly into my own eyes, dissolving into white, bubbling pools in their sockets.

Somehow, the emerging skull emanated a feeling of hate that I had never experienced. The jaw dropped open as muscles turned to ash, and the head went lax, setting surprisingly lightly on the ground just outside the flames. I watched as his clothes smoldered, letting the flames eat the exposed flesh, which ignited as if marinated in oil. Within a minute, he was mostly a blackened skeleton with dried tendons holding joints together. Some meat had survived, though charred, but I knew by his burnt skull that he was gone.

In the distance, I could hear the frantic citizens approaching the smoking alleyway. I couldn't let them find Ulric's fanged skeleton. I would have to remove his remains and bury him.

I looked around, desperate for anything to put the roaring flames out.

An idea struck and I walked up to the flames, feeling the heat threaten to conflagrate me. I stuck my arms out to either side, like a bird stretching its wings before flight. I was going to slam my hands together at supernatural speed to put out the fire. That's when I remembered my broken wing, which had stopped spurting precious blood, but remained, well, gone. I commanded my body to start the healing process as I figured out a different plan. An idea struck across my mind.

I slammed my only palm flat on the cobblestone with enough force to send out a shock wave. I was thrown back into the opposite wall of the alley, where I was briefly stunned. The air also smashed into the fire and scattered flaming debris in all directions in a beautiful explosion. Captivation took hold as I watched it rocket toward the heavens. Doubt and then worry replaced the awe I experienced as the firestorm slowed in midair, stopped, then changed course, heading back down.

Time was running short, but I couldn't help but watch what I had just done. A sickening feeling bloomed in the pit of my gut.

"Shite..." was all I could manage as flaming wood landed on nearby buildings. With helpless eyes, I watched as they began to ignite. They were going up faster than a painstakingly prepared campfire. Within a few ragged breaths, the entire block was smoking.

Screams began then. Men who were already approaching the alley called out an urgent warning, but the flames were growing rampant, feeding on the buildings with an insatiable appetite.

Footsteps approached.

I snapped myself out of the horror of my impulsive action, scooped up Ulric's charred remains, and ran. There was a vague awareness, and even awe, that my arm was healed up to the wrist now. I continued to run as my eyes drifted to my hand, which was beginning to sprout.

I ran with Ulric's shrunken frame curled in my arms; partly out of practicality, and partly out of the loss I was trying to fight back in my head. Though he was going to kill me at the end, he was all I had known for the last almost two hundred years. Even if I hadn't been aware of the passage of time, that was still a hell of a long time to travel the world with one companion. It was like the stories I had read where the protagonist was forced to kill their abusive spouse or parent. They felt a crippling grief at having to take that kind of action against someone they loved, no matter the reason.

As I reached the edge of the city, I turned and was hit by a brick wall of guilt. Just north of the River Thames and west of the Tower of London, the city was glowing orange. Even in the blackness of the night I could see the billowing smoke blotting out the stars, creating a divide in the heavens. I felt like an evil doppelgänger to the righteous Moses.

After what could have been hours of watching the glowing in the city grow, I was met by the first tendrils of the sun. It was time to finish this.

I dragged Ulric's corpse to a nearby tree and dropped him at the base. Lifting my freshly grown palm, I sent out my blood into the dirt, creating two shallow graves. While holding the dirt in the air, I looked at Ulric with a frown.

"You may have lied and manipulated me, but you also made me what I am. Your part is over. Rest now," I said solemnly. I pulled his smoldering body into the grave and laid the dirt on him.

I climbed into the other hole and let the dirt rest on top of me just as the sun peeked over the horizon.

My mind raced with the surreal events that had just taken place. I forced my thoughts to settle into reality. This had happened. Ulric was dead.

I was free. The world was mine.

But with Commander Godwin dead, what was I to do? What was the point of existing with no hope for vengeance? Hating Godwin had become a part of me, and with him gone, I had redirected that hate toward my maker.

A tear freed itself from its prison and absorbed into the dirt as unconsciousness took me.

Chapter 19

PRESENT DAY

I followed the screams of terror. Most of the time, mortals disregarded supes as a trick of the mind—they'd see a glimmer of an apparition, or a giant fur-covered beast dash between the bushes, then quickly tell themselves they were just seeing things. But when a giant, hulking monstrosity was rampaging down the street just after sunset and ripping people apart, the dread sank in.

This didn't happen often, of course, as there were rules against revealing yourself to mortals. Rules that were punishable by death. But demons didn't give a damn. This one in particular seemed to revel in the limelight.

I bounded down the street, passing half-eaten bodies with looks of horror permanently etched into their faces. Sporadically, I passed by a supe whose human skin had fallen away with their demise. Trolls, faeries, goblins, ogres, and even rebellious demons were strewn about, all trying to stop the mortals from gathering proof of our existence.

Then, I saw it.

It stood the size of a house. *"Holy shite!"* I yelled in panic. It was the demon from my nightmare. I skidded to a halt and started to hyperventilate. The creature heard me and began the long process of turning around. Terror gripped my body and filled my muscles with concrete. I couldn't move.

Its sunken, red-fire eyes spotted me, and its giant maw slowly turned up into a smile. Within its massive body, a deep rumble began that moved up its throat and escaped its mouth.

"Mos-qui-to," it rumbled, barely audible with the sheer force of its voice. Windows shook and car alarms went off. I peed a little.

It charged impossibly fast at me, intent on doing its master's bidding and killing the last vampire; or so I assumed by the sparkle in its eye.

Instinct took over, and I crouched while leaning to one side, making it look like I was about to run in that direction. He took the bait and changed course like a speeding train on a curving track. I went the opposite way and willed my blood through my palms, joining them together and forming a giant Viking sword. I swung with all my might at the creature's back as he passed, trying to stop his momentum. The bloodsword struck armor and shattered. I cried out in shock as the moderate power required to create the weapon was lost. A flash of doubt entered my mind, as I either hadn't used enough energy or the demon somehow canceled my power. I would have to be more careful, and as Ulric had taught me, use a clear head.

In my moment of bewilderment, the monster swung its massive, bone-spiked arm and hit me dead on. Bone spears pierced my torso and face at my cheek. I flew what had to be several hundred feet down the street. But luckily, a sturdy panel van made of solid metal broke my momentum. A giant, me-sized crater bent the van nearly bumper to bumper, forcing the ends to try and meet like a folded piece of paper. Stuck in the middle, I pried my limbs from where they had imprinted and forced myself into a ball. I wriggled until I was facing one of the sides and found purchase with my feet and hands, pushing the van apart. Once there was enough room, I let myself drop to the ground and muttered, "...Jell-O..."

My intestines were hanging out of one of the holes in my stomach, so I did what any normal person would do and pushed them right back in. After a moment, the holes knitted themselves shut. I felt somewhat of a relief that he hadn't used hellfire with his attack.

The brief reprieve was short-lived as I both felt and heard the monster's footsteps approaching.

I turned with a new focus. I refused to be beat by some pawn of a demon in *my* town. Teeth clenched and eyes narrowed, I stared at my opponent and tried to find any weaknesses in his armor. There were gaps between the plates, about six inches apart, to allow for movement and bending. As big as he was, he wasn't as agile as me, and those gaps provided a perfect place to focus my attacks. But I would have to be in close range to be effective.

Through my palms, I manifested two gladius swords that were made for speed and stabbing rather than blunt force. I stood my ground as the creature confidently approached. A toothy smile twisted its face.

Closer and closer it came, crumbling the cement beneath its monstrous feet. I bent my knees.

Only a few more steps and I would be within its reach. I crouched lower and moved my center of gravity to my legs.

It took a deep breath that sounded like the wind from a tornado, and bellowed directly at me, throwing me slightly off-center. My eyes blurred and ears rang, but I held fast, feeling its movement beneath my feet. Once it thought I had been incapacitated from its verbal assault, it ran the remaining steps.

I acted. My eyes refocused, and I sprang forward with enough force to high-five the clouds had I been going straight up. The street shattered beneath my feet as I propelled myself impossibly fast in the direction of my prey. The monster had a brief look of incredulity before adjusting and reflexively swinging its massive arm in a wide arc.

As the arcing limb was about to hit, I leaped and landed on its wrist, then started running up its arm toward its center. The demon leaned back to avoid my approach, but this only helped to widen the gaps between his torso plates. Still running, I pulled my arms back into a striking position and then lunged forward, jumping off the appendage and toward his house-sized center mass. My left blade struck the corner of a plate and shattered, causing me to gasp at the permanent loss of energy, but my right blade found purchase and drove into the demon's chest, close to the heart. The creature roared in immense pain and momentary panic. Viscous black oil spurted from the wound, spilling the creature's blood.

I hung from his chest like an ornament, still stunned from the loss of the first gladius. This gave the beast time to recover, and he grabbed my entire body, from chest to knees, with the massive meat hooks he called hands. I recovered just in time for his hands to close around me, squeezing my body like an ancient, gargantuan serpent.

The focus I had was melting away as fear crept its way into dominance. My head shot back and forth, desperate to find any way out.

He brought me up to his rows and rows of shark teeth.

"Oh great," I panted. "Now you're going to bore me to death with your master pla—"

He shoved me into his mouth and started to chew.

Chapter 20

LONDON, 1666

As night began to swallow the light, consciousness trickled back into me like water dripping through the ceiling and into a bucket. Once the sun had fully retreated, the rest of my mind sprang back into place.

I lifted myself out of my shallow grave and rubbed the dirt from my eyes. After shaking my head and slinging earth from my hair and ears, I looked at Ulric's small mound.

"Sleeping in tonight, I see?" I asked the mound. Reality fell upon me like a crumbling brick wall, and my face and heart dropped with an unseen force that threatened to push me back into my hole. I stuck a dirt-coated hand out and set it gently on the mound, afraid to disturb the remains.

As I looked at the grave, a flickering of orange light on the grass caught my attention. I looked out over the River Thames and noticed that even more of the city was ablaze.

My heart stepped off the ledge and plummeted into the depths of my guts, and my throat tightened to the point where I was confident that, if I had to breathe, I wouldn't be able to.

I stood up, letting a mass of dirt fall to the ground. Light brown clouds rose from the buildings and were carried off by the wind, freed from the earth.

Looking at the orange city, my first instinct was to help. But what could I possibly do? My last attempt had created the situation. Not to mention the fact that fire was to vampires what dry land was to fish; our archnemesis. Well, that and sunlight. And not consuming blood. Okay, so it wasn't our only archnemesis, but it was one of our nemeses.

Flames plus vampire equal dead. D. E. D. Dead. And now, there was only one left in the world.

Realization pierced my heart: I was the last of my species.

After a few moments of wallowing in self-pity, I set my jaw and rushed toward the inferno that had once been the heart of London.

As I crossed the Thames, I let my senses flow freely. PS was telling me to run from the situation, making it harder to utilize my predatory senses. In my mind, I grabbed PS and shook him with vigor.

This is MY body and we will do as I command. Now pick up that feck'n rein and let's do something good for a change.

With hesitation, PS grabbed one of the reins, and my senses flooded with preternatural energy. We were aligned for a common goal.

I scanned the area with my eyes, looking for heat signatures, but the heat from the flames made that unreliable at best. Letting my eyes close, I focused on my hearing, taking in sound from several blocks away.

Footsteps came first, accompanied by the sound of sloshing water. Several hurried steps followed close behind. I opened my eyes to see a line of men carrying buckets of water, running as fast as they could without spilling their precious cargo.

Closing my eyes, I focused further out. The whimpering of a dog caught my attention, and I zeroed in on where it was coming from. Running at blinding speeds, I leaped and exploded through a second-story window. Smoke filled the upstairs, making it hard to see. Another whimper. I burst through the thin wall separating the rooms and found a puppy curled up in the corner, scratching at the wall with all its might.

A few hurried steps and I was scooping the puppy up in my arms and jumping through the window. I leaped a few times and was on the bridge again, away from the fire's reach. I set the puppy down and quickly petted his head. I noticed my arm was wet, and I looked down to see a small ring of urine forming at the edge of my fancy coat. I scowled at the puppy, who wagged his tail and yipped at me, then smiled. How could I stay mad at that?

A child's scream pierced the night's air. Turning on my heels, I ran in the general direction of the sound and came to a building that was fully engulfed. Another shriek rang out. It was coming from the center of the top floor. A woman fought against two men who were restraining her from entering the building. With each scream, the woman's eyes went wider, and the men had to use everything they had to keep her from running into the beckoning flames. It was as if the conflagration had set up a trap and was willing as many victims in as it could in its short lifespan.

My eyes vigorously searched for a way in that wasn't a gateway to a room on fire. An idea struck, and I turned and ran back to the bridge.

The puppy was still there, trying to shake the water from his fur. He looked up and saw me run and jump over him into the river below. The cold enveloped me in an embrace that would have stolen the breath of a mortal. Floating to the surface, I reached out with a bloodwhip and caught the bridge, pulling myself up with one solid tug.

The puppy ran up to me, tail wagging and yipping his excitement as he did.

"Stay here, my friend. I will return," I told him before starting my run back to the building.

With a few bounds, I was back and flying through the air right into the mouth of the raging inferno. The screaming had stopped. With a quick glance, I took note that the woman had collapsed to the ground and was sobbing uncontrollably into her hands.

The fire embraced me as I landed in the top floor in a crouch. The heat was immeasurable to my supernatural skin. Clenching my jaw, I crawled on my hands and feet toward where I had thought the sound came from. Within a few moments, I found a room where the flames had just started to lick. I blew out the air I had stored in my lungs and extinguished the door for a few moments. Reaching for the doorknob, I pulled back at the contact with the superheated metal.

I began to steam as my protective layer of water began to boil on my skin. My hair and beard started to singe, sending white smoke into my nose and signifying time was running out.

I manifested the first thing that came to my mind, and slammed the bloodhammer down on the doorknob. It broke off, clattering to the ground and bringing a chunk of the dried wood with it.

I yanked the door open and was met by the odor of cooking flesh. With the smell came the associated memory of my mother, and for a moment, I was paralyzed with the flood of emotions. Even though it had been almost two hundred years ago, the memory hadn't degraded, and it felt as fresh as the night it had happened. It was an unexpected flaw in becoming a vampire that the books never mentioned; perfect memory recall without degradation. When a mortal lost a loved one, time eased the pain by dulling the memory.

Tiny, bloodshot eyes looked at me from beneath a blackened forehead, freeing me from the prison of my memory. I picked up the bald child, with one hand behind her neck and the other behind her knees, and rushed through the flames and out the window. I landed in the alley, where no one was standing, and an idea came to me.

With my mother still stinging my heart and mind, I said, "Please work," as I willed blood from my palm and over the girl's exposed skin. It covered her entire head, including her blistered lips, leaving little holes for her nostrils. A moan escaped her throat, and she began to writhe ever so slightly. I focused the blood flow over her arms and legs, willing my own energy into her skin. I was careful not to throw too much of myself into her, as I wasn't sure what would happen. Plus, I was still exhausted after my battle with Ulric. I hadn't fed yet, and fatigue was knocking at my door. PS nodded at me in my head, and I focused on returning the blood to my body.

As the crimson life left her skin, a beautiful little girl, complete with a full head of hair, was lying in my arms. Her eyes fluttered open but were unfocused. I ran the back of my hand over her cheeks and said, "It's going to be all right. You're all right." She shifted her head to me, put one fresh hand on my cheek, and asked in the sweetest voice I had ever heard in all my years, "Are you an angel?"

I was stunned by the question. Though it was a blatant lie, I looked her in the eyes and said, "Yes, my child. I am an angel, here to save you. Now, close your eyes."

As she did, I ran to the street and yelled at the gathered group while pointing down the alley, "There's a child here!"

The group of people, who must have all lived here, rushed to the alley. They ran past me without a second look and toward the child. The mother led the pack. A different cry filled the alley; one of joy and unimaginable relief.

For the first time in a long, long time, I felt peace bloom in my heart. A smile forced its way onto my face, and I didn't fight it.

After searching for the rest of the night and returning to the bridge to make sure the puppy was doing well, dawn was approaching again.

Before I returned to my shallow grave, I picked him up and traveled to where survivors were being held. A quick walk around the perimeter of the room and I located the little girl, who was asleep next to her mother. I walked up, leaned down, and put her new best friend in her cradled arms. Tired eyes opened and spotted the bundle of adorableness. A tiny gasp left her nonblistered mouth, and she embraced the puppy. Eyes already wide, they flicked up to me and grew impossibly large with delight.

"You're the angel," she whispered.

I nodded while smiling and caressing her hair, astonished at how my blood had healed her. In my mind, I noted that Ulric had made me drink his blood in order to become what I was. Good trick to know.

"Will you promise to take care of him?" I asked.

The little girl nodded enthusiastically while bringing the puppy up for a kiss on the head.

I left them like that, embraced in the happiness that only a child with a new puppy could have.

Climbing into my hole next to Ulric, I looked over at his mound and wondered what the future would hold without my maker and guide. My parent's killer was long since dead. I briefly entertained the notion of draining his descendants, but thought better of it. The son would not be punished for his father's crimes. I could sleep, but that would only delay the inevitable.

The little girl with her puppy flashed through my mind, as well as how good I had felt. I had saved them both and could have easily perished. No one would ever know except for her, and that was enough.

That's what I would do; I would exist to help those in need. Perhaps I would spare another family my fate. Lowering the dirt onto me, I had to remind myself that I was smiling before earth went into my mouth.

Chapter 21

PRESENT DAY

The pain was immediate and blinding. White-hot lightning shot through every limb with each crunching motion. The breath was squeezed out of me. The bleeding began, and I was sure I would die from losing my precious blood energy before I even met his stomach. The only reason I wasn't dead already was because my head was at the back of his throat and the body armor Depweg had given me prevented my upper torso from being punctured.

An idea hit me, and I willed all the surrounding blood to form a protective barrier around me, solidifying into plates of bloodarmor. This gave me a valuable few seconds to gain my bearings. I grabbed at the creature's uvula and pulled myself down his throat. As I did, I forced my bloodarmor to grow into spikes, lodging them in every direction in his esophagus.

The beast started gagging and tried to reach its fat, stumpy fingers down its gullet then started clawing at its own throat when that failed, tearing chunks of flesh as it did. I started wriggling my body, turning it slowly, cutting its tender flesh as I did. It tried to scream, clawing even more fiercely at its neck.

Finally, it tore through and grabbed one of my feet, yanking me backward and taking even more of the throat with me as I went.

As he pulled me through, leaving me hanging upside down, I let the shield drop and sucked in as much of the blood that had energy left as I could, letting the rest drop. I then reached at my lower back and pulled out my Glock, keeping my hand hidden until the time was right.

The creature pulled me up to his eye level while he grasped his throat with the other hand. Anger was clearly written all over his face. Though he couldn't speak, his intentions were clear. No more playing around. He was going to end it now.

He let go of his neck and started reaching for me, ready to tear me in half. I pulled my hand around, aimed the Glock right at one of his sunken fire eyes, and pulled the trigger.

I saw it all in slow motion: there was an explosion out the front of the barrel with white smoke and yellow flames, then the bullet was released. The slide was thrown back, and my hand recoiled. The iron-and-silver round flew through the air, directly at his fire eye, and smashed through it, extinguishing the flame like a candle being blown out with a leaf blower. The bullet expanded on impact, and the iron and silver pellets bounced around inside the demon's head, ripping its brain apart.

Its grip loosened on my leg, and I dropped to the ground, doing an awesome flip in midair and landing on my feet. The monster dropped on top of me.

After several seconds of struggling, I was able to slide out from under the thing. I stood, patted the dust off my tattered clothes, and then looked at my handiwork.

The other eye was still alight, though barely flickering. I pointed the Glock at it and said, "*Hasta la vista*, baby."

Anticlimactically, the light extinguished and the body started to become wet. The skin turned transparent, and the mass started falling in on itself, turning back into ectoplasm. It reminded me of the end of *Gremlins 2*. I almost expected the thing to start gurgling out, "New York, New *York*..."

But it didn't. It dissolved away into nothingness as the ectoplasm was returned to the ether, leaving behind a trail of destruction and dead bodies. I holstered the Glock at the small of my back and took in a deep breath of relief.

A voice called out, "Jonathan, I thought I told you to stay out of it."

I turned around, trying to locate the voice.

"I warned you, blood bag. Now you'll pay!"

The source was coming from on top of a nearby three-story building.

"What's up, Hufflepuff? Got out of potions class early?" I taunted Locke. "Where are your hired goons?"

As soon as I asked, giant lunch-box hands grabbed me from behind, and I was pulled in tight against a brick wall of a chest. The other goon walked out from the shadows and stood in front of us, fists clenched.

"Fellas," I said, "don't make me blow my rape whistle!"

At that, the fisticuff goon pulled back for a power punch to my torso. I let him. His hand hit the iron-infused Kevlar and shattered the bones of his hand into dust. He recoiled with a look of disbelief.

With my right hand, I reached behind, grabbed the gun, and pointed it at the crotch of the hired muscle holding me in place. Like magic, he let go the second after I pulled the trigger, letting a whispered moan escape his lips.

I slipped through his loosened grip and stuck the gun in his face, squeezing the trigger at point-blank. He blinked as the back of his head exploded, while only a dribble of blood leaked out the dime-sized hole in his forehead. He collapsed to the ground.

I turned and shot the other goon in the heart, and watched the life dwindle in his eyes. I felt no remorse or pity for taking their pathetic lives. They'd chosen the path of evil and had paid for their decisions. Play stupid games, win stupid prizes.

Sirens wailed in the background, snapping me back to the present. I looked up and saw a group of SWAT cops making their way down the street. They had spotted me covered in blood, holding a Glock, and standing in the middle of the devastation—as well as executing two men right in front of them.

I put my hands in the air and called out, "Guys, this isn't what it looks like!" I forgot the gun was still in my hand, and they didn't appreciate my slight oversight.

They opened fire. I stood there, flabbergasted, as bullets ricocheted off my skin.

"*Really?*" I asked. "What about him?" I pointed at the now empty roof where Locke had just been.

They stopped shooting and looked at each other in amazement as their bullets had no impact. One of them adjusted the body cam on his chest to get a clear view of me.

"Oh, shit!" I said to myself and bounded down the street away from them. It didn't hit me until after that I probably shouldn't have gone mock supe while being filmed.

In due time, I made it back to my hidey-hole and descended the stairs to catch Da watching *South Park* on an iPad.

In my best Jack Nicholson voice, I said, "Honey, you'll never believe what happened to me today."

Chapter 22

GERMANY, 1945

I retracted my bloodknife from the liver of my latest SS officer, careful to not get blood on his sexy black leather trench coat. Excuse me, *my* sexy black leather trench coat. His drained body collapsed to the snow, cheeks sunken and eyes rolled back into his head, exposing only the whites.

Sliding the coat off his body, I slung it across my back and inserted my arms. My fingers expanded as they passed through the sleeves in a gesture of victory. A tiny aura of steam emanated from my warmed skin. I took in a breath and exhaled, marveling at the torrent of vapor that rushed out. It was one of my favorite party tricks.

The long coat flapped in the frigid breeze as I twirled around, careful to not trip over the plethora of bodies around me. After having their bodies drained of the warm blood, the snow was already adhering to their faces, blurring the features of the men. I continued to dance to the music in my mind, feeling the rush of power and elation flood over me. I may have giggled once or twice in my blood-induced delirium.

After a few more minutes of unabridged delight, I focused and brought myself back down to reality, though a much more enjoyable one.

I gave myself a once over and removed the medals, sleeve, and anything else that identified the wearer as a Nazi.

"Wonder how long you'll last, Mr. Coat," I said while running my fingers down the fine leather. I felt the ridges and appreciated the craftsmanship involved.

An unfamiliar smell snatched my focus, and PS immediately sprang to attention. It was blood, but something was wrong with it. The aroma of metal intermixed with something...powerful. I closed my eyes and sniffed the freezing air, trying to get a fix on the location. A fresh gust of wind brought an intense concentration, and my head turned into the wind. Predatory eyes opened and sought a heat signature.

Going against the wind, I quickly crept through the snow with my head on a swivel. With each gust, the scent grew fresher. Whatever I was hunting was hurt, and I had to restrain PS from completely taking over. The blood was intoxicating and not like any I had ever smelled before.

Dense snow started falling with a relentless vendetta against the ground, threatening to swallow the world. Fierce winds ripped through the trees, tugging at my new trench coat while teasing my nose with the alluring aroma. My hair was whipped unrelentingly behind me; I could feel the strands slap my ears at random intervals.

In the distance, my preter-eyes saw as a red blur came into view. Still in predatory mode, I crouched down and started crawling on all fours, using the trees and growing snowbanks as cover. As I neared, the blur focused into a man sitting against a tree. He had something in his hands and was lifting it to his mouth every few seconds. I could see him breathing heavily from the steam that escaped his mouth and nose.

Charting a path, I started circling around the perimeter, trying to remain out of sight. The wind started blowing against my back, threatening to lift my coat and wave it like a warning flag.

The man stopped moving and his head shifted toward where I hid behind a fallen log; he appeared to sniff the air. I closed my eyes and listened from where I hid. It was tough to make out any sound through the raging winds. Opening my eyes again, I slowly raised my head and was met with scowling eyes a few inches in front of mine. A tiny yelp of surprise escaped my lips as I fell backward into the thick snow. A large man stood straight up with a puzzled look on his face. He sniffed the air again while keeping his gaze locked on me.

The goliath of a man was covered in deep slashes that had cut through clothing and skin. Blood leaked out of the fresh wounds, staining what was left of his shirt and pants.

"What are you?" the huge man asked in German. My eyes flicked to his hands and I froze in place. He was holding an arm that had been torn off at the elbow. Ribbons of flesh and tubes of veins hung out; but that wasn't what had caught me off guard. There were obvious bite marks in the flesh of the forearm, with chunks of meat missing. With an open mouth, my gaze shifted back to the face of the man who had a vast ring of maroon around his lips. Some dripped down his chin and into the white snow, staining it crimson where it hit.

"What am I?" I began with an uncertain voice. "What are you?"

In response, the lumbering figure kicked the fallen log that separated us. By pure instinct, I kicked my feet at the ground and flipped backward into the air, letting the log fly under me. Landing on my feet, I let PS take the wheel, and prepared for a fight with my unknown opponent.

My fangs grew, and I hissed a warning at the cannibal in front of me.

"Vampire!" he cried while still speaking German. Letting go of his lunch, my knowledgeable friend reached for his belt to a long blade inside a sheath. I chuckled to myself and let him pull the weapon, knowing no mortal blade could pierce my skin.

A feeling of uncertainty built inside me, washing away my smirk, as the metal cleared the leather sheath. It hummed with unseen power, causing PS to squirm in my mind.

Kicking up snow toward my attacker's face, I lunged with an overhand right and landed a solid blow to his solar plexus, sending him tumbling several yards. The cry of victory bellowed from my core quickly morphed into one of intense pain. My fist, which was still in front of me, quickly retreated to grab just above my neck in instinct. Fresh, steaming blood coated my fingers as I lifted my hand to my face. I could feel warmth spreading down my neck and into my new coat. My eyes grew wide and my brow furrowed at the realization that he had actually fucking cut me, and deep. Fingers trembled, and my breath came in ragged bursts.

A war cry pulled me out of my daze, and I looked straight ahead to see the man charging, his bloody weapon poised and ready to taste more of my blood. He should be dead. No mortal could have survived an attack of that magnitude.

I threw my hand out and aimed at the rushing man, sending a dagger attached to a bloodchain from my palm. The supernatural man dodged my impossibly nimble attack, forcing me to pull the blade back with a snap. As it flew back toward me, the blade barely nicked one of the giant's shoulders, which protruded from his stressed shirt. No blood emerged.

Shit! I said to PS. *His skin is tough like ours!*

The man continued his charge. I was vaguely aware of blood reaching my waist. He slashed the air at stomach level, and I leaped backward several yards, sliding in the snow to a stop. A curse snuck out between gritted teeth as I couldn't force my wound to close. Precious blood continued to seep out at an alarming rate.

Now I was pissed. I threw the blade with enough force to create a shock wave, and the beast of a man deflected it with the side of his glinting blade. As it came into contact with my blood manifestation, power was evaporated where they touched. This stunned me for a moment, but the feeling of self-preservation kept me focused. Plus, he had only taken a fraction of my energy.

Willing the weapon back into my palm, I strode over to an adolescent sapling and ripped the trunk from the frozen ground. It was about a foot in circumference and perhaps fifteen feet tall.

Letting the attacker draw closer, I lifted the tree until I was holding the roots and then swung with all the might of a pissed off vampire.

It hit home and the man went flying, the tree breaking on impact. His blade tumbled to the ground, and I walked over to where it lay and inspected it. Reaching down, I lifted the weapon by the handle to my face. It hummed loudly to my ears and promised unyielding pain should it bite me again.

"Silver..." I said to myself. Shifting my focus from the weapon, I leaped to where the man had fallen. He was attempting to right himself when I landed in the snow in front of him, blade pressed to his throat.

"Do it," the man said in English, his eyes meeting mine. With my peripheral vision, I could see the man's left arm was broken where the tree had impacted. His wounds still oozed on his torso.

"How did you know I spoke English?" I asked.

Wincing, the man said, "Heard you say 'silver.'"

"You heard me whisper from way over here?" I asked, unbelievingly.

He nodded weakly. I noted his skin was losing color.

"What are you?" I asked.

"A werwolf," he responded.

"You mean a werewolf?" I corrected, using the English phrase.

"No," he said, "I'm German. We prefer werwolf." I noticed he had emphasized the first "w" as a "v" sound, but not the second.

"Very well, Mr. Wolf," I said as I extended my hand out to him. I was taken aback when he took it without hesitation.

"Why did you attack me?" I asked.

"Thought you were a Nazi," he said. "That, and you smelled...off."

"Seems reasonable, Mr. Wolf. I am, in fact, not a Nazi. I just like their coats."

"Please, call me Depweg," he said, a smile forcing its way on his pain-stricken face.

"John," I said, sticking my hand out for a proper shake. He grabbed my forearm, Viking style, and we shook. I wondered at that moment how old he was.

Chapter 23

PRESENT DAY

O kay, seriously, when the hell did we get an iPad?" I asked. I had it on my to-do list to purchase one of those X-boxes the cool kids went on about, or maybe a smart TV. Film was a big part of who I was and it was near painful to no have ready access to the newest content.

"Oh, this old thing?" He pushed the sleep button and closed the case.

"So, all those times I said out loud that I missed TV...?" I asked, hands outstretched toward the iPad.

"You were mentioning your night?" he segued.

"Dude! I've had the craziest day."

"Night," he corrected.

"Oh, I'm sorry. Did you want to tell the story that happened to me and not you?"

He didn't respond, only glared in annoyance.

I recapped the past few evenings, with Depweg basically saving my life, the demon terrorizing downtown, and Locke showing up. I left out the part where I was swindled into getting a tanning membership so my car would be ready in time—which hadn't even mattered in the end! I needed a watch.

"Let me get this straight, John. While being filmed, by an officer no less, you showed off your supernatural speed?" He paused, considering. "The other members of the supernatural society are not going to take this lightly, you realize."

"It crossed my mind. But honestly, almost all of them have fled to different planes."

"So, it's true." Da looked at the ground in deep contemplation.

"What's true?" I asked.

He continued to stare at the ground, not answering.

"Da, tell me what's going on. Now!" I demanded.

"I must go." He folded in on himself and retreated to a different plane, leaving behind a micro-shock wave as the air rushed to fill the void.

Staring at the place where he had just been, I said, "Abra-ca-fucking-dabra."

One of these nights, I was going to get Da to teach me that trick. Damn faeries.

I decided to take the rest of the night off and catch up on some reading. Climbing into my iron Fortress of Solitaire, I felt it best to read some more *Sandman Slim,* where the hero got to do whatever he felt like, good or bad, and didn't give a damn what anyone else thought. Helped relieve the stress of the night.

It was a well-known fact that the best sleep came from procrastination. Have a report that's due in a few days? Take a nap!

It didn't take long before I drifted off into a deep sleep.

Chapter 24

GERMANY, 1945

Helping Depweg walk, we found an abandoned shack on the edge of a lake that had probably been used for fishing. As we crossed the distance to the small building, a black cat darted from the porch and into the bushes at the shoreline. Poor fella must be freezing.

We entered and I set Depweg down on the cot in the corner of the room. Noticing that he had begun to shiver, I went to the small cast-iron furnace and threw in some pre-cut logs. Crouching down, I focused on a small portion of wood and ignited it. The flames slowly grew, bringing with it heat that slowly edged most of the cold out of the tiny shack.

"I'll give it to you Germans, you know how to build stuff," I said while looking around at the structure and nodding. "Speaking of, why did you try and kill me if you thought I was a Nazi?"

"They are evil, and I have sworn to stop those who harm the innocent." I was beginning to like this guy.

"Why don't you have an accent?" I asked, squinting at him.

"Why don't you? Your red beard indicates Irish or Scottish de—" he started.

"Irish!" I corrected immediately.

"I stand corrected. However, my point is still valid."

"We all have our gifts, I suppose," I said while nodding and casually looking at the ground, letting what he'd said set in my mind. I had never met another supe before.

Depweg moaned and reached for his oozing torso. I stepped closer to him and said, "Let me try something." I extended my hand and touched his skin. It was cold, and that worried me. Letting blood flow out from my hand, I focused on his injuries. As the blood inched its way to his cuts, I was met with a bolt of lightning that coursed through my arm, making it go numb for a moment.

"Lilith damn it! What was that?" I asked while shaking my arm out, letting the feeling seep back into it.

"The...silver," Depweg said weakly, as if he were out of breath. "It left a residue. You'll...have to burn it closed." As he finished, his eyes shifted to the furnace. I turned my head, following his gaze, then nodded in understanding.

I grabbed a quartered log and opened the furnace grate. I stuck in the end of the log and let it catch fire. Once it was sufficiently blazing, I stood and walked to Depweg. He took his shirt off and then rolled the fabric, sticking the lump between his teeth. Looking me in the eyes with full knowledge of what was about to come, he nodded once.

I stuck the end of the log to the bottommost wound and left it there for a few seconds.

Depweg bucked and screamed through clenched teeth, the cloth dampening the noise. The smell of burning flesh filled the small room, reminding me of the girl back in London. She was long since dead now, but hopefully she had had a full life with a family. Maybe her puppy had had a litter of its own, continuing the cycle of life.

"It's closed. *It's closed!*" Depweg yelled. I was snapped out of my train of thought and moved the log further down the wound, careful to keep it in place only as long as was needed.

In short order, and after a lot of muffled screaming, all of Depweg's wounds were closed. The skin blistered around the slashes. He let the cloth fall from his mouth and took in several ragged breaths. Snot hung off his chin, and he wiped it from his face with the back of his huge forearm. He looked at me and smiled.

"Your turn," he said, smirking.

"What?" I asked, standing up and backing away.

He pointed at my jawline, right above my neck. I lifted my hand and was amazed to feel fresh blood still flowing.

"Look, ah, me and fire don't really get along," I said nervously.

"No choice. It will not heal on its own," Depweg said while lifting himself into a sitting position with his good arm. I noticed his broken arm had already straightened. Interesting.

He stood up and reached out a hand, gesturing for the still burning log. With a mountain of reluctance, I handed it to him. I was fairly sure a whimper left my mouth at one point. Depweg's smile widened. It was his turn.

I backed into the corner and Depweg followed. Turning my head, I closed my eyes and waited, hoping I wouldn't explode into flames.

Ulric flashed in my mind, wailing in agony and thrashing his limbs while coated in merciless flames.

"Wait!" I said, placing a hand on Depweg's massive chest. I manifested the sharpest blade I could imagine in my right hand, placed it at my jawline where my ear connected, and then sliced. I removed skin, muscle, and even most of my jawbone. Blood cascaded from the horrific wound, coating my torso in a sheet of crimson.

Depweg stepped back, wide-eyed and openmouthed.

"What are you doing?!" he almost screamed. Disgust morphed his features.

Closing my eyes, I sent all my will and focus into my face. I saw the artery stop gushing, then the bone filling out. Muscle grew over my jaw and skin started advancing from both fronts, meeting in the middle. A few moments later, I was as good as new. My beard finished the picture by sprouting to its former glory.

Depweg still stood holding the burning log, and wordlessly marveled at what he had just witnessed.

"Can't have any residue if you cut it all out," I said with a smile. My fingers ran over my beard and the new skin underneath.

"You heal with incredible speed," he said admiringly.

"Well, I had a big lunch," I indicated by patting my stomach.

Depweg touched his own stomach, which seemed to growl its jealousy.

"Hungry?" I asked.

"Always. But after sustaining these injuries, I must feed to gain my strength back."

"Ooh, ooh!" I shouted while jumping up and down. "Can I drain the Nazis and you eat their flesh?"

"That, my friend, sounds like a plan."

We headed back out into the night, coming across another small unit of SS soldiers.

"John," Depweg said while stripping off his remaining clothing, "Want to see a magic trick?"

Having lived through the old-world era of magicians being regarded as royalty, I nodded enthusiastically.

He dropped to the snow-covered ground on all fours. Limbs popped and extended. Hair, no, *fur* started sprouting from every inch of exposed skin. His jaws cracked and grew out from his face. Teeth elongated into fangs that looked like my piercers, but it was all of them versus just my two.

After a minute or a minute and a half—I'm bad with time—the transformation was complete. Snow started collecting in his fur, and he shook his entire body, clearing it.

Lifting his head to the sky, a bellow erupted into the night that almost made me jump out of my skin. It was a howl unlike any I had ever heard any creature make. Hairs prickled on my skin, and I shuddered. It seemed, even to my ears, that there were multiple sounds emanating from his throat, and it was off-putting. It sounded like someone had used all their outstretched fingers to create a single chord on a piano, but the sound wasn't unified. Some would argue it was minor, others would say it had to be diminished or augmented. Either way, it was unnerving as hell.

Depweg let the howl linger in the air after he stopped, and it had the desired impact. The camp grew silent, and every soldier came out of their ramshackle buildings and stood near the large fire in the center.

With a chuff, Depweg sprang forward and rushed toward the camp. After a moment of awe, I realized what was happening and joined in the chase.

Depweg barreled through one of the flimsy wooden buildings that had been hastily built and out the other side. I mentally took back my statement of Germans building quality structures.

I slowed to a fast walk as I watched this giant wolf, who had somehow doubled in size, rip men apart.

"Save some for me!" I yelled as I started running again. I pulled out a bloodspear and threw it at the men who were frozen in place with fear. It pierced two of them and gashed the leg of a third. I willed blood from the two men before their hearts could stop beating, feeling the rush of life energy flood into me. I started laughing at the top of my lungs and running in place, barely able to contain the energy.

Depweg leaped on the men as they died and began rending massive chunks of flesh from bone. I pulled back my spear and willed it into a sword, letting another sword grow from my free hand.

Bloodlust engulfed my world as I vaulted from Nazi to Nazi, stabbing at swollen livers and inhaling every ounce of liquid flowing through their arteries as quickly as inhaling a deep, chest-expanding breath. Bleached bodies fell to the ground where my new best friend, pun intended, tore into the meatiest of body parts before going to the next.

Gracefully flying through the air in a magnificent summersault, I was in awe of how fast this gorgeous monster took entire thighs in one bite, followed by calves, arms, and then the chest; all the most protein-dense cuts. He seemed to almost swallow the meat whole, allowing for an excellent time-to-kill ratio. PS took note of how powerful the beast was, and stored it for later reference.

Letting my bloodblades absorb back into my palms, I picked up the quivering frame of the last man standing—rather, last man in a fetal position. Holding his neck and pulling his back to my chest, I used my free hand to dive deep into his mind, searching for a particular memory. Letting myself slide down the tendril into his skull, I effortlessly found the part of the mind associated with stored information. Like flipping through a book, I searched his recent memories until I came across what I was looking for, letting myself slide behind the eyes of his past.

I was a passenger in his memory, unable to alter anything. My eyes surveyed what he had seen; my ears listened to what he had heard. Unfortunately, this man suffered from tinnitus, and I could only make out what was directly around me. That was one of the subtle gifts that I'd most appreciated once turned; total silence from the ringing that plagued any who worked around loud animals, machinery, and gunfire.

We were in a room, possibly a large tent, with several seats pointed uniformly to a large map of Europe. On the map were several red arrows, each of which marked a camp and the progression of the spreading army. In an instant, I knew everything I had sought to learn, and let my essence flow back into myself.

"Thanks," I whispered in his ear before sinking my teeth into his neck. It was fun to go back to the tried-and-true methods of feeding from time to time. I didn't inhale everything he offered. Instead, I opted to enjoy each frantic heartbeat as it spurted otherworldly ecstasy into my being. My eyes rolled back, and a primal moan emanated from somewhere deep inside my chest. The Nazi fought at first, but grew weaker with each betraying beat of his heart. Once the organ began to pound an erratic beat, I sucked the remaining life in one gulp.

My eyes rolled back into focus, and I was momentarily stunned at the enormous, salivating wolf in front of me. I stood unmoving as the beast chuffed and stepped forward a pace.

Realization dawned as a glob of blood, mixed with saliva, fell in a string to the ground. I held the drained body out in front of me, lifeless limbs hanging loose and head bobbing with the motion. Depweg whined.

"You want this, huh? Do ya boy?" I teased, moving the body back and forth in front of the monster.

Depweg answered with a growl that reverberated through the ground and up my feet. Fangs were bared, and the point was made clear.

"Only a joke," I said apologetically, dropping the body and raising my hands up in placation.

Keeping his slit eyes on me, Depweg lowered his head and rammed his point home. He bit off the arm of the man then began eating it, bones and all. He might as well have been eating a fresh loaf of bread. His gaze never left me as the last of the fingers went down his throat in a dramatic display.

"You and me, we're going to be great friends. I can feel it," I said with a smile.

After he finished his meal, Depweg trotted over to one of the buildings, stuck his head in, then moseyed on to the next. After a few buildings, he chuffed and walked inside. From outside, I could hear the popping of bones and ligaments, accompanied by a controlled, muffled whimpering.

I crunched through the fresh snow and into the lukewarm building to find Depweg removing clothing from a large backpack. I noted the burns on his torso were healing up nicely. He donned the contents of the pack, starting with the full body long johns and finishing with the boots that were a half size too big.

As he finished, I asked, "Hey, you just ate at least thirty kilos of meat. Where did it all go?" I gestured to his flat abdomen.

"How many gallons of blood did you just consume?" he returned the question, staring at my own stomach. I looked down, patting it.

"Touché, sir." I had always wondered where the surplus went. Ulric had theorized that it was instantly converted into energy, but had had no insight as to where the physical blood went.

Depweg was now wearing a full Nazi soldier's uniform while I wore the shit out of an officer's coat, albeit without the medals and sleeve.

"What's the plan, Deppyweg?" I asked playfully.

"Well, Jonathan—"

"It's just John," I provided with a rehearsed interruption.

Putting emphasis on the first word, he continued, "*I* plan on taking out as many of these bastards as I can for using my body in their experiments."

"That is the keenest thing I've ever heard. Thank you for sharing that with me," I said in awe.

His stern look was both assessing and annoyed.

"That is whacky of them, though. But hey! I happen to know where every one of those jerks' camps are, and what directions they are going. I could show you?" I was less than confident that he would bite, if you'll excuse the pun.

"What, like a couple of spooks?" he asked. His features softened.

"Pardon? I haven't heard that lingo before," I said, confused if I was in or not.

To answer, he said in German, "Better get used to modern slang if you're going to be in cahoots with me."

I answered in perfect German, "I don't know what 'cahoots' means either."

"Your German is too perfect. There are nuances to each region. Tell me, where is the next encampment?"

I told him, and we were off. As we trudged through the snow, he provided information on the accents of the different regions, and told me of his horrific backstory. After I told him my own, we walked in silence, feeling each other's seeping wounds that drove us to eliminate the villainous cancers of the world. A comradery was born that night, and it felt good to walk alongside another supe with a moral compass that aligned with my own.

Chapter 25

PRESENT

I awoke to cold water dripping on my forehead. My eyelids felt like weighted steel and were almost impossible to open. The muscles in my body felt like concrete, and it took a massive effort to move. I drunkenly pawed at the LED switch on the side, and the lights came on.

The trickling sped up as water found new cracks to enter through, meeting in the middle and rushing to kiss my face.

I pushed with all my might on the lid, but my muscles couldn't bear the weight. Water started pouring in like a cascade into my coffin.

I wasn't worried about drowning, but the water was starting to burn from the iron residue being dragged in and mixing into a John soup. "Good to know," I murmured, trying to force myself awake. It was taking all my energy to stay conscious.

Placing my hands on the iron, I tried to move it sideways, upward, and downward. Nothing worked. I lay back in the burning water and started to panic. I knew it had to be daytime outside, but I shouldn't be weak enough that I couldn't even lift my damn lid! An image of me wearing Uggs and holding a Starbucks coffee while yelling, "I can't even!" shot through my mind.

The iron-infused water was now up to my ears. I raised my head and became aware that an alarming amount of my hair was now floating, unattached to my noggin.

Water filled the coffin up to where the switches were, and sparks exploded in my face. Darkness swallowed the light in an explosion of blackness, leaving me alone with only my gasps of panic and sloshing water for company. The iron would soon snake its way into my blood, ensuring I would die an incredibly painful death inside my own coffin.

In my best (given the circumstances) Bill Paxton voice, I said, "Game over, man. Game over!"

There was an impact on the lid, moving it slightly, but then fell back into place. I lifted my burning head and screamed, "Da? *Da,* is that you?"

I could barely make out a voice from outside the coffin saying, "Who else would it be, you dolt? Now *push*! I can't move this thing alone."

"On the count of three!" I yelled, gurgling water as it neared the top. "*Three!*"

There was another impact, and one of the hydraulics broke apart. Inside the coffin, I flattened my back, which dunked my head under the corrosive water, placed my palms and feet on the lid, and pushed with everything I had left.

My eyelids were starting to be eaten through, and my lips were unable to hold their seal. Acidic water poured into my mouth, sending a renewed hysteria through my core. I shifted my hands and feet to the side that had the broken hydraulic and pushed. It was unlife or death. There was an impact on the bedroom floor that was felt just as much as heard, even with my ears underwater. After that, the lid came up easily on the remaining hydraulic.

Da peeked into the coffin as I was jumping out, and I trampled him as we both fell into the water that was invading my home. I made my way to my knees and pulled myself up to wobbly feet. There was a giant boulder lying next to my bed with a ton of dark dirt everywhere. Looking up, I noticed a SUV-sized hole on my ceiling.

Drunkenly, I asked, "The fuck is going on, Da?"

"We are being attacked," he said while climbing up one of my drawers to try and dry his clothes. "I think it's Locke. Perhaps it's time to test out your bat exit, yes?"

"Wait," I said while reaching back into the burning water of the coffin to grab a few bags of sealed blood. With them secure, I said, "Okay, let's go."

We made our way to my bookshelf—me stumbling like a Russian on any day of the week. I ripped open a bag and sucked it dry, feeling instantly better, but the damage was still severe. I needed as much blood as I could to fight off the detrimental iron particles that were making their way to my bloodstream. The blood wasn't even a fraction as effective as straight from the tap, but anything helped.

I drank the other bag, threw down the container, and flipped the head of the bust on my bookshelf. Underneath was a button, which I pressed. There was a click, and the hidden door swung inward. We moved through it, and Da closed it behind us as I stumbled through the waist-high water in the tunnel. It was big enough for two men standing shoulder to shoulder, and tall enough to accommodate my six-foot frame.

After a hundred feet, it started to curve upward at a slant. In short order, the water was down to my knees, then ankles, until we were finally out of it. We continued moving at an angle away from my home. My legs still moved as if fully submerged in water, and the tops of my eyelids fought to hold on to the bottoms, like a scared mother and child huddling in the dark with iron grips.

"How the hell did he know where my coffin was?" I drunkenly asked Da.

"Probably because it's the only spot in the compound that he couldn't see," he suggested.

In my best Bob Peck impression, I said, "Clever girl..."

We made our way to the ladder constructed of 2x4s and climbed the ten feet up to the cover we had hidden with a fake bush at the edge of the property.

"Hey, what time is it. Do you know?" I asked Da, looking down at him.

"Do I look like I wear a watch?" he asked.

"Oh, I'm sorry, Mr. iPad," I mocked.

I placed my hand on the cover and lifted extra slowly. My muscles still had concrete inside them, so I had to put some force into it. So instead of inching the lid up, it shot up all of a sudden when I put in too much uncontrolled effort.

Thank Lilith for the shade that the bush had provided, but the sunlight still shone through, scalding my face and blinding me.

A scream escaped my mouth as my eyes melted in their sockets. I clamped my hands around my mouth to dampen the sound, and I dropped the metal cover on my head, knocking me down to the ground ten feet below. Da barely dodged out of the way with a curse, dropping down after me.

"Are you alright?" he asked in alarm.

"Sun: 2. John: 0," I said, barely conscious.

"I think it's daytime, John," he remarked in response to my earlier question.

My head slowly turned toward his voice with, what I imagined to be, an obvious look of annoyance.

"Let's just hope they don't find my supersecret exi—"

An explosion of wood sounded deep in the tunnel behind us.

"You had to say something," Da said with a sigh.

"Well, shit," was my only response. "What now? Grab a walking cane and attack Locke with it?"

The sound of sloshing water was barely audible in the distance.

"They're coming. Can't you use some magic to collapse the tunnel behind us?" he asked.

"It's day, man. I'm having trouble just staying awake, let alone use any of my focus. Plus, being kissed on the forehead by sunlight isn't fucking helping at all. Not to mention the freaking iron dust in my Lilith-damned body!" My voice started to rise at the end.

"Alright. Alright. Let's calm down," he begged.

"Calmer than you are," I said.

"If we can't use your magic, then let's *outthink* them," he said with hope in his voice.

I heard tiny hands digging in the dirt about six feet away from the ladder, where it would still be dark even if the cover was taken off. I grasped what he was doing after a moment, and blindly crawled on my hands and feet to where he had already dug—I was assuming—an adorable little hole.

My hands dug into the cool, damp earth, which I scooped into a big pile.

The sounds of trudging through the water became quicker as they moved up the tunnel into the shallows.

"Climb in," Da said. "I'll throw them off your trail. But first..."

I heard him fly away and up the ladder. There was the sound of the cover coming loose. Warm light flooded the tunnel and stayed that way for a couple of heartbeats. Then the cover was replaced, and Da flew back to me.

"Now, this may hurt a little," he warned before stabbing me in the chest with what I could only assume was a piece of molten metal forged in the depths of Mordor itself.

With a pitch reserved for little girls, I sharply inhaled to scream again, but the agony wouldn't let me exhale.

"John, I need you to scream with all your might," Da said, and then used another piece of white-hot metal to cut off my arm at the elbow. I obliged his request.

The scream shook the walls, and loose dirt rained down. The sound of footsteps stopped.

"What...?" I started, at the edge of passing out.

"I stabbed you with iron to prevent Locke from finding you via divination. Then I cut off your hand to place it at the edge of where the light is."

"So that they think I died trying to escape," I finished through clenched teeth.

"Exactly!" he said triumphantly.

"I think I already had enough iron in my body to prevent that," I remarked as he moved the mound of dirt on top of me and then spread the excess around the tunnel.

He briefly stopped. "Better to be extra sure, then!" he said.

After he was finished, I heard the plop of my arm, and then the tunnel cover was opened again, letting the edge of the light sear the end of my arm to a smoldering ember. With that, he did his disappearing act right as the first goon made his way up the tunnel. The cover went back into place, leaving behind the smell of burnt and rotted flesh behind.

The goon walked all around the tunnel, looking for any clues he could find. He stopped at my arm for a moment, then stepped forward to the ladder. I could hear his dull footsteps on the wooden rungs as he made his way up, then the sound of the cover moving. Another few moments passed before the goon moved it out of the way entirely and then climbed back down, grabbing my arm. With that in hand, no pun intended, I could hear him retreat down the corridor toward my underwater home.

With the tunnel spinning and no longer able to keep my nonexistent eyes open anymore, I succumbed and let the black tendrils of unconsciousness grab hold and pull me under.

"Jonathan," I heard in my dreams. *"I know you are not dead. Well, more dead than usual."*

I snapped back into reality, aware of a darkness near me.

"John-a-thon..." Locke purred, only feet away from me. "I can smell you, still. You aren't dead, are you?" His footsteps wandered back and forth up the tunnel, stopping periodically.

I kept as still as inhumanly possible, which was incredibly easy with the iron stabbed into my chest.

He chanted something under his breath, and I could feel an ethereal hand slide over me without pausing. I felt it rest at where my arm had been lying. Smoke from the freshly seared John flesh still drifted in the air where the arm had been burned with the light.

After a moment, Locke took in a deep breath and said, "Well, that's anticlimactic. Died like the coward you were. Your father would have been ashamed. At least *he* died like a man."

I was stunned by what had just pierced my ears and ricocheted throughout my brain.

After realization set in, rage built in my chest, and my remaining hand, which was resting on my stomach, clenched into a fist, moving the dirt as I did.

Locke took notice of the sound, but couldn't locate exactly where it was coming from.

"I still remember how he begged for your mother's life, and yours. He didn't care how much we tortured him as long as we let his wife and son go. I lied, of course, and promised I would free the both of you the instant he gave me his confession. He gave me everything and more."

The weight of what he was saying crushed my chest and turned my guts into sludge. The only reason I wasn't shaking with anger was simply because I had nothing left in me, plus the iron that had eaten most of my skin and pierced my chest kept me barely not-alive. All I could do was lay there, listening to his taunts about how he had killed my fucking family.

He continued, "After his official confession, I leaned over where we had him strapped to a table, and whispered in his ear *exactly* what I was going to do to your mother. I'll give it to him though, Jonathan. He did not cry. He didn't even tear up. Your father simply turned his gaze to the ceiling and stayed that way, jaw set, as we pulled his intestines out inch by agonizing inch." Locke finished and stood still, expectantly.

Pressing his point, Locke continued, "I still remember the smell of searing flesh as your mother screamed and clawed, futilely," he was almost laughing as he spoke, giddy with delight.

Tears welled and mixed with the dirt at the bottom of my eyelids, where the light had just stopped eating my flesh. My bottom lip trembled slightly.

"It was an amusing game, the cat and mouse we played. But then, one day, you just stopped playing. I was so disappointed. Didn't you get all the clues I left for you? No? You don't think," he gasped in mock surprise, "that your companion, Ulric, found them before you and hid them, do you?"

Everything went still in my mind. My body went numb. I saw Ulric in my memories, always insisting on spreading out when searching for information. The only good leads coming from what I found. I knew he had prevented me from discovering the passage of time, but to actually *hide* information from me...to prolong the chase intentionally. That was a fresh bag of bullshit.

"Hmm. Oh well. I suppose this game is over too soon as well," he said, and then started to make his way to the ladder. A foot stepped on my face, packing the dirt and mud into my empty sockets. I heard him climb the ladder and remove the cover. Then he was outside.

His words ran through my head over and over, etching themselves permanently in my brain. That son of a bitch had killed my mother and father. Tortured them first. Given my father false hope before crashing it down and prolonging his death. I had finally found my parent's killer, something that Ulric had denied me for so long.

The sounds of the night filled the tunnel. I needed fresh blood with blinding ferocity. With Da still MIA, it was up to me—*blood*—to get myself out. I started moving my fingers up my chest like a man crawling on the ground. *Kill.* It took what seemed like forever—*hungry*—until I reached the white-hot iron that was stabbed into my chest. It didn't budge. *Now! Now! Now!* The thirst was too much to bear. *Throat, anyone's throat, everyone's throat.* It was getting increasingly difficult to focus—*feed, feed now*—but I managed to push one of my nails underneath the metal sticking out of my skin and lift it forward a fraction of an inch. This gave me new vigor, and I moved my hand closer for better leverage, placed my finger underneath it again, and pushed with all my strength. The nail popped out, and a rush of energy flooded my body. *Kill now! Kill now! Eat now! Eat now!*

PS shoved me aside and grabbed the wheel, daring me to try and take it back.

I burst through my cavernous grave, oriented myself toward the ladder, and jumped *through* the ground, exploding to the surface and into the air for several feet. Once I landed—*blood nearby, find, kill, eat*—I smelled what I craved for survival.

My eyes were still gone, but my other senses were sharper than any mortal predator. I used them to guide me. When in full hunter mode, I could *see* the blood of my prey in any light. The energy and heat given off pulled at my senses, like a snake tracking its next meal.

Hunt. There! Kneeling at the cold rock, holding the strong-smelling plants. Eat her.

I got closer, stalking her from behind. I leaped through the air and tackled my prey to the ground, sinking my teeth into her neck. I wasn't delicate, and bit through half her neck. Blood sprayed out, coating the gravestone. Even in my literal blind rage, my consciousness, which had been thrown into the back seat, could read that the gravestone was for a young man of about twenty-five due to the outline of the still warm blood on the stone.

Changing position and moving my mouth to better catch the arterial spray, I drained every last drop. It wasn't enough, so I pushed on the gaping hole in her neck and sucked with everything I had. Her body shriveled in my hands. I had to spit out chunks of vascular tissue that were ripped out, and dropped the body. The hunger still had control of me.

There was a car running on the path, and I leaped over to it, grabbing and then ripping the door off its hinges. My eyes were growing from the fresh blood, as was the stub at the end of my arm, which grew longer by the second.

As my eyes healed, I could make out a child sitting in the back seat holding a superhero action figure. He lifted the hero in defense, eyes wide and streaming tears. Snarling, I ferociously crawled into the car and reached into the back.

A small, powerful hand grabbed my belt and yanked me backward with enough force to send me tumbling in the air several feet. The seat I had been clutching came with me, ripped from the metal frame of the vehicle.

"*John!*" Da's voice screamed at me. But not just at me. *Inside* my head. I always hated it when supes did that.

The booming voice stunned me, allowing my consciousness to wrestle the wheel back and gain control of my body. The horror of what I had just done started seeping in as the primal part of me receded into a corner of my mind.

In a booming voice, Da commanded, "Look at me, now!"

I lifted my head to see Da glowing white with plumes of energy blooming off him, arcing upward like a Jacob's ladder.

He. Was. Pissed.

My eyes had fully healed, allowing me to see as my bloodlust wore off. I turned my head and spotted the shriveled mummy of a corpse sitting in front of...

"Her husband's grave, John. In front of their *now* orphan child, no less," Da scolded. The child was whimpering in the back seat. The air carried the smell of urine, furthering my shame. "Now this boy will have to endure losing both his parents with what you did this evening, causing untold psychological damage. You," he pointed right at me, "are a monster."

I sat there with my blood-soaked mouth hanging open in wordless surprise.

"I—"

"*Don't. You. Dare!*" Da screamed.

There was a flush in my face, and I wasn't positive if it came from the fresh blood or my overwhelming feeling of embarrassment and shame. With my tail tucked between my legs, I stood up and started walking away, head hanging low. Tears brimmed in my eyes as the surreal events that had taken place cemented into reality. It was all too much. Locke surviving the centuries and revealing Ulric's betrayal sat at the forefront of my thoughts, making me dizzy.

I stopped walking and looked up from the ground with an expression of anguish blossoming on my face. I had just done to that boy what Locke had done to me...Locke had made me into a monster.

No. I had done that on my own by letting PS off his leash. In my mind's eye, I turned to stare at PS, who was hiding in the shadows. Only two rubies glinted where his eyes were. He was regretful, but for the same reason a dog was after being punished by its master for chewing the couch; he didn't know what he had done wrong, only that the master was angry.

I looked up into the sky and vowed to never let PS take full control like that again. I would also have to find a way to ensure that child had a good life, declaring it my responsibility to make it right.

With both of my hands in full functioning order, I placed them in my pockets and sullenly walked away from the cemetery toward the church.

A montage of thoughts rushed into the theater of my mind, and I bore witness to the complete puzzle, now that the missing pieces had been found. Ulric hiding valuable information from me and knowing Locke had survived the centuries, if he had, as Locke had stated, left clues.

Locke. My modern-day bully. The pain in my ass that no cream would calm. I thought about all of our interactions since my move to Houston back in the '90s. He had to have known who I was and what he had done to me.

I clenched my teeth and shouted at the ground, "He fucking *knew* who I was the whole time!" My fists where shaking in the air now with fury. "It was all a damn joke to him, and I was the punch line!"

I took in a deep breath and wrestled my emotions back to Zen. I was not going to let Locke control me, especially after what I had just done in the cemetery. I was in control, not that murderous fuck.

It hit me again, and I stopped in my tracks. Looking up to the black, starless sky, I asked myself, "Am I any better?" The wind blew cool across my skin in answer, further drying the blood of the innocent that matted my beard.

I became aware that I was walking down a public road looking like I had just pigged out at an all-you-can-eat BBQ which had run out of napkins. Bringing my hand up to my face, I willed blood through my palms and used that to coat my entire face, letting it hydrate the dried blood and intermingle with mine. After a moment, I willed all the blood back inside my hand again, leaving my face crimson-free. I ran my fingers through my beard to straighten it out, and adjusted the gray beanie still on my head. A slip of hair escaped through one of the bullet holes, and I mentally noted that I should see my dry-cleaning guy soon.

A few minutes after walking while lost in the thick forest of my thoughts, I looked up and realized I was approaching Valenta's.

"Sign taken," I said to the building.

Brushing the excess dirt off my coat, shirt, and pants, I put on a fake smile and entered the saloon.

There were two tables occupied by supes that stopped all conversation as soon as I entered. Valenta stood behind the bar with a scowl on his face, making a point not to look at me. I could feel all the other eyes moving up and down my body, piercing my upbeat facade.

I quietly walked to the bar and sat down in front of Val. His eyes were closed tight, and he inhaled deeply. After a few moments, I spoke.

"Hey, man. How's business tonight?" I meekly asked.

His eyes opened and locked on mine. There was a white fire that blazed behind them, pulsing with the vein in his forehead.

"Ya stupid, undead fuck," he spat. "You've any idea the shitstorm you're in, boy?" His voice increased in intensity as he went on. "You let mortals see you, boy!" He slammed his fist on the bar, forming a crack down its length and sending glasses careening to the ground. I dropped my face toward the worn wood of the floor, defeated by those I called friend.

The other supes quickly got up from their chairs, dropped some money on the tables, and left. Murmurs lingered in the air until the door closed behind them, leaving only a fierce Valenta, and me.

His voice returned to its normal cadence and volume. "You're dead, ya realize. Hope ya packed your bags, 'cause you've bought a one-way ticket off this mortal plane."

His words stung, like a father telling his son how disappointed he was.

I clenched my jaw and leveled my gaze at him.

"Let them try. All of them. I'll tear each and every one of those fuckers down. If they kill me, I'll drag as many as I can down to the pits of eternity. And when I'm in Hell, I'll slap the Devil in the face. Now give me a Lilith damn drink, Valenta!" I yelled and slammed down enough money to get the job done.

After the silence grew awkward, Valenta reluctantly poured my first drink. As he started to pull the bottle of my special mix away, I commanded, "Leave it."

A show of disappointment crept into his face as he studied me. His eyebrows lifted, and his shoulders slightly shrugged in placation as he moved down the bar, picking up pieces of glass as he went. To him, I was already dead. Well, deader.

I floated the entire bottle within an hour, getting super schwifty wasted. Getting up to leave, I glanced over at Val, who was still ignoring me.

Trying to keep my balance, I pointed my finger at the spot where now two Valentas were standing behind the bar twirling in circles around each other, along with all the stools and the bar. My mouth hung open, unable to speak with the room spinning like a kaleidoscope.

I pushed my mouth closed with my hand and slowly turned to the door, teetering to one side or the other the whole way.

In the parking lot, I looked around and noticed it was completely empty.

"Schit," I slurred, "Bhasterd had mah car towed," not realizing in my hammered stupor that I had left the car back at the Batcave.

The walk to the church was challenging. Did I say walk? I meant hammered stumble. Even drunk me questioned my decision to imbibe as much as I had, and Val had just let me do it. Of course, he had been operating under the assumption that this might be my last night undead. It wouldn't take long for the footage to go viral and for a bounty to be put out on my head by the wardens of the supernatural community.

"Lhet dem come," I said to a featureless black cat that was watching me from the shadows. Its eyes reflected the moonlight. "And when I dead, ill chock slahp tha Debil...wit mah dhick...on the fhace...wit mah dhick." The cat yawned and sauntered deeper into the shadows, unamused with my antics.

While spinning to face the street again, I lost my balance and fell on my back.

"Dhidn't fheel hit," I said, turning my head to try and fight the dizziness.

Footsteps approached. I lay still, trying to triangulate on their position. They came closer, growing more prominent. When they stopped close by, I leaned up and threw my hands out yelling, "Boogity boogity booooooooo!"

There was no one in front of me. A hand rested on my shoulder from behind, and a familiar voice said, "Your friend told me where I could find you."

"Fhather T? Is that ye?" I said as everything went black.

Chapter 26

PRESENT DAY

My eyes fought to open. Usually, my preternatural sight let me see in the pitch black, but even after a few moments, my vision was filled with complete darkness.

I was lying on an old, twin-size bed that smelled of a forgotten closet filled with thick clothing. Sitting up, I tried to swing my legs off the bed and onto the floor when noticed a weight attached to my ankle. My hands explored the cold rock of the wall and found a metal loop where a chain was attached. The metal slightly burned my exposed skin as I grasped it to follow its length. It ended at my ankle, where a metal ring wrapped around a leather cuff.

"I wouldn't play with it too much, my son. It's iron," an elderly, calm voice informed.

"F-Father Thomes..." I stammered, "What's going on?" It was impossible to hide my confusion and building fear. The clergy had hunted vampires for millennia, so I knew Father Thomes could end my existence with little trouble, especially if I was chained to a stone wall with iron. "Why am I so weak if the leather is protecting me from the iron?" I asked almost breathlessly, exhausted.

"It's day, John. This was for your own protection, as well as that of the innocent."

I didn't respond, knowing exactly what he meant.

"A grieving wife and mother, John. In front of her child. Thank the Almighty that you were stopped before you took his life as well," he scolded.

A light was switched on, blinding me for a moment. I shielded my eyes, not only from the light but to hide the tears that had sprung.

"I am afraid what you have done has set you back substantially," he said.

Clearing my eyes and wiping my nose, I pleaded, "It wasn't *me*, Father. I had no control."

He stood up fiercely, glaring at me, and boomed in a commanding voice, "And you think that matters, abomination?" The fear must have been evident in my face because his posture relaxed and he regained composure. "John, we are free to make whatever decision we want on this plane. It's the consequences we cannot avoid. No matter our intentions, we will always pay for our sins in the end."

I turned my head away from him, ashamed.

"I am tired of everyone else telling me what I've done." I turned and looked right at him. "I fucking know what I've done, old man, and you couldn't possibly comprehend the eternal struggle that battles inside of me Every. Single. Night. The thirst that clutches at my every thought, clouding my judgment at the best of times, and taking the wheel of control away at the worst."

Tears brimmed in my eyes again, and fury rose in my chest. I matched his ferocity as I stood. "How dare you pretend to know what it's like, mortal. How about I throw you and a small child into the churning ocean with a tattered life vest and we see what decisions a drowning man makes."

With that, his posture straightened and he wordlessly turned and left the room, flipping the light off behind him. The sound of heavy metal locks clicked into place. I was his prisoner.

The urge to scream after him to free me was almost overwhelming, but the futility of it kept my mouth shut. I knew he would never set me free unless I could assure him no other innocents would be hurt. The truth was, I didn't mind hiding in his basement. None of the other supes would find me here, so it was just as good a spot as any to lay low.

My mind repeated the events of the night with Da, Val, and Father Thomes over and over. I was almost impressed with myself. Having the ability to alienate three out of the four people whom I could call friends was reserved for made-for-TV villains.

"Note to self: send an edible arrangement filled with meat to Depweg," I said to the air as I lay back on the bed. The day was still holding my energy hostage, dampening it.

I closed my eyes and let the little death come.

Chapter 27

PRESENT DAY

Night came. While the sun slept, my vision became supercharged and I surveyed the room, searching for anything I could use. The room was empty besides the bed. Though I couldn't touch it, I could feel the door to my prison was made of iron. It only took an hour—or half a night, I have no sense of time—to give up and put all my eggs in the basket of Father T eventually freeing me.

There was no sound that my ears could pick up, nor a single smell that my nose could detect that was out of the ordinary. If the father was in the building, he was being remarkably quiet. Either that or I was deep in the catacombs beneath the church. Which, if true, would be exceptionally impressive for a church in Houston.

I sat in my cell throughout the night, staring at the ceiling. As the hours dragged on, I could feel dawn approaching, even though there were no windows. My vision began to diminish and my energy dropped, filling my limbs with concrete.

When morning was fully upon me, I let myself slip into unconsciousness. I awakened again at dusk to the same scenario, and felt the first pangs of the thirst. I decided to try and free myself with fresh eyes and a more determined mind. Thirst was a powerful motivator.

I spent the better part of the night trying to figure out a way to free myself. Yanking was fruitless. He must have blessed the metals, effectively canceling my preternatural strength. I tried piercing the stone wall and digging around the restraint, but it, too, would not budge.

"The hell is on these walls? Iron paint?" I asked, realizing that's exactly what it was.

A sinking feeling in the pit of my stomach began to form as the realization that he had made this room specifically for me crept into my mind.

Nights passed without any semblance of the father being home. Hunger started to overtake my every waking thought. Even my dreams were erratic and focused on blood, creating imagery that I had only seen in movies where the hero started tripping after imbibing an unknown liquid.

PS crept from the shadows, threatening to take charge if I didn't feed. I hadn't had my fill after my encounter with Locke, or even the demon before that, and I was weaker than a newborn kitten.

"Locke," I exhaled through gritted teeth. My train of thought locked onto his gaunt, smiling face. All other thoughts were held hostage from the raw hatred that bloomed from the seed long since thought lost in time. The memory of my parents being brutally executed was all-consuming, replacing all reason and logic with pure, unbridled rage. I lived to wrap my hands around Locke's skinny neck and crush the life out of him. I wanted to rip his head off and then laugh in his blinking face before he went to Hell. Hating him became a part of me again, and that piece slipped right back into place, like an ample ass returning to its favorite recliner. No matter how much time passed, the indentation was always there, welcoming.

I allowed the hate train to pass, focusing back on my predicament and the events that had led me to it. Damn Da. Damn Val. And damn the mortal that kept me as a prisoner. I was tired of trying to do what everyone else wanted me to do. I was going to get out of here.

Following the chain with my eyes, I muttered a curse and decided what I was going to do.

I stood up and moved far enough from the bed to tighten the chain. I reached down and shredded the leather cuff that prevented the iron from touching my body, then rolled up my pant leg, exposing my skin to the enchanted iron. As I did, jolts of lightning and waves of fire shot up my leg and into my core. My breath was taken away as every muscle constricted in agony.

Shaking, I picked up some of the leather pieces and put them between my teeth. Biting down, I brought my leg back toward the wall, shut my eyes, and kicked forward with everything I had.

My ankle exploded, with bones splintering through the back of my leg. The chain dug into my skin, bringing with it a new existence of excruciating pain. I collapsed to the ground, spasming violently and whimpering with each reflexive breath.

The leather muffled my sobs. My vision blackened to a pinpoint. I forced myself to relax and take in deep breaths, which was purely a mental relaxation technique, as I didn't actually need to breathe.

I commanded my hands to find purchase underneath my body, which now seemed to weigh a shit ton. After a couple tries, I was finally able to push myself up and rest on my hands and knees. I pivoted and looked at the damage.

The chain was halfway through my ankle, but what alarmed me was that the iron had started to make my flesh necrotic, and it was quickly spreading up my calf. Panic provided all the strength I needed to get up on my good leg. I expressed this verbally with a barrage of superb vernacular efficiency that would have made Sir Shakespeare jealous.

"Shit, shit, shiiiiit!"

I leaned forward, brought my leg back again, took a deep breath, and kicked as if I were trying to knock down a bank vault.

The kick carried through and the momentum threw me into a backflip, where I landed on my stomach. The electricity stopped flowing through every nerve in my body, and I just lay there, lightly shaking.

After a few moments, I was able to get up on my one good foot and look around. My foot had landed on the bed behind me, still in its shoe. The flesh looked as if it had come from a zombie—the appendage completely consumed by death.

Looking down and balancing on one foot, I lifted my pant leg to see that the decay had spread all the way up to my knee.

"Oh, shit!" I said to myself at the realization that if that last kick hadn't been successful, I wouldn't have been able to move my leg a third time. I would have died in one of the most agonizing ways a vampire, or any living being, possibly could. At least the sun was quick compared to this necrosis.

As I continued to watch, the decay spread over my knee with insatiable appetite.

"Oh Lilith!" I cried out in horror. "Damn you, holy man!"

I looked around the room for anything to stop the expansion. My eyes landed on the chain, and I laughed as my panicking brain desperately tried to convince itself that it would make a good tourniquet.

The deterioration continued to creep up my leg. My knee had already withered, exposing the bone. The tendons snapped and the joint crumbled away, dropping what remained of my leg to the ground, where it evaporated into powder.

I was not about to let this thing take my junk...and my life, of course. I focused on my palms and forced blood through the skin, congealing into a giant pair of bolt cutters.

Placing the living flesh of my thigh between the crimson jaws, I cried out, "Green Lantern ain't got shit on me!" in reference to my blood manifestation, and slammed my hands together, severing the leg just below my pelvis.

The rest of my stump fell to the ground, where it was quickly ravaged by the holy enchantment. I watched in fascination as the once plump and supersexy flesh blew away like a dried-out sandcastle on a windy day. Still holding the supersized bolt cutters, I let the blood liquefy as I brought my palms to the gaping wound that was spilling my life force. I wasn't able to grow the limb back with my lack of energy, but I managed to at least close the wound before the blackness completely swallowed my vision.

I let myself fall to my hands and knee, shambling to the bed. Once I climbed onto the mattress, I turned to face the door while my vision regained control and fought back the darkness. After several minutes, my head stopped swimming, and I pushed myself up to my remaining limb.

"I'll never model for Victoria's Secret again," I said to my now lonely foot, whose workload had just doubled. I hopped over to the door and placed my hand on it, feeling the iron exciting my molecules. "Feck'n knew it," I muttered to myself, letting some of my mother tongue slip through.

I turned in circles, which I was confident looked hilarious, looking around the room, trying to spot the giant sledgehammer that I must have missed before. Alas, there was still no superconvenient tool just lying around. Not even a gas-powered jackhammer.

"Yelp will hear of this atrocity! One star!" I yelled to the ceiling.

Turning to look at the bed, an idea sprouted through the packed earth of my mind filled to capacity with movie facts and references. I stepped forward, eager to fulfill my plan, and then fell on my face.

"Right. The leg...situation," I reminded myself.

My eyes latched onto the door hinges. They were also made of iron, but the peg through the middle had to be a different, stronger metal to support the door.

I got back up and hopped over to the bed, where I grabbed the old comforter and threw it in front of the door. Tossing the mattress to the side, I grabbed the wooden frame of the small twin bed and ripped it in half. I repeated the process on the edge of the frames and took two of the wooden legs in my hands. I awkwardly hobbled to where the comforter now rested as if oblivious to its upcoming fate. I set the two wooden pieces against the wall and picked up the comforter, tearing it into shreds and setting the pieces aside.

I picked the legs back up, placed them together, and started rubbing them against each other. Slowly at first, then faster. After a few seconds, I was rubbing faster than a teenage boy discovering his first porn site. Smoke started to drift from the wood, and I accelerated to supe speed, causing a bright flame to burst from the legs. I set one down and started wrapping the comforter above where the flame was, careful not to catch myself on fire. After I set the torch on the ground under the bottommost door hinge, I repeated the process for the other leg, which I propped just under the middle hinge. Hopping back to the bed, I grabbed a third leg, returned to the door, and used the fire from the first to ignite the wood. After it was wrapped and blazing, I held it up to the topmost hinge, and waited.

At that moment, I heard the big doors of the church entrance swing open then shut again. The sound was faint, but I would recognize the front doors I had entered countless times from anywhere. I could tell that I was, indeed, far beneath the church.

A lump in my throat grew, as I was past the point of no return. I was in his domain, and he could easily extinguish my life. Had you asked me yesternight if I thought Father Thomes had it in him to execute me, I would have heartily laughed. But now, after revealing the monster inside me and killing an innocent, I was just as sure that he would.

After what felt like an eternity plus one, the bottom hinge expanded and broke the casing. A few seconds later, the middle one exploded and went flying, ricocheting around the room. I nervously chuckled at the thought that an iron door hinge could end my life if it hit just right.

Another door lock above was forcefully turned. My eyes were focused on the last hinge, licking my lips in anticipation. Sweat would have beaded on my forehead if such a thing was possible. At that moment, I wondered how I could cry and salivate, but not sweat.

Footsteps started to descend a large, stone spiral staircase.

My face was inching closer to the flame as I slightly bounced on my one good leg.

"Please, please, please, please, please," I pleaded with the hinge.

As if on cue, it exploded, skimming my forehead as it flew past. I grabbed the door and pulled back with all my might, feeling the iron singe my hands. It gave way and I ripped it away from the wall and let it drop on the ground with a thunderous bang.

The footsteps stopped.

I dropped to my hands and ran like a three-legged dog in the opposite way the steps were coming from. I had no idea where I was or what I was going to do. I just kept running, desperate for a window or a...

"Fireplace!" I cried out in happiness as I approached a dark reading room filled with ancient books and scrolls. I leaped over a red velvet chair and slammed into the empty firepit and looked up. The flue was standard metal, so I grabbed it and ripped it off, bringing down a torrent of ashes.

Father Philseep ran through the hall and stopped in the room, looking frantically at me.

"John, I can't let you leave!" the father said sternly, with urgency creeping into his voice.

"You *really* need to clean your chimney more, Father Asshole. It's a fire hazard!" I said before starting my ascent through soot-encrusted darkness.

After a few feet, I heard Father Thomes chanting from below, and then there was a small, fierce fire growing at the base of the pit. I looked down and watched it increase in ferocity, changing colors until it filled the entire base with red, white, and blue flames; very patriotic of him.

The heat was immense and immediate. My remaining pant leg started to singe, which was my cue to hurry the fuck up.

Running on fumes, I hauled ass up the chimney, slipping constantly. The growing flames below attempted the most uncomfortable rim job I'd ever had. Each tongue lashed out with the promise of oblivion if I slowed down.

I reached the top with a photo finish, the flames struggling to reach that high but giving it their all. I clawed at the chimney cap and tore the metal apart like aluminum foil, freeing me from a fiery doomy-doom.

Climbing out, I fell onto the slanted roof and lay there for a moment, my head clearing from the blazing heat. He had actually tried to *kill* me.

There was a sting at my good ankle. I looked down and noticed my smoldering pant leg had just caught fire. I quickly sat up and patted it out with a curse. Earthen fire was terrifying enough, but holy fire? That was something I wasn't curious in the least about testing with my own flesh.

A giant, cold stone hand grabbed my shoulder and turned me around effortlessly. I was paralyzed to see one of the grotesque angel statues had come to life and had unsheathed his sword, hefting it above his head in preparation for a fatal blow.

My predatory instincts shoved me out of the driver's seat and took control. I darted to the side and used my new favorite leg to sweep the angel's own out from under him. He fell on his back and started to slide down the slope of the roof.

The golem shoved his sword into the roof and used it to slow his descent, tearing a long crevasse along his path. He must have weighed a literal ton. Maybe even a shit ton.

I wanted to jump down the other side of the roof and run away, but PS had the wheel, and he was pissed. Exhausted and with no mortals around, I let him.

I jumped right at the statue as he attempted to find purchase with his feet. Pivoting in the air, I landed on his back, digging my claws into the stone. The rock monster was tough, but I was still strong enough to crush old, crumbling stone. After my fingers dug in, I made fists and yanked out chunks of the angel, then repeated the process. The golem made no noise or indication that he was in any pain, which was creepy as hell.

Unable to reach me, the statue simply let go of the sword, and we started plummeting down the roof. I stopped attacking and jumped off him. But as I did, he grabbed my leg with a vise, forcing me to fall the several stories to the ground with his added weight.

Normally I wouldn't worry about heights, but I was severely injured and drained of energy—seemed to be my luck as of late. I had also been starved for several days, which normally wasn't that big of a deal, but I had already been hurt and in need of energy. We fell, and I briefly wondered what would happen once we hit the ground.

As we fell through the rushing air, I struggled, but had no leverage. What was worse was that the golem was steadily pulling me under him, making sure his weight would land on top of me. Both his hands were on my leg now, squeezing tight. Tight enough to shatter bone. The thought of someone wringing bubble wrap came into mind as my last leg crumbled. The pain was a distant memory as I panicked, trying to prevent my assured death.

My spider-sense tingled, and an idea came to me. I reached my open palm toward the rushing windows, ledges, and statues, and forced a bloodrope out. It found purchase around the neck of a gargoyle statue, and I gripped the rope with both hands as tight as I could. It went taut, and I felt a dull thud and heard a ripping sound that reminded me of a turkey leg being pulled off at Christmas dinner. There was a thunderous crash from below that shook the dirt from the windowsills as I swung freely through the air, smacking into the wall of the stone church.

White-hot pain shot through my body like a bolt of lightning splitting a tree, stemming from where my new favorite leg was no longer there.

Dangling from my rope and trying not to pass out, I said in a half-assed Arnold voice, "I nheed a vhacation."

I noticed the stone wall in front of me was moving downward. I looked up, and to my chagrin, the gargoyle whose neck I had wrapped around was yanking me upward to his gaping maw and clawed paws.

"No, gargoyle! Bad gargoyle! That's a bad rock monster!" I weakly yelled at it, on the verge of passing out.

I had two choices, and both of them sucked: I could disconnect the blood from my palm and drop to the ground, which would mean losing all the precious energy left in the rope forever; or I could face the monster head-on while weak from lack of feeding and missing both my damn legs. Oh, and I was bleeding from the new wound. This situation was what the Himalayan monks called, bullshit.

PS had given back control of the wheel, and shrugged at what to do next.

Concentrating on my hand, I closed my eyes and prepared for what was about to come. I healed the wound and disconnected the rope, dropping to the ground. Losing the energy was like being struck in the solar plexus, rendering me momentarily stunned on the ground. It could have also been plummeting to the ground that had stunned me, but more than likely, it was a combination of the two. I promised myself I would buy a lottery ticket the next chance I got because my luck had to change sooner or later.

I was staring straight up and noticed the gargoyle was looking down on me from above. Both it and the church swirled in my vision. I could barely make out that it was perched at the very end of his platform and was shaking his tail in the air behind him, like a cat about to pounce.

There was a rustling sound several feet beside me, and I struggled to turn my head to see the angel golem pulling himself out of his crater. His lower half had shattered, and he walked on his hands toward me, slime-covered stone face expressionless but intent on me.

Seeing him crawling on his hands, I wheezed out, "Welcome to the club, McNubbins."

Feeling exhausted and with everything broken or missing, I struggled to turn onto my stomach and start crawling in the opposite direction of the handicapped angel. The thought of two snails racing entered my mind, and a delirious smile upturned the corners of my mouth.

That's when the handi-capable gargoyle decided to jump off his perch and land in front of me with an impact that made me bounce off the ground. All four of its paws imbedded deep into the earth, and he struggled to pull free, his eyes never leaving me.

I shifted course and crawled perpendicularly to my new stoner friends. Black dots drifted in my vision as I exerted myself. As I turned, I became aware of wet grass behind and under me. Precious blood squirted out of my torn leg. As quickly as I could, I focused everything I had in closing the grievous wound. The cords on my neck stood out, and my eyes were shut so hard I thought my cheeks and eyebrows were about to high-five. I felt the artery closing, but that was all I dared to do while in a high-speed pursuit with the golems.

There was a sloshing sound from behind as one of the paws was freed from the earth, breaking my concentration. Dread sunk in as I knew I wouldn't be able to stop whoever was the winner of the "Murder John" race. I shook the fear out of my head momentarily and turned to start crawling again. I was barely able to keep my eyes open. My eyelids were so heavy, and promised a quick nap would fix everything. Only my ravenous hunger kept me on the verge of consciousness, refusing to give up before seeing if it was possible to drink an Olympic-sized pool full of fresh, steaming blood.

Keeping my head down, I put everything I had into escaping. My arms were made of jelly. My fingers could no longer flex, forcing me to rely solely on my palms. The world around me was becoming black around the edges.

There was another slosh from behind, and another. I dared not look back, keeping my focus on the ground directly beneath me.

My hand landed on a steel-toed boot, and I struggled on a popsicle-stick neck to look up. There were tree trunks of pure muscle attached to the boots. Even through the 5.11 tactical pants, I could see the sweeps of massive quads. My eyes kept climbing upward to a barrel chest and bulbous arms interlaced with veins the size of the Alaskan pipeline. Perched on top of the chest was a chiseled, well-groomed jaw.

"Dep...weg..." I sobbed in a burst of relief. Tears blurred what vision remained. I just wanted to roll him on his back and pet his belly until my hands fell off.

"You should have called, John," Depweg said in a strong, deep voice, eyeing the statues.

"New phone...who dis?" I managed to get out before letting my face fall onto the grass.

There was another freeing sound from behind, followed by a gallop that reverberated through the ground, making my head bob up and down slightly.

The boots stepped over my disfigured body and walked confidently toward the approaching statue.

I propped a weakened forearm underneath my chin and looked over my shoulder as best I could, struggling to focus on Depweg.

The creature oriented on the new threat and continued to charge. All I could do was watch, helpless, as the giant stone monster grew closer. It had considerable size and immeasurable weight on Depweg. He should have just picked me up and ran.

When it was within pouncing distance, it leaped in the air, stone claws outstretched.

Using supernatural speed, Depweg grabbed one of its paws and turned 180 degrees, like a lumberjack swinging an axe at a downed log, and slammed the creature on the ground in front of him. There was a tremor at the impact, and the gargoyle shattered into grapefruit-sized rocks that tumbled in all directions. One rolled right up and smacked me in the Almond Joys. All I could do was laugh and say, "No way, man. No way," as I gently rocked back and forth on the ground, grasping my supernaturally crushed gonads with my free hand.

Depweg, still holding the now severed, solid paw of the crumbled gargoyle, turned to the crawling angel. Without a moment's thought—or even a witty remark—Depweg stepped forward with one leg and threw the paw at the angel with monstrous force, like a baseball pitcher who was also a freakishly strong werewolf. His aim was true, and the head of the angel exploded into dust. The rest of the body became motionless where it lay, hands still reaching out.

Relieved and still holding my downstairs mix up, I gave in to the demand of my eyelids and let them close, allowing the blackness to overtake me.

Chapter 28

PRESENT DAY

I awoke to a bright light above me. My eyes fluttered, and I looked around to see a white, clean room with stainless instruments lying on small cloth-covered tables. The smell of fur hung heavy in the air, masked with cleaning supplies and bleach.

Depweg approached and laid a hand on my shoulder.

Squinting up at him, I said, "I thought they only took injured friends to the vet in the movies."

"What, you thought you were my only friend, John? Typical narcissism. Doc," Depweg said while shifting his gaze across the room, "guess we need to put him down."

There was a chuckle from the other side of me, and a balding, white-haired man with glasses looked down at me. As he did so, he said, "Well, I guess I do have some garlic bread left in the fridge."

"Ha!" I said victoriously, "Doesn't work." I noticed I had my energy back, which was curious. I still felt like an empty shell, but it was infinitely better than what I had just been through.

"In that case," the doc said while turning to his instruments table, "maybe this will." He showed me a glinting bone saw. "Infused with iron, of course."

"Yeah, that'd about do it," I said, shifting my gaze back to the light, completely aware I wasn't in any form of control in this situation. I pulled my hands to my face and dragged them from my forehead to my chin, exhaling as I did. An IV stuck out of my hand, and I followed the red line up to a bag hanging from a metal stand.

I propped myself up on my elbows and looked down at the rest of me to assess the damage. My legs weren't fully healed, but that was to be expected from blood that wasn't straight from the well. However, they had grown several inches and had started sprouting tiny feet.

"Look at it this way, John," Depweg started, "Think of all the money you'll save from only having to buy Barbie shoes now."

He took in a deep breath and bellowed a throaty laugh that could be felt as much as heard. Doctor Glasses giggled in short titters while covering his mouth with a closed fist.

Feeling stronger, I kicked my baby foot out and placed it under his nose in a fraction of a second. He was still laughing with his eyes closed when he stopped, nostrils flaring. He opened his eyes, and they grew wide with disgust.

"Kiss it," I said, wiggling my microtoes, tickling the tip of his nose.

He shook his head and swatted at my foot while stepping backward, trying to flee from the horrible sight and delicious smell of my fetus-like appendage.

"Ah, Deppyweg, you know just how to make me feel sexy," I mocked with pouty lips.

Depweg's demeanor straightened as he said, "Glad to see the bags did their trick. We were concerned you were going to wake up in a blood rage."

As he said it, the doctor put away the iron-infused tools. I stared with morbid understanding, and gulped.

"Me too, buddy. Me too," I said. "Thanks for saving me, man. You're the Westley to my Buttercup."

"You're a terrible man, but I'd hate for you to die," he mocked.

I didn't smile or correct his movie reference. I just laid my head back down on the cool metal and closed my eyes. I *was* a terrible man.

Depweg's voice interrupted my self-loathing, "Aren't you going to ask how I found you?"

"How did you f—"

"Glad you asked," Depweg interrupted. "Got a call from your bartender friend. It would seem that you've spoken about my canine sanctuary, openly, in his bar. A quick Google search and he had my business number."

"Well, I only talked about you to him. Not like I have a lot of friends who hang out there," I said, defensively.

"For future reference, I would appreciate not being mentioned in a supernatural hangout. My kind is considered a trophy, and there are some who would test their metal by hunting us," Depweg informed. I looked at him, feeling embarrassed, and didn't respond.

"But..." Depweg said, "this one time, I'm glad you did. I would have been your only pallbearer, and that would have been difficult." He smiled warmly.

"I'm surprised Val called you. He seemed pretty upset with me," I said.

"He was, but when no one had heard from you for a few nights, he decided it was time to bring in the big guns," Depweg said while flexing his massive twenty-inch arms.

I laughed, and it hurt my everything.

"Knew I'd get ya to smile, bloodsucker," Depweg said, punching my arm playfully.

"Bone licker," I countered just before a thought entered my mind. "How did you know I was at the church?"

"Val told me the direction you were heading based off his security cameras, and mentioned the only other place you openly talk about is the church. I followed your path and found some scent trails. Then I saw a building that could only be the church you had so fondly described. It definitely looked as if it had been made just for little ol' you," he finished with a smile.

"How did you know he had me in the catacombs?" I asked, perplexed. "Your nose can't be that good, man."

"I'm not telling if it is or isn't, for fear you'll go and tell everyone who will listen!" Depweg joked. "The truth is I searched the grounds until I was certain your scent ended at the church. Then I waited."

"Why didn't you try to break in?" I asked.

"I could sense the traps the father had placed. Plus, I knew he was your friend, and I didn't think you were in any real trouble."

My mind flashed to the special John Room that was my cell, and I shuddered.

"Imagine my amazement when I saw you flying off the roof with a freaking statue, of all things," Depweg said, amused. "They really wanted you, brother."

"They were obviously girl statues. Happens all the time. Sometimes I'll just be walking down the street, and a mob of women—"

"Will cross to the other side of the street?" Depweg finished, interrupting me.

"Oh, Depweg, it's almost as if we finish each other's..." I said, leaving a moment of silence at the end and waving my hand in the air like reeling in a fish.

"Sandwiches, I know," he said, rolling his eyes.

I sat up on the table, letting my baby feet dangle off the side, kicking to and fro. My eyes fixated on the floor in front of me. "Did..." I began, "Did Val tell you anything?"

"No," said Depweg.

I breathed a sigh of relief.

"But Da did," he said while staring directly at me, expressionless.

I looked up at him in shock, mouth open.

"I went by your house first, just to cross it off my list. Da was there, cleaning up what looked like a night to remember."

"What did he say?" I asked, afraid of the answer.

"The truth," he replied. "That you lost control and made some mistakes. He was pretty upset, but was also worried. He confirmed that you could only be at the bar or the church."

"Am I really that boring?" I asked. "I mean, sometimes I go to the movies, and stuff."

He rested a hand on my shoulder. I met his eyes. There was understanding in them.

"You aren't mad at me? Everyone else is," I said, defeated.

"I'm a werewolf, John," he said, using the German wording again. "Losing control is something I know a lot about. To feel the call of the primal rip you from the pilot seat."

I barked out a quick laugh and pointed at him. "I use a similar metaphor!" I told him with a beaming smile and wide eyes.

Depweg smiled again and patted my shoulder before letting his hand fall back to his side.

"Now then," he said, "how about you rest at my place while Da fixes up your house? I have the newest *John Wick* movie on Blu-ray."

"Lair," I corrected him. "House sounds so...white picket fence and stuff," I said, trying to find the right words. "But a lair, mmm, yes."

Depweg paid the doctor with a stack of cash, shook his hand, and headed for the door. I put on my coat, which dragged on the floor behind me, like a kid wearing his dad's clothes. The doctor gave me a medical bag filled with bloody rags and bandages.

"Figured you'd want to dispose of these yourself, personally," the doc said with a smile and using a terrible Sylvester Stallone voice.

"*Judge Dredd*," I said without hesitation. "Give me a challenge next time," I finished with a wink.

I hopped off the table and landed on my adorable little nubs and started walking, swaying to the sides and pivoting at the hip until my knee caps grew back.

As we walked, I looked up at a now towering Depweg and asked, "Seriously, why didn't anyone tell Stallone that his redundant statement was, well, redundant?"

Depweg smiled and chuckled a few times, always entertained by my theatrically based commentary.

We got into Depweg's reinforced Jeep and took off. I was ready to relax. But first, I needed a drink.

Chapter 29

PRESENT DAY

P ull down this street and slow down," I told Depweg. He did so with a wrinkle in his brow, compliant but confused.

"I need to eat," I informed him, pulling my legs up with my hands and wiggling my baby toes. "This is one of my favorite parts of town. I call it the ol' fishing hole."

We crossed an intersection with a group of savory characters standing around a car listening to loud, verbally suggestive music. "Pull over here and turn on your emergency lights."

Depweg did, trusting me. "Pop your hood, and for Lilith's sake, stay in the car. You'll scare the fishies!"

I got out of the jeep and wobbled adorably to the front, cringing as my ancient duster dragged on the ground behind me. Climbing up on the bumper and lifting the hood, I stared at the engine and cursed.

"Ah, jeez!" I said loudly. "The gosh darn flux capacitor is busted!" I normally wore a reflective Movado watch made of tungsten when I fished, showing it off by keeping one hand on the hood and letting the sleeve of my duster slide down. Since this had been an impromptu hunt, I'd left it at home in my hopefully not-flooded dresser. Fishies loved shiny things.

Instead, I pulled out my wallet and fanned out my cash and asked loudly, "How much is it for a tow truck?"

The fishies, who had been pointing and laughing at my nubs, stopped talking. I reached out with my senses and could feel them behind me. One had been sitting on the car but now was standing up, looking around at his friends to make sure they were all on the same page.

"That's it," I whispered. "Come to mommy...I mean, daddy."

"Heard that," Depweg stated from the driver's seat.

"Shit," was my only response.

"Yup," he said while audibly unlocking his cell phone, uninterested in the outstanding citizens approaching from behind.

With my back to the gentlemen, I let my wallet fall to the ground and loudly cried out, "Oh noes! My wallet full of monies! Can anyone help me!"

"Say, homie," said one in perfect elocution. "I think I can help wit dat." He bent over to scoop up my wallet.

A smile spread across my face, and then I let it drop to feigned sorrow. I dropped to the ground and turned to face them. I reached out my hand palm up, giving him the chance to return the wallet.

He smiled at me instead and asked, "What else you got, McNubbins?"

The irony was not lost on me with that comment.

In a sheepish voice, I said, "No...nothing, sirs. I just need my wallet for my grandma's operation." My hand was still outstretched.

The thug pulled out my cash and pocketed it, handing me back my wallet and saying, "Here ya go, fool. As requested." His posse laughed and spread out, surrounding me. There were five of them. The leader had a bald head with tattoos on his face and neck. He wore a white hoodie and Adidas athletic pants.

The others had on various clothes that had clearly been bought at the same shop, or taken from someone's house. Tattoos were prominent, as were gold necklaces. I was somewhat impressed that the races were mixed. *Progress,* I thought to myself.

One of the blood jugs reached down and seized my arms from behind while another kneeled down and started riffling through my clothes.

A toothy, predatory smile crossed my face, and I headbutted the fool in front of me, sending an eruption of blood in all directions around his nose. His hands reached up to grasp his broken smeller, and the other gents pulled out switchblades, except the leader. He pulled out a Springfield 1911 and pointed it directly at me.

"Can we hurry this up, John?" Depweg asked from the driver's seat, followed by laughter and the sound of the *like* button being pressed. "Puppies playing with a tennis ball," he said to himself while chuckling. "That ball's too big for you, fella."

Two of the thugs went around the side of the car, one on each side, knives ready.

My arms shot forward, breaking the fingers of the punk that had been holding me from behind. He inhaled sharply as he held his fingers in front of his face. His eyes were the size of cue balls.

Turning to him, I tilted his head to one side with a finger, then pretended to put a napkin in my shirt while licking my lips.

I could sense the leader behind me, frozen in surprise, still holding the gun on me.

Whispering in the tax-paying citizen's ear, I said, "Now, this may sting a tad," and bit into his neck, letting the blood flow from him to me. My nerves were alight with renewed energy, and my legs started healing. The bruised feeling over my body withered and was replaced by strength and energy.

The Big Gulp started sinking to the ground, weak in the knees, as I started to rise, growing at the knees. His eyes rolled back into his head and his cheeks became sunken. I let him drop, lifeless, to the ground, skin matching the color of his wifebeater.

I stood on brand-spank'n-new legs and turned to the leader, who was rubbing his eyes muttering, "It's a bad trip, man. A bad trip!"

His gun barked as I stepped toward him, his free hand unironically clutching a crucifix that hung from a gold chain around his neck. My acting classes paid off as I did my best Bugs Bunny impersonation of when he was shot. I made "oooh" and "ahh" noises while stumbling around jerkily, my face contorted in hilariously dramatic poses.

"Get out of the car! Now!" one of the men barked at the werewolf.

"It's a jeep, not a car," Depweg said as I heard the door open.

"Stop playing around," Depweg commanded as one of the goons flew toward the front of the jeep, landing next to the leader. Confident footsteps walked around the back of the vehicle and approached the remaining moron. This was followed by a shaky voice screaming a machine-gun succession of noes that were interlaced with the growing epiphany that a mistake had been made. His body flew onto the street in front of where I stood.

Shocks protested as Depweg walked back around and got into his jeep.

Taking my cue, I grabbed the leader and pulled him close with one hand. With the other, I plucked the cheap, gold-painted cross from his chain and brought it up to his bulging eyes, where it was crushed between forefinger and thumb. By reflex alone, he kept the gun pointed at my chest, barking until empty. Even as I drained him, the clicking sound could be heard as the trigger was squeezed repeatedly. The clicking slowed and eventually stopped, along with his heart. I let him drop and finished off the other two morsels with my bloodwhips, draining them completely before climbing back into the jeep with Depweg.

"Feeling better?" Depweg asked.

"Oh, man, I am stuffed to the rafters!" I claimed, rubbing my stomach with enthusiasm.

"Did you have to scare him so bad with the cross?" Depweg asked, only half accusingly.

"First, how the hell did you see that? And second, yes. He clearly wasn't the churchgoer he pretended to be. Otherwise he wouldn't be in his current predicament, now would he?"

Depweg pointed forward and I followed his finger to the hood, which was still up. At the bottom, I could see the gap that had allowed Depweg to view my theatrical performance.

"Oh, sorry about that. Didn't think you'd see me go all antihero on him."

"Not that," Depweg started, "The hood. Close it."

"Right. The...the hood," I said as I slid out of the passenger's seat and walked to the front, slamming the hood down.

As I got back in, Depweg looked at me and said, "They deserved their fate. They made the bed, now they sleep in it." As he finished, he looked forward and started the jeep up, continuing on our journey.

As if to further cement his approval, Depweg broke the silence and said, "Well, I see you got your shoe holders back," while nodding at my legs.

Taking the lifeline, I said, "To the shoe store!" while pointing forward, relieved to have him on my side.

Depweg smiled, and we were on our way back to his cabin in the woods.

Chapter 30

PRESENT DAY

Depweg and I had a long talk about different things, resolidifying our bond as supernatural brothers from another mother...and species. We hadn't spoken as much since Father Thomes and I had begun our missions, and it felt good to catch up. Though I knew I had been doing the right thing with Father T, it had caused me to separate myself from my only true friend. I mean, Da and Val are—or were—friends, but they didn't understand me like Depweg did. He was my hetero soulmate.

Depweg filled the time by further explaining about his canine shelter and how he had built every kennel himself—he had used wood he'd chopped down from the trees on his vast property. He had enough stories about the dogs and how they had come to be in his care that the car ride felt like minutes instead of the hours it actually was. The most heartbreaking was Tiny Tim's, who had been abused by his drunken master for being different, culminating with the piece of shit throwing a cinder block at the poor pup and snapping its little back. I wanted to pay a visit to the bastard, but Depweg assured me it had been taken care of. I wasn't entirely sure if he meant by the mortal authorities or by the justice of the food chain.

He asked about the father, and I explained how we had met during a time when I had felt aimless in my unlife. I had been doing good things, but on a small scale: stop a murderous cartel ring here, catch a serial killer there. There had been so much more good I could have been doing with my abilities, and Father Thomes Philseep had provided just the direction I had been looking for. Plus, it hadn't hurt to be doing favors for an emissary of the Big Guy upstairs.

All caught up on what we had been doing since we had last parted, we discussed our next plan of action, which meant grabbing some of his arsenal from his house/lair. The silver-and-iron bullets would make our lives so much easier when dealing with what was coming. There were semiautomatic rifles, bolt-action sniper rifles, shotguns, and varying sizes of easily concealable handguns we could use. Plus, body armor that could cover us from head to toe. Nothing would be able to stop us!

At one point, I asked Depweg to pull over. I picked up a nice, baseball-sized rock, and heaved it across the road into a certain tanning salon/auto repair. Chuckling to myself, I got back into the jeep to face an astonished Depweg.

"He'll fix it," I said confidently. "He's good with glass."

Shrugging, Depweg pulled back on the road and toward the beginning of the end.

As we turned to pull down his long gravel driveway, we saw the black smoke drifting into the sky. Depweg saw it first, eyes growing wide with dread.

He slammed on the gas, throwing us back in our seats. We traversed the gravel driveway with highway speeds, bumps and potholes threatening to dismantle the undercarriage.

The smell of burning wood, grass, fur, and flesh grew denser in the night air as we closed the distance.

I could hear Depweg next to me crying out in dismay as the wind let up, allowing the sound of whimpers and piercing howls to fill the vast expanse of his violated property.

Depweg smashed on the brakes and we skidded to a halt. I used the momentum of the braking to propel myself forward, and sprinted on bare feet toward the burning house. The fire raged red and orange with highlights of green hellfire. The heat forced me to slow and shield my face. I was intent on getting the silver weapons though, and pushed forward.

From the house came a barely audible whimper over the rolling thunder of the hungry flames.

"*Tim!*" I screamed in gut-wrenching panic. That gave me all the motivation I needed, and I ran full speed at the engulfed cabin, veering at the last second to jump through the rainwater collector attached to the side of the house. I burst through the white plastic and came out drenched from head to toe in cool water.

I could hear Depweg behind me, running for the kennels. His breath came in raged, panicked gasps, as if he were barely holding on to his sanity.

Leaping through the flames and the already broken window of the living room, I called out to Tiny Tim. I was met with the deafening roar of flames as they consumed everything in the house. I ran through the house at preternatural speed, looking for my little buddy. The sound of pure anguish being screamed at length into the night from outside made me pause. Depweg had made it to the kennels.

Water evaporated in plumes off of me at an alarming rate, snapping me back into focus.

Feeling the fierce strength of the hellfire threatening to eat my protective layer and burn my essence, I continued my search, desperate to find Tim. A fresh scent of singeing fur caught my attention, and I followed it into the bedroom where the bed was a pit of dancing fire. Throwing myself on the floor, I found him. There, underneath the inferno, was Tiny Tim, wheelchair overturned and fur smoking and shriveling before my eyes. His breathing was quick and shallow, and I grabbed him by the chair and pulled him out. I stood, pulling him to my chest, and leaped through the bedroom window onto the back porch. Twinkling glass rained down around me like the stars winking in the night sky.

I set down Tim, who was limp, and noticed he had stopped breathing. Dropping to my knees, I frantically started CPR, trying my best to not blow out his little lungs. Between breaths, I placed my index and middle finger on his sternum, pressing in and letting up in quick succession.

"Come on, little buddy! Don't leave me!" I begged between breaths.

I put my ear to his chest, and I could hear his little heart fluttering erratically. I placed my lips around his snout and continued administering CPR. After a few more breaths and compressions, I leaned down again and listened.

His heart slowed, and then gave up, beating for the last time. I lifted my head up and looked down on him in dismay. His little mouth hung open with his tongue hanging out the side. His eyes were half-closed, with only the whites showing. The fur on his body was black around the edges. I leaned down and kissed his little nose, which had split open from inhaling the blistering smoke of the hellfire.

My head shook back and forth in disbelief. I swallowed hard and said to myself, "No. It's not fair. It's not fucking fair!"

After a few moments of staring down at the lifeless body of Tiny Tim, I removed him from the constraints of his blackened wheelchair and clutched him against my chest. I raised my head and saw Depweg slumped on his knees in front of rows of burning kennels. The sound of crackling flesh and the smell of burnt fur lay heavy in the air, competing with the black smoke from the house on which could be the first to choke one of us. Depweg's chin rested on his chest, and his arms lay motionless in front of him, the backs of his open hands resting on the ground. There were red plastic gas cans littered around the grounds.

Through the crackling of the fire, I could hear the deep sobs emanating from my friend. The only friend that understood me and the constant, unyielding battle between my conscious and predatory sides. I had alienated everyone else in my life; Da for losing control and feeding on a grieving mother in front of her child; Valenta for breaking the rules and putting a target on my head; and Father Philseep for both reasons. Now, the only person who was in the same boat as me had been targeted and attacked simply for being my friend and helping me.

I looked back down at Tim and said to him, "This is my fault."

My jaw locked in anger, and I could feel myself starting to shake with unbridled wrath. I jerked my head to the side and sent sheer energy empowered with anger into the ground, exploding a hole big enough to bury the form that was now lifeless because of my actions. I placed my little buddy in the hole and covered him up with dirt, whispering my last goodbyes to him, promising to punish the person responsible.

It hit me like a kick in the nuts. Lifting my head with wide eyes and yelling through clenched teeth, I screamed, "*Locke!*" Spittle flew and speckled the ground.

Depweg, weak as if the will to live had been syphoned from him, turned his head to look at me. His head bobbled and swayed, like he was ready to pass out from pure anguish. My words hit him and everything in him tensed. He rose a few inches as his legs tightened at the command from his brain telling him the time for grieving was over; it was time for bloodshed. Depweg stood up from where he sat and turned his body toward me, eyes blazing—literally. The flames that were consuming his home were reflected in his eyes. I didn't know what to expect as he started to approach me, but whatever he was about to do, I deserved it.

There was power in his steps as Depweg strode over to me. Shadows danced on his features from the house fire, while crackling flames roared behind from the kennels. I sat there, staring at him like watching a car crash in slow motion; helpless. This wouldn't have happened if I hadn't come here. Whatever was about to befall my head, I wouldn't fight back.

Depweg stopped in front of me and stood for a moment, fists the size of lunch boxes pulsating with barely contained rage. I waited for what was coming.

He unclenched a fist and extended his arm to me, fingers spread. He must have seen the look of confusion cross my face, for he shook his hand, signaling me to take it. I reached out and grabbed his forearm. Depweg's monstrous fingers clasped around my own, and he pulled me up. We stood, face to face, grasping each other's forearms as he spoke. But what came out of his mouth was made by an animal's vocal chords, deep and rumbling.

"An eye for an eye, and a tooth for a tooth." As he spoke, his eyes shifted to yellow slits, and his teeth elongated into long rows of razor-sharp fangs that faced slightly backward, all the better for grabbing you with, my dear. A vengeful smile creased my own face, and I let my own eyes shift to their predatory aspect, and my canines elongated into surgical points.

Chapter 31

PRESENT DAY

We spent the remainder of the night hashing out ideas as we buried each of Depweg's canines. I created the holes, and he used a shovel and a bucket to keep the charred remains together so they could be buried in one piece. Blackened bones pierced the ashes, reaching out to the stars.

Depweg sobbed off and on, as if losing a war with his emotions. I caught myself frozen as the thought of Tiny Tim flashed through my mind, reinforcing my resolve to punish Nathanial Locke, the warlock. Lilith, what a stupid made up name. Oh how I hated everything about him.

After the house fire died out, we searched his cache and found that the hellfire had melted the silver with its anticelestial heat. With no weapons aside from the remaining rounds from my Glock, Depweg and I would have to rely on our brains.

I know what you're thinking, and you're right, so I'll naturally be leaving most of the decision-making to the military mind of Depweg. My brain is mostly filled with movie trivia. For instance, did you know that Jack Nicholson didn't take a salary for the 1989 *Batman*? Instead, he opted for a percentage on the back end, including merchandise. Up until R.D.J. reprised his role as Iron Man for *The Avengers*, Jack had made the most money of any actor in history. Neat, right? Locke doesn't stand a chance against me!

As we finished the ceremony of respect, I handed the gun and spare magazine over to Depweg. He looked at it and then back at me, smiling.

"Won't be needing that." He gestured with his human hands and wiggled his thumbs. I caught on. He wouldn't have opposable thumbs once he transformed. Werewolves had supernatural strength that rivaled that of ogres and outright beat vampires', but they couldn't open a jar of pickles. When choosing their attributes, werewolves put everything they had into strength and let dexterity slide to the wayside. I liked to think vampires were a healthy mix. Though I was faster than any werewolf, if I were to be cornered, there would be little I could do to stop a fully transformed were from mauling me to death and feasting on my assumedly tasty meat.

I placed the Glock back into my waistband at the small of my back and pocketed the spare mag.

Depweg grabbed the handle to his back door, turned the knob, and pulled. The entire door came off its frame and crumbled into pieces at his feet. Still holding the knob, Depweg looked at his hand and let the brass piece fall from his opening fingers. Watching this happen gave me a ping of regret and I flinched, knowing that the simple action personified him losing everything he had.

Depweg stepped through the threshold and looked around at what had once been his home. I walked up beside him and placed my hand on his shoulder, saying,

"I'm sorry, man."

"Nothing to worry about, buddy. They were just things. The walls and ceiling were wood, as was the furniture. I made them all and can remake them, with time," he said.

He stepped away from my hand and walked to the kitchen with purpose. He stopped in front of the scorched refrigerator and grabbed one of the handles. As he pulled, nothing happened. He put some force into it, and the fridge opened with a wail of protest. The smell of cooked meat, veggies, and melted cheese escaped, along with the odor of melted plastic. Inside, the shelves looked like a Salvador Dali painting. All that was missing was a melted clock on one of the shelves.

Depweg crouched, grabbed a warped shelf, and pulled it off its hinges, letting it hit the ground at his feet. With ease, he ripped the top of the shelf off and reached in to pull out something wrapped in butcher's paper. It was seventeen inches long and slightly curved, similar to a banana.

He turned and set it on a small piece of his countertop that still remained, and began to respectfully unravel it.

Wrapped in the paper was a kukri blade sheathed in old, worn leather. The handle was five inches in length and made from a dark wood. It had been well cared for over the years, with the handle being treated with oils. He grasped it and pulled out the blade, which was a full foot long and hummed with power.

"Is that...?"

"The silver blade," Depweg finished for me. "The same one I got just before we first met while in the middle of WWII. A Nazi werwolf hunter came after me and left me with these." He lifted his shirt, revealing the road map of thick, zigzag scars I had seen as fresh gashes so long ago. Even after burning the wounds closed, the silver had still left its mark.

"There was a Nazi werewolf hunter? You never told me that!" I said, mocking a hurt expression. "Seriously though, shit sounds like an '80s straight-to-VHS movie. Neat."

He chuckled at that, thought for a moment, and said, "Felt more like a Christopher Nolan film as it was happening. But that's a story for another time."

"What, like a spin-off? You think you're there in terms of character development yet?" I joked.

"Oh, so this is a story about you then, is it?" he jabbed right back.

"Everyone's the star in their own movie."

"Everyone's the hero in their own story as well. Don't forget that," he said.

That struck home. The actions I had partook in of late had been more than questionable, even downright inexcusable. Just because my intentions had been pointed in the right direction, it didn't make me a good guy.

Depweg noticed that I was deep in self-reflection and added, "Always time to change the narrative." With that, he smiled. After a moment, the weight of what he had just gone through pulled his smile down at the corners of his eyes and mouth, as if an elephant had been tied to his face and thrown off a cliff. He looked much older in an instant.

Now it was my time to console my friend.

"Did you know that in *Terminator*, um, Arnold's iconic line 'I'll be back' almost didn't, ah, happen?" I said shyly.

Depweg looked up at me. Sadness was replaced with confusion.

"Yeah. Arnold argued with James Cameron that a machine wouldn't use a contraction like 'I'll.' So, we almost got 'I will be back,' which I don't think has the same gravitas and flow."

He continued to stare at me in disbelief, though he had cut the strings holding the elephant, letting it plummet to its death, alone.

"I...did not know that," he said slowly, still confused.

I mentally high-fived myself for changing his emotion. I was a master manipulator.

I pulled up the sleeve on my leather duster, revealing a naked wrist, and said, "Would you look at that, it's murder time."

After another moment of looking at me as if I were speaking in tongues, Depweg vigorously nodded his head, snapped his fingers, and said, "Instead of Miller time. I get it. I understood that reference."

"Okay, Captain America. Shall we go seek some revenge?"

"I'm from Germany," Depweg stated.

"Lilith!" I said in exasperation. "I need to take you to a damn movie."

"I don't put out," he remarked seamlessly.

After Depweg grabbed a few provisions from what remained of his house, we set off down the dirt road. The night was cool, or maybe it was just warm around the remains of the flame. The air smelled fresher the further from the graveyard we drove. Wind rustled the leaves, and it sounded like a stadium full of fans applauding in the distance.

There was a crack as a branch was broken. Depweg let off the accelerator and we coasted to a slow stop. After glancing at each other to confirm that we had, indeed, both heard that noise, we went to work. He smelled the air while my eyes scanned the darkness, searching for any heat signatures.

"We are upwind of the tree line. I can't smell anything," Depweg whispered.

Another crack further down the line from the first. My eyes locked onto the area of the noise, and I could barely make out a line of blurry red spots. Something was off about them, like they were behind a thick wall or coated in some sort of infrared-dampening clothing.

"Get down!" I half yelled, half whispered at Depweg.

I leaped out of the jeep and Depweg followed out my side, putting the vehicle between us and the trees. An explosion of suppressed gunfire erupted and slammed into the driver's side of the jeep. The impact of the bullets on the metal frame sounded like cracks of lightening, while the actual reports of the guns were muffled whispers in comparison.

Depweg huddled on the ground while I used the jeep's giant tires as a blockade. A bullet found its mark and hit Depweg in his exposed calf, splitting the skin on the side. Though it was a glancing shot, it dug deep. Depweg called out in pain and grabbed his leg, his head facing the sky in agony. This presented the back of his skull as a prime target, so I leaped from my position and tackled him to the other tire just as a hail of bullets ripped the seat apart where his head had just been.

"Si-silver," Depweg stammered. "The fuckers are using silver rounds." Blood was seeping through his fingers where he held his gaping calf.

The jeep provided minimal cover, and they were going to flank us soon. Looking left and right revealed that there was nowhere to go. We could head for the trees behind us, but the jeep would stop providing cover if we got up and ran. We had to fight.

"Depweg," I said as I grabbed his shoulders, forcing his gaze to shift to me. His eyes held pain and anger, but there was no fear. "They killed your pack," I said pointing to the tree line. With that line uttered, his breathing slowed and became deeper. The pain around his eyes withered and was replaced with fury. "Time for dinner," I said with a smile. As I did, my canines elongated and my eyes shifted to crimson. I willed my fingers to sprout thick, razor-sharp bloodclaws that covered my nails.

Depweg took the cue and fell on all fours, with the tire still blocking his bulk. He threw off his clothes and let the change take over. He gulped in a deep breath and held it for a few heartbeats. His bones started to pop as they began to grow. Sinew and muscles were lengthened, and Depweg let out a bone-chilling howl that was part human in agony, and part wolf free of his human prison. His legs bent backward with deafening cracks. Hair sprouted all over his body; human at first, then growing thicker into a wolf's dense pelt. Depweg's face expanded outward. His eyes closed tight in pain. The jaws extended outward while teeth grew into saliva-covered fangs. When he opened his eyes again, they were pure yellow orbs with black slits. They reminded me of the color of a bright full moon when it was low on the horizon.

A giant, five-hundred-pound, eight-foot-long wolf stood on all fours and howled into the night. The sound was like a haunted locomotive carrying twelve thousand tons of rage. He looked at me with his yellow eyes, chuffed, and nodded once. I took my mark and turned toward the tree line, with my hands pointed at the ground before us. I sent spears of blood deep into the ground, underneath and in between the jeep and the trees.

Shifting focus, I spread out the blooddiggers to either side for several meters in a crescent moon shape. The ground rumbled audibly. Pebbles danced on the surface. After I had extended far enough to be uncomfortable with the amount of energy I was about to use, I stopped and took a huge breath.

The gunfire had ceased at the howl, and now the sound of magazines being ejected and replaced filled the night's air. Bolts were slapped into place, and footsteps sounded on the foliage.

I squatted down to the ground, like a powerlifter about to deadlift the world. With a gargantuan amount of focus and will, I sprang up and threw my hands to the sky above us.

The explosion was immediate and intense. Rocks, clay, dirt, and mud shot through the air straight up, creating a curtain of earth. At the cusp, the debris hung in the air as if frozen in time. Before gravity could take hold again and return it to its rightful place, I leaped on top of the jeep and slammed my hands together with enough force and speed to break the sound barrier. A thunderous shock wave expanded out in a sphere, throwing me backward several yards. I landed on my ass and tumbled tits over feet until my momentum slowed. The desired effect was achieved, however, as chunks of earth were propelled at the tree line in a blitzkrieg of streaking rocks.

Startled cries pierced the night as several men were torn and shredded. I propped myself on my elbows, still recovering from the sonic boom and expenditure of energy, to see Depweg diving into the fray. He targeted the men who were left standing and dazed. It was a magnificent slaughter.

Claws raked body armor, leaving rivulets of blood, as black-clothed men in masks struggled to recover. Salivating jaws tore chunks of gore and flesh from throats as gurgling men collapsed to their knees, holding what used to be their necks.

Depweg then located the last man standing, his finger squeezing a trigger that clicked empty. His jaws engulfed the helmeted skull and tightened. The man screamed and tried to punch the giant wolf, forgetting about his gun and spare mags entirely in his panic. The helmet started to crack and dent as the man clawed at the straps under his chin with clumsy fingers electrified with adrenaline.

The man shrieked in panic as the helmet started pushing its way into his skull. Bones cracked, and a high-pitched scream escaped the man's throat. The front of the helmet had been bent over his eyes, and only his face below the nose stuck out. Streams of blood started spilling down his face. His hands abandoned the chin strap and now frantically pushed upward on the helmet, slipping on the blood that was increasing in volume until there was a scarlet waterfall pouring down his face.

After a few more moments, the helmet was three quarters the size it had started as. The man's hands slowly began to sag as the life left his body. Sound didn't escape his wide mouth anymore, but it continued to open and close like a morbid ventriloquist's dummy. The final crunch came and the man jerked once, then went limp. Depweg dropped him to the ground, where the man's body twitched at random intervals, as if hit with a malfunctioning stun gun. I made it up to my feet and over to the tree line, where Depweg and I methodically tended to the wounded.

I could see a man whose legs had been crushed by a boulder the size of a paint bucket. His feet stuck straight up at an awkward angle, with the rock crushing his shins and knees into the earth. The assassin struggled uselessly to move the rock. He stopped when he saw Depweg stalking his way to him. The man looked around in fear and spotted his gun a few feet from where he lay pinned to the ground. He reached for it and then screamed in agony at the movement, his cry muffled by his balaclava. His bloodshot eyes locked on Depweg again, and he stretched his arms to the weapon a second time, wailing as he did. His fingertips had barely touched the gun when Depweg walked up behind the man and grabbed his neck in his jaws. A quick bite and jerk of the head, and the man fell limp.

Another assassin was leaving a trail of blood mixed with mud as he tried to pull himself away on his forearms. I stood on his lower back and pressed down. He sucked in air in surprise and pain and then moaned, letting his face drop to the dirt.

Reaching down, I flipped the man onto his back with ease and looked him in the eyes, letting my bloodclaws pierce his shoulders.

"Locke?" was the only thing I asked.

The man didn't answer, only stared at me with barely controlled panic in his eyes and a gaping mouth. Pulling the man up to my face while digging the claws deeper, I said, "Don't make me ask again, blood jug," revealing my fangs as I did. The man continued to stare, not answering.

I felt breath on the back of my neck as Depweg pushed his head past my shoulder and into the man's face, jaws drenched in blood and gore open and dripping.

The man's eyes went wide enough I thought they were going to pop out of his head and flee into the night.

"Ye-yes!" the man stammered.

"Thank you for your cooperation," I said in my best RoboCop voice, and sank my fangs into the man's neck. The life rushed into me, and I felt like I could scale the highest mountain.

After all threats had been eliminated, Depweg and I sat on the ground in relief. I lay back and let my gaze shift to the night sky, watching gray clouds pass.

"That," I paused for emphasis, "was close."

Depweg whimpered, and I turned to see him licking his lower back on his right side. I pulled myself up and walked behind him. There were three blood-soaked holes in the shape of a half moon that were matted with fur. Blood flowed freely with no signs of stopping.

I reached around him while whispering in his ear, "No homo." I felt his stomach and around his torso, but couldn't find any exit wounds.

"Shit," I said. "Gonna have to dig those bastards out."

Depweg whimpered and turned his head away.

I willed little chopstick-sized spears of blood from my fingertips and touched the first gaping crater.

"Now, this might sting a bit," I said as I slid them into the bullet hole. Inch by inch I went in, all the while Depweg slightly trembled and whimpered.

"Shit," I muttered, "that's in there pretty deep." As I finished talking, the tip of one spear touched the silver fragment, and then broke. A jolt of electricity went up my arm and I fell back. The manifestation fell from my hand and melted like a popsicle in the sun.

Waving my hand in the air to pointlessly abate the pain, I said out loud, "Right, silver."

Looking around, I noticed the jeep and got an idea. "B-R-B," I said, enunciating every letter.

I jogged over to the jeep, where I found Depweg's bag, and then rummaged around until I found the kukri. I removed it from its sheath, letting the moonlight glint off the reverberating blade.

Making my way back to where Depweg sat, I held the knife—very carefully, I might add—out in front of me. Last thing I needed was to trip over a gopher hole and stab myself through the face. Depweg looked over and shifted his eyes immediately to the glinting blade. His ears lay back and his eyes became yellow billiard balls while shaking his head in negation.

"Gotta do it, buddy. Only way," I said, trying my best to sound reassuring.

He turned his head away and lowered it, clearly unhappy as to the upcoming addition to his road map of scars.

Standing over the wounds, I placed the blade over the hole and sliced into it, cutting in a few centimeters. Depweg whined through closed jaws and flexed his paws into the earth.

I set the knife down and stuck my index and middle fingers into the hole as gingerly as I could, and slowly pulled the hole wider. The slit allowed the skin to part evenly and cleanly. After further opening the wound, I started to slide both fingers into the bleeding cavity until I could feel the reverberation of the silver fragment. Letting my delicate digits slide over the bullet, I pinched and smoothly pulled it out.

As the bullet cleared the hole, I dropped it to the ground, ready to repeat the process two more times.

Second round removed, I moved on to the third, which was deeper. I was forced to pull out and, apologizing to Depweg, cut even deeper into his flesh with the blade. I was confident Depweg had loved it because he tried to turn and give me a love bite with razor-sharp fangs.

I spanked his nose and said, "No. Bad Deppyweg. Bad."

He turned his head away again with a growl and let me finish my task.

With the last bullet out, I looked down and noticed the wounds were still flowing with blood.

"Hey," I asked, "are these wounds going to be small enough to heal?"

Depweg turned his head and inspected the wounds. He licked them, as dogs do, and looked back up at me. A shake of his head confirmed my suspicions.

"So, fire then," I said with a sigh of frustration. At the mention of fire, Depweg jumped forward a bit and turned to face me with his whole body, growling.

"Dude, I get it. I no likey fire as much as the next supe, but that's our only choice. Now, do we do this in wolf form or what?"

Depweg paced back and forth, whimpering with each pained step.

"Human form?" I asked.

Depweg stopped, looked at me, and nodded.

"Alrighty, then. Convert away. Or is it revert?" I asked.

He nodded his head, but then looked up at me and chuffed once.

"What is it, boy? Little Timmy stuck in the old well?" I said while crouching down slightly and putting both hands on my knees. The realization of what name I had said struck home, and it took me off guard for a moment.

After looking at me for a moment, seemingly in the same thought, he chuffed again and turned to one of the bodies and started eating.

"Oh, right. Food to heal. Hey, you could have eaten them in human form and I wouldn't have judged. I do it all the time," I joked, forcing humor to swallow my grief.

After every one of the corpses had the thick muscles from their nonarmored arms and thighs eaten, Depweg lay on the ground and began the transformation. Fur began to thin until it was humanlike hair, then fell out. His snout shortened with the sound of a truck's tires slowly driving up a gravel road. The fangs in his mouth fell out, and human teeth grew in their stead. His knees popped back into place, and claws were swallowed by growing tan-colored skin.

After a minute, the transformation was complete, and Depweg lay shuddering on the ground. Blood continued to pour down his wounds, which had not shrunk with the rest of him. They were actually bigger on his body now. The silver had prevented whatever magic flowed through his veins from working on the holes.

Depweg reached behind and felt the trauma with a trembling hand. He pulled his fingers away and brought them in front of his face, inspecting the dark blood.

"Whatever you are going to do, John, please hurry," Depweg said with fading, pained breaths.

Looking around, I got another genius idea. I strode over to one of the hit men and removed his balaclava from his face. As I walked back over to where Depweg was bleeding out, I ripped the mask into three even strips. Once I reached where he lay, I crouched and said, "Sorry man, but gotta do this," and stuffed the strips into each of the holes as deep as they would go. Depweg gasped in pain and tensed, but only a little, which worried the hell out of me.

"Hold on, man," I said with growing worry as I focused on the strips. One by one, I excited the molecules of the fabric all the way into the wounds, which started to smoke and then smolder. The blood fought to keep the strips from igniting. I took in a deep breath and then focused on the strips with all the force of my will. Veins stood out on my head as I concentrated. They continued to smoke, but did not burn. This pissed me off, and I used my anger. I wasn't about to let my friend die, especially considering it was my fucking fault.

I regathered my will and focus, and stared at the first strip. After a moment, it blazed up in a tiny pyre, reaching fruitlessly for the sky.

Depweg moaned loudly and tried to reach a hand back. I grabbed it and moved my focus to the next strip.

After they were all lit, I let them burn for a moment, and then blew them out using my preternatural strength to force the air out of my lungs like a quick shotgun blast. The flames blew completely out, leaving behind ashen skin. I sat upright and admired my were-birthday cake.

"There ya go, buddy. Let those people digest in your tum-tum, and you'll feel right as rain soon enough," I said, trying to convince myself as much as him.

After carrying Depweg back to the jeep, I dressed him, intentionally putting his jeans on backward. As I buckled him into the seat, I snickered to myself at the thought of him waking up and being all, "Why are my pants on backward?"

I let the seat lay as far back as possible, to provide him as much comfort as the jeep would allow. With a wince, he shifted his body weight to his good side, relieving the pressure on his brand-spanking-new collection of scars.

After securing him and putting the cleaned off kukri back in his bag, I sauntered over to where the dead men lay and rifled through their gear. Most of the guns had been damaged in the earth blast and almost all the ammo had been expended, but I was able to grab a few Sig Sauer MPX's with full auto option and suppressors. I whistled loudly, as I knew they were expensive weaponry. I emptied all the partially used magazines into one of their duffle bags, and saw there were about three full mags worth of ammo. I grabbed three empty mags and threw them in with everything else.

As I started to walk back to the jeep, I heard a muffled voice coming from one of the hit men's headsets. I stopped, pivoted on one foot, and walked over to where the dead man lay for his final rest.

"You must have been the leader, huh?" I asked the decimated corpse, lightly kicking the chest as if expecting a response. He looked odd with his thighs and arms eaten away, leaving behind calves, forearms, and a plump torso. His glinting blood looked black in the moonlight.

I bent down and removed his headset, placing the earpiece in position over my head. A voice chimed over.

"Parker. Parker, do you copy? Over," the voice asked methodically.

I pushed the switch on the earpiece, putting on my super scary voice, and said, "Parker's...indisposed." I glanced down at the mutilation that had once been a human. "Maybe I can help. Where are you?" I let the last syllable linger in the air.

Silence was the response I got.

"Oh, ah, over," I said, finishing the appropriate radio etiquette.

An unmistakable voice came over the line and violated my ears like they were a pair of roofied prom dates, "Is that you, Jonathan?"

"It's just John. And you didn't say over. Over," I said to Locke.

"I assume that your dog survived?" Locke asked absently, already knowing the answer.

My mind flashed to Tiny Tim and anger grew in my chest, white-hot and deep. I couldn't let him know I was affected. In my best cheery voice, I half lied, "Nope. But he did eat your men while they were still alive. Their screams, oh, their screams. Most of them even pooped themselves." Growing ballsy, I said a little louder, targeting the other people surely listening in the room, "I ate a few myself. Got to read their minds and learn their secrets, like where your base is."

Locke called my bluff, "And where is that, exactly?"

Damn it. I knew I should have dove into the last-man-standing's head. With Depweg over my shoulder, I had wanted to look all cool and stuff. Shit.

"Oh, you'll see soon enough. It was bad enough you were on my shit list, now you have two of us hunting you. Everyone who works for you will be food for us. Then I'll—"

I was cut off by a voice next to Locke. "Got him, sir."

"Show me on the map," Locke said from further away, as if he had put the microphone down.

"Here, sir," the man responded.

"Excellent," the voice grew louder again. "Hey, Jonathan, don't move."

A sickening feeling grew in my stomach, and I instinctively dropped the headset and started to run. Several bounds in, I cursed myself and turned around, running back to the body. I grabbed the bag containing the weapons and noticed there were shadows dancing on the ground. They grew longer, causing me to stop and look around. The ground grew lighter, and I looked up to see a small, bright moon growing larger.

"That's no moon," I whispered to myself and turned to start sprinting back to the jeep.

As I ran, the ground around me turned as bright as day. I slowed for a millisecond as I looked around in awe. I hadn't seen the world lit up like this in hundreds of years, and for the first time since my transformation, I was in wonderment at how much I actually missed the sun. The greens and browns were vibrant all around. I hopped over a body that was in my path, and I stared at the ruby-red blood with my mouth agape. Even with the brightest LED lights on the market, blood could never be as red as what I saw.

Snapping out of it, I risked a glance over my shoulder to see the ball of light was the size of a house and plummeting toward where the dead men lay.

I picked up speed and leaped into the air, dropping the bag into the back seat. Landing in the front seat, I fumbled with the keys that were still in the ignition. Grabbing hold of them, I turned them and was rewarded with clicking that sounded like an empty machine gun. I let go and turned again, but was met with the same result.

I leaned out the jeep and looked at the engine block, which looked like swiss cheese, and yelled, "*Fuck!*"

I turned in my seat and grabbed the bag, slipping the strap over one shoulder and across my chest. Pulling the strap tight, I leaped out the top of the jeep and onto Depweg's side. I reached in and undid his seat belt while chancing a glance at the ball of death. It was hurling toward the trees with the ferocity of a falling star.

With renewed vigor, I threw Depweg over my shoulders in a fireman's carry and started sprinting down the dirt road in the direction of the highway. A moment later, I saw my shadow extend out in front of me, growing tall in the falling light. It was about to hit.

There was an earsplitting boom and a shock wave that propelled me forward, almost launching me off my feet. I felt the heat creep up as I ran, and my once long shadow started to retreat back toward my face as a ball of fire erupted into the sky. Depweg moaned at the movement and probably the burning air as well. Luckily, his girth was keeping most of the immense heat off of my shoulders and head. But man, oh man, did my ass and legs burn!

I made it to the edge of the road and looked back. The fireball had diminished to black smoke, violating the night sky. The woods around the area were blazing.

Depweg moaned, and I turned my face just in time for him to vomit chunks of man-flesh all over my face.

"Sorry," was all he could manage before passing out again.

I stood there, with my face scrunched in disgust, and spit out a dribble of flesh that had flown into my mouth. I turned my head and wiped my face on his jeans, clearing my vision.

When I dared to open my eyes, I looked around and tried to figure out what to do next. A beautiful sight came into view as I spotted the twin, white commercial vans sitting on the side of the road a quarter mile up the side of the road. I chuckled to myself and started walking toward them.

As I got closer, I could see orange traffic cones around both vans and the official-looking equipment on top. "Locke's City Services" was printed on either side of both vans. Sonofabitch was humble.

I walked around to the back of the first van and grabbed the handle. Locked. I was sure there was a pun there somewhere.

"Shit," I said, knowing there was no key left in existence after that firebomb had incinerated the remains of the hit squad.

I pointed my index finger at the lock and willed my blood into the keyhole. Once it was filled, I pushed on the tumblers and twisted, unlocking the van. The blood retreated back into my finger, and I opened the door with a little, "*Yes.*"

Inside, the work van was an organized treasure trove. Cabinets ran along one side of the van with a bench parallel on the other.

I stepped in and laid Depweg down on the bench with his wounded side facing up.

I turned and saw that most of the cabinet doors were open. The first revealed hard foam slots where the automatic weapons had been. I closed the empty cabinet and moved on to the next. Boxes of silver rounds were stacked on top of each other. I counted ten unmarked boxes of the expensive ammo and mentally smacked my forehead for not grabbing more magazines. After closing the ammunition door, I went to the final cabinet that was at chest height and mentally unsmacked myself once I saw the spare magazines lining the wall. Most were gone, but three remained, bringing my total magazine count to six. I closed the last door and kneeled down to the lower cabinets, which were situated under a work bench.

The first had a red cross on it, and I opened it to find a well-stocked first aid storage unit, complete with operating tools, bandages, and even pharmaceutical vials. I found some burn ointment and grabbed it. Turning to face Depweg, I lifted his shirt to reveal the blackened holes, which were a reddish pink around the edges. I liberally applied the burn medicine to his wounds, which Depweg met with a quick jerk and a gasp, followed by him relaxing and laying his head back on the bench. His breathing went back into a deep rhythm a minute after that.

I turned back to the cabinet, grabbed a large bandage, and removed the adhesive covers along its perimeter, laying it over the wound and smoothing it out.

The other cabinets contained slots where body armor had been at one time, radios, and even one full of MREs and water bottles. I was sure Depweg would appreciate those once he woke up.

Before getting in the driver's seat, I did a quick search of the other van for supplies. I grabbed the first aid kit, thinking it could be useful at home in case of an emergency, and grabbed the other mags and spare ammo. There wasn't as much as the second van, suggesting the lead vehicle had contained the bulk of the force.

After throwing the supplies in the back of the second van, I made my way to the front and settled in the driver's seat. Reaching for the ignition, I noticed the keys weren't there. A quick check of the glove box and center console revealed nothing.

"That's odd," I muttered to myself. "What if the driver went down in battle and was, like, eaten or something." My brow was furrowed in confusion, and then I remembered every movie ever and grabbed the visor. A set of keys fell into my lap as I did.

"Neat," I said as I picked up the keys. "But, why was the van locked?" I looked at the driver's door next to me and noticed the indicator in the up position. "What a confusing bunch," I said out loud as I put the only key on the chain into the ignition.

After adjusting my mirrors and clicking my seat belt (you know, for safety), I threw the van into gear and did a U-turn. Destination, Houston.

Chapter 32

PRESENT DAY

Locke was going to pay. Besides revenge and the obvious, he just wasn't a good guy at all. I bet he snapped at waiters and told retail employees to go get their managers. I'd be doing the world a favor by sending him to the pits of Hell to roast like so many assholes before him. He had haunted me for far too long, and now I was going to return the favor.

A question tickled just behind my forehead; how had he survived for so many centuries? I had never heard of a warlock being able to extend their life for more than a few decades.

Depweg rousing in the back broke my train of thought.

"Heeeeeyyy," I said with an elongated syllable. "How we doin' back there, champ?"

A long, drawn out moan was his response as he pulled himself up to a seated position.

In a voice that's usually reserved for a parent trying to lift the spirits of their sad child by telling them they had made pancakes, I said, "There are MREs in the cabinet, sweetie."

Without looking back, I could hear Depweg rummaging through the cabs.

"Bottom left," I said.

"Mmph," was his response.

The next sound I heard was a package being torn open and consumed greedily. The noise sounded like an old '80s zombie movie where they zoomed in on the body being eaten to gross you out. I'd always laugh at the production quality.

We drove like that for some time, starring me as Morgan Freeman in *Driving Mr. Deppyweg*. In short order, Depweg had consumed all of the MREs. Once he was done, he made his way up to the passenger seat, waving his ass by my face as he did, and let one rip.

I thought my face was going to melt off from the heat. The ball of fire Locke had thrown was nothing compared to the unholy abomination that emanated from Depweg's rusty starfish. Thank Lilith I didn't need to breathe oxygen or I might have thrown up. My eyes did water, however.

After sitting down, Depweg looked at me and said, "'Ode to Ass' by Johann Sebastian Bach."

I turned my head toward him slowly with a deadpan look. We sat in silence, looking at one another. We both burst out laughing at the same time. Unfortunately for me, the process of laughing involved air going in and out of my lungs, and I got a shotgun blast of were-fart in my mouth and nose.

I started coughing, heartily. This only increased Depweg's mirth, and he bent over laughing. He stopped with a gasp and grabbed his side.

"That was...sidesplitting, wasn't it?" I said with the taste of refried man-flesh sitting on my tongue.

Depweg looked at me and tried his best to control his laughter at my dad joke.

A rain of gunfire barked in the night, startling Depweg and myself. Bullets slammed into the van on the passenger side. Looking at the side mirror, I saw two similarly decked out white vans with black-clad men hanging out of the vehicles.

The window shook violently, looking like giant rocks covered in white dust had been thrown at the window.

"The van's bulletproof," I said to Depweg. "Grab one of the Sig's in the back and slap in some mags. We are in for a bumpy ride."

As Depweg moved to the back, a battering ram slammed into the passenger side. Depweg was thrown into the bench, reminding him quite abruptly about his perforated, well-done side. He cried out in pain and collapsed to his knees, clutching his wounds.

"Get up!" I yelled, looking at him in the rearview mirror. "Now is not the time for your 'play dead' trick."

Depweg moaned angrily through clenched teeth and grabbed the countertop for support.

Another ram nearly threw us off the road, forcing me to overcorrect back and forth until we leveled out.

"Damn, this bitch has a fat ass," I said, fighting with the wheel. "How much do you weigh, Depweg?"

"Two-fifty with my pretty face on," he replied, slapping a magazine into an MPX and priming the bolt.

"Go for the tires and the grill," I told him while letting the van slow, watching the others match our speed. After we dropped to fifty, I slammed on the gas, giving Depweg a clear target.

Depweg grabbed the handle of the back door with a smile and pulled. Nothing happened. He jiggled the handle several times in confusion.

"Oops," I said, pressing the unlock button next to my arm. "Child safety locks, for your protection."

With that, Depweg threw the back door open, though his action smile had disappeared and had been replaced with a scowl. With one hand braced against the roof and half his body protected by the other door still closed, Depweg let loose a volley of gunfire that ripped into the front of the first van. He kept the gun in control with three-second bursts, allowing him to better control his aim. We were traveling at almost a hundred miles per hour at this point. I was impressed at the modifications the men had done on the seemingly innocuous vans.

A few of the rounds struck home, and the van started to smoke out of the hood, slightly obscuring the driver's vision.

In front of us, a semi-trailer was coming on the opposite side of the four-lane road, and a delicious idea popped into my head.

"Semi coming. Blow out their driver's side tire on my command," I said.

Depweg took aim but didn't shoot, waiting.

"*Now!*" I yelled.

A quick burst of fire hit the intended target, and the tire blew out with an explosion of tread. At the speed we were going, the van lost control immediately and was thrown into the oncoming lanes, where it was met with a fully loaded semi-death machine.

There wasn't an explosion like in the movies, only the sound of crunching metal, like someone crushing a beer can right next to your ear. I was really getting sick of how much the movies lied. The howling of tires followed as the huge semi slammed on the brakes.

I watched the carnage unfold from the side mirror, smiling widely. The van mimicked an accordion while the massive semi only suffered damage to its extended engine block, leaving the driver relatively unharmed, though a little rattled.

"I love it when a plan comes together," I said in my best Hannibal Smith impression. Depweg turned his head toward me and smiled.

A pair of headlights squared up in my rearview mirror and then grew in size, fast.

Looking down, I noticed I had rubbernecked and let my speed drop back down to eighty, giving the second van a chance to move into position.

"*Hold on*!" I screamed right as the other van slammed into our rear. "Lilith damn it! I said *no* anal on the first date! No means no!" I slammed on the gas, but didn't pull away. There was a moan of metal, and I realized we were stuck.

Depweg cried out from behind, "We're stuck!"

"I know, I know! *Watch out*!"

The driver's side back door was pinned open, allowing a front-row view of my sitting ass. One of the hit men was casually sticking his gun out of the passenger window, with only his hand exposed now. Everything we could see of the piggybacking van was bulletproof, leaving us like fish in a barrel. Depweg turned and hid behind the closed door, leaving me as the lone fish.

From the rearview mirror, I saw, as if in slow motion, the gun barrel pointing in my direction. It appeared to be the size of a cannon as I looked down its length, and it ended in the black nothingness of my oblivion. He squeezed the trigger.

Blinding strobe lights broke the darkness, and someone punched me in my left shoulder, hard. It threw me forward and to the right, making me let go of the wheel. The silver burned white-hot, stealing my breath and making my arm hang lifeless at my side. I felt warmth slowly spread over my jeans. Looking down, I could see blood streaming from my fingertips and onto my leg, creating a blossoming crimson circle. What concerned me was that I couldn't feel the blood passing over my arm.

"*John*! *Are you still with me, man*?" Depweg asked, panic growing in his voice.

Slurring my words, I said, "Bastards ruined my pants." With my good hand, I touched where the impact had been and felt the mess of flesh and torn leather. "And my coat!"

I pulled myself into the passenger seat, letting the caboose van blindly steer for us. Perplexed that the sting of the silver was dwindling so quickly, I looked down to the front of my shoulder and noticed an even bigger hole. My eyes shifted to the driver's side of the van, where a Jackson Pollock painting coated the van's white interior and windshield.

Black bugs swam in my vision like flies on a carcass. I was losing a lot of blood, and with it, my life force.

"Dep...weg," I managed.

From behind, another volley of gunfire ripped through the interior, ricocheting off the bench and shredding the driver's seat. One bounced a few times and decided my leg was a good place to call it a day.

I gasped in pain, the black bugs being replaced with solid darkness encompassing my vision at the periphery.

Looking down at where the bullet was stuck halfway out of my leg, I said, "Damn...it." I moved my good hand to where it sat like an unwanted wart mocking me.

Grasping it with my fingers, I pulled, but didn't have the strength to hold on and my fingers slipped with all the blood pooling around the wound.

"Little help?" I cried while fighting to stay conscious. The pain crept up my leg toward my core.

Depweg quickly, and carefully, made his way up the right side of the van and leaned around the seat. He saw what I was doing and reached down and flicked the bullet out of my leg. The ache that was growing up my body slowly ceased its progress and dulled.

"The bullets...are coated," I told Depweg.

"I can't stop them, John," Depweg said, concern evident in his voice.

"There's a way, but you're not gonna like it," I drawled.

"If it means getting out of this alive, I'm game."

I started whispering at a barely audible level, forcing his ear down closer to my mouth. I whirled on him, grabbing the other side of his head with my good hand, and sank my teeth into his neck. He struggled for a moment before relaxing, realizing what I was doing.

The blood was rich and powerful, like drinking an entire busload of humans at once. His ancient blood flowed, bringing with it power I hadn't felt since Ulric had let me feed on him for the very first time.

I could feel my wounds start to close, but they didn't heal all the way. My left arm was still just for cosmetic purposes. Would probably have to clean the silver traces out completely before it would heal all the way. Everything else felt powerful. The white insides of the van became bright and glowing. The lights passing overhead had the aura of little suns. I could smell the cordite in the air from the spent ammunition.

Depweg's heart fluttered, and I grabbed my mental wheel again, throwing Depweg backward into the van.

With my good arm, I effortlessly smashed out the bulletproof passenger window, which fell away in a single mass covered in spiderweb cracks. I crawled outside and to the roof. I walked the length of the van, eyes almost glowing red and teeth elongated into surgical fangs.

The passenger had reloaded and was sticking his hand out the window again as the driver frantically pointed inside to where Depweg lay still.

I forced a whip out of my hand with a blade at the end and cracked the air at the gun. It tumbled to the asphalt below with a hand still attached. I saw eyes grow wide in the balaclava as a spurting stump was pulled back from the window. The other men froze while staring at the geyser of blood as it smeared the interior.

I commanded the whip to straighten into a spear and hefted it above my head.

"Hey, assholes!"

The driver turned his head and leaned forward to get a better view, and I slammed the spear through the glass and into his top shoulder, right at the neckline. It went deep into his torso, and I willed his blood into me. I put all my effort into sucking every last drop before he finally died, which made his body shrivel into a husk right in front of his buddies. I yanked the spear out of the man and broke dried bones as I did, like pasta being broken before being thrown into the boiling pot. I laughed maniacally with a wide, tooth-filled mouth.

Screams erupted as the professionals lost their composure. Both vans began to decelerate at a noticeable pace.

I leaped on top of the attached van, willing my spear into a sword, and cut right down the middle of the roof like a kitchen knife on an empty soda can. With the blade still inside, I forced it apart like a pair of crowbars, forcing the roof to peel open like a surgeon operating on a patient. Once open, the men sprayed gunfire. I had anticipated this and had already moved to the back of the van.

Both vans had slowed and veered off the side of the road into the grass. Once the gunfire had started, the vans had stopped. I jumped off the side of the van and turned to the doors.

Using my stolen supernatural life force, I focused on my good hand, bending my body slightly like a pitcher about to throw the fastest ball of his life.

The back doors flung open in unison as I dropped to one knee and threw my hand forward, willing a gargantuan bloodserpent to erupt from my hand and into the van. The tail tapered off and ended at my hand, while its enormous mouth swallowed men whole, one at a time. Screams of terror reverberated throughout the metal van and escaped into the night.

Shots were fired into the beast, and it sent electric currents up my arm, forcing me to clench my teeth to the point where I thought they were about to shatter into pebbles.

Two of the three remaining men were swallowed, and the third pointed an empty submachine gun at the serpent, as if maybe the gun had forgotten it still had unspent rounds left.

The serpent snapped its jaws at the man's kicking feet and caught one. As it began to slide up his leg, he placed his other foot on the beast's snout and pushed. The snake quickly opened its jaws wide and let the other foot slip into its mouth. The man, having dropped the gun, pounded on the nose with his fists and gulped in air with wheezing panic.

I commanded the serpent to stop at his waist, and then walked up to him.

"How did you find us?" I asked.

The assassin, still in panic mode, only looked at me with wide eyes.

"I don't have time for this shit," I said to myself and tried to lift my other arm to take control of his synapses. At that moment, I was reminded of my lifeless arm and rolled my eyes. There would be no mind-diving on this night.

"The hard way it is," I said with annoyance while rolling my eyes.

I forced the digesting bodies of his buddies, who were in the girth of the animal, to pass beside him and onto the ground on either side of the man. I had already sucked all their juices and had no use for the remaining meat.

The man whimpered at the sight of the bodies, which were now dry husks of man-jerky. I felt him relieve himself in the snake's mouth.

"Aw man, gross," I said. I had to focus on the foreign liquid and separate it from the blood. I let it drop to the grass below.

"I'm going to ask you one more time, and then I'm going to eat you. Then, if I'm not happy with your answers, I'll find your family and eat them too. Aunts, uncles, parents, your spouse, and even children. Heck, I'll eat your family dog if you piss me off," I said with authority.

"Now, how the *fuck* did you find us?" I demanded.

"Trackers, on the vans," the man said through sobs.

"Thank you. Was that so hard?" I said as I willed the snake to suck him in with one quick movement. The man held his breath with cheeks puffed through the balaclava and sent his hands and feet in all directions, desperate to find an escape. I closed my eyes and willed my blood to enter through his skin, freeing the prisoner that was his own hemoglobin. The life force seeped out of him from every pore, and within seconds, the man went still, letting out his last bubbles of air.

I let him drop next to his friends and willed the serpent back into my being. Snake back in its home, I went to check on Depweg. As I walked past the passenger side of the rear van, something flailed through the night and struck me in the back of the skull, knocking me flat on my face.

Pulling my good hand up to where I had been hit, I could feel a massive, hot piece of metal imbedded in my skin. I pried it off, losing only a bit of blood before the skin knitted itself back together.

Still holding the nonsilver bullet, I got up and turned to see the one-armed man holding a smoking, chrome-plated hand cannon revolver through the passenger side window. It was bigger than his own head and pointed directly at me.

I flicked the bullet at his remaining hand, which exploded in a mass of bone and tissue.

With a devilish smile, I walked up to him and said, "Guess they let you bring your own handguns, didn't they? Didn't spring for the silver rounds, huh?"

I grabbed the door and ripped it off its hinges, throwing it onto the grass behind me. I reached over him and undid his seat belt and dragged him out of the seat. In his shock at losing both his penis grabbers, he didn't fight back. Letting him drop to the ground where he lay barely conscious, I walked to where the vans were connecting and kicked the rear van backward.

"Give me a hand, will ya?" I asked of the downed man. "Oops, never mind."

Using my body as a brace, our van stayed put as the rear one rolled backward a few yards, crushing one of the jerky boys I had left behind.

I climbed into the van and stood over Depweg, who looked pale. Terror gripped my heart as I realized I had drained more than I had intended.

Leaning down, I lightly slapped his cheeks and said, "Stay with me, man. I got some fresh food for you."

His eyes fluttered open and his mouth opened a little. I got the signal immediately. He was too weak to change, so I would have to feed him.

I jumped out the back and walked to where the no-armed man was, grabbed him, and walked back to the van. I tossed him on the countertop and started removing his gear. From the waist up. He barely protested as his wide, glazed eyes searched for focus all around him, finding none.

Taking out his own blade, a standard issue military knife with half serrations and a razor edge, I hastily began cutting strips of flesh off his body.

After a few had been cut, I leaned down and carefully dropped the thin strips into Depweg's mouth. He closed it and started to chew. After several seconds of chewing, he swallowed, and then opened his eager mouth again. I dropped another strip and he half opened his eyes.

Blood dripped down from the countertop and striped the cabinets. I cut the man's bicep completely off and handed it to Depweg, who grasped it with both hands before taking greedy bites. Color was starting to come back to his features.

The man on the countertop took one last breath and slowly let it go.

I helped Depweg up on the bench and handed him the knife. He got to work on the once assassin as I reached for the cabinet with the red cross on it. Inside I found iodine solution in a squeeze bottle. I took a deep breath and jammed it into the front hole on my left shoulder and squeezed, hard. The cleansing fluid rushed through the entire wound and out the back, taking with it most of the silver dust that had coated the rounds. I squeezed again and almost emptied the bottle before pulling it out and sticking the tip in the broken skin on my leg, repeating the process.

After a few moments, my leg started to stitch itself up. I looked at my shoulder and could see it starting to slowly rebuild itself as well.

Within five minutes, Depweg had eaten almost every muscle on the man's upper body and started on the lower half. Feeling returned to my fingertips in the torturous form of pins and needles. I sighed a breath of relief, and let my head rest on the van's wall.

"We need to go soon," I said. "It won't take long before they realize something is wrong, and I don't want any more of Locke's fucking fireballs coming our way."

Depweg nodded and quickly cut both the man's quadricep muscles off with practiced precision. "For the road," he said as I looked at him.

We started walking down the highway, just on the outskirts of the woods, and I said, "Forgot weres could eat people with their pretty faces on. Pretty neat."

"To be honest, I hadn't had to do it since we first met. Usually shifting to wolf when injured gives us a better chance at survival." He looked at me and continued, "Never had my blood drained before. Didn't know vamps could drain supes."

"Then we are both learning new things about ourselves tonight," I said, remembering the rush of power and life I'd felt.

"This is taking too long. Can you shift yet?" I asked.

"I think so," he said while starting to strip off his clothes.

I walked to the edge of the tree line and stared down one side of the highway, and then the other, keeping a lookout for work vans at this late hour. Or early, depending on whom you might ask.

A few minutes passed as I stood watch, letting the events of the evening replay in my mind. There was a chuff from behind and I turned to see the giant wolf staring at me with yellow eyes. His tail wagged in delight at his successful transformation and resulting energy. He dropped his front paws and extended them, leaving his rear legs straight. His tongue stuck out the side of his mouth, and he barked in excitement.

"What?" I asked. "Wanna play fetch or somethen?"

He cocked his head to the side, tongue pulling back into his closing mouth, and growled at me with half sincerity.

"Whoa, boy. That's a bad boy," I scolded.

He stood up tall on all fours and walked to me. His eyes the same height as my own.

"*Just* kidding!" I said with a high pitch while throwing my hands up in placation.

He stopped, his snout less than an inch from my face. I could smell the woods on his fur and the meat still on his breath.

He stood there for a moment, with me all but pulling a Michael Jackson by leaning so far back I thought my ass was going to touch ground. He licked my face and chuffed at me before bounding off into the woods, heading in the direction of Houston. I leaned down and grabbed his clothes, stashing them in the duffle bag. I thought about leaving his pants behind, but the joke would be on me; I'd be the one who would have to look at him later.

There was a distinctive car beep in the road. My jaw dropped open as I looked and saw the Fae, Lily, standing next to a hot-pink Rolls-Royce. She was applying makeup from a handheld mirror while she leaned against the driver's side door, which had the window down.

I turned to where Depweg last was and whistled, loud but short. As I started seductively walking toward Lily, I heard romping in the distance, which quickly grew louder until Depweg was right next to me, staring at Lily.

"Looks like we got a ride after all, buddy," I said as I scratched him between the ears. He responded by pushing at my lower back with one of his massive paws, causing me to stumble forward and almost fall on my face.

"Hey! Bad dog!" I said as I righted myself and turned to face Depweg with a scowl. He ignored me and, instead, sniffed the air in the direction of Lily. He snorted and started sneezing, rubbing his nose into the grass as if something had invaded his nostrils.

After a few more sneezes, he jerked his head sharply to stare at Lily. I pieced the puzzle together.

"Lily," I said with authority, "cut it out. He's a friend."

"Oh, I know," she purred. "I simply wished to greet him, in my way." She paused, considering. "Curious. His reaction was not what I was expecting for a man-beast. How intriguing."

After a few moments, the new info settled in and was filed for later use, snapping Lily from her train of thought.

"Time to go," she said, opening the driver's door and getting in.

Depweg and I looked at each other.

"It's in her best interest that we stop Locke, and that's good enough for me," I reassured Depweg.

After a few heartbeats, Depweg nodded ever so slightly. I pulled his clothes back out and laid them on the ground. He picked them up in his jaws and sauntered to the tree line. Once he was out of sight, I could hear the transformation taking place.

Lily looked at me from the visor mirror that she had lowered to finish her makeup and did a "what's taking so long" gesture with her face and free hand. I lifted my index finger, indicating it would only be a moment longer.

A minute later, Depweg came out of the woods, pulling down his black band shirt. This one said "Tool" on it.

"Hey," I said while pointing at his shirt once he got close, "aren't they the 'Barbie Girl' group? Catchy song."

He rolled his eyes so hard that they almost did a complete revolution around their sockets. He continued past me to the passenger side of the Rolls.

"Shotgun," he said.

"Ah, man!" I cried out in legitimate disappointment.

"He did call it, Jonathan," Lily gloated.

In unison, Depweg and I said, "It's just John."

She giggled and motioned for me to climb in the back with her thumb. I obliged. It was ridiculously luxurious in the back seat. There was a TV screen coming out of the center console that had the news on mute. The seats reclined and even offered vibrating massages and heat. She even had a damn minibar. I did a double take as I noticed a crystal container of a dark, red liquid.

"Is that..."

"Just for you, lover," Lily said while glancing in the rearview mirror as she pulled onto the highway.

At the comment, Depweg flicked his ear so slightly that a mortal's eyes would have missed it.

I didn't say anything and focused on pouring myself a drink. Lily was staking her claim and making sure Depweg was aware of her presence on the food chain. Depweg turned his head to stare out the window, much the same way a passenger would do if a tone-deaf driver started belting out lyrics along with the radio. As if turning away abated the awkwardness of it all.

The tension was palpable. *Should have let me take shotgun, buddy,* I thought while taking a drink. It made my tongue tingle as it passed over it and washed down my throat. My eyes closed and my hairs stood on end, a moan of pleasure escaping my lips before I could stop it.

"Tell me, boys, what is your plan for stopping Locke?" she asked, breaking the tension.

"Go in, guns blazing!" I said with abnormal delight.

"Well, it's a bit more complicated than that," Depweg said while glancing curiously in the rearview mirror at me.

"You're both crazy," Lily said, bemused.

"That's what my therapist says!" I said. I was met with silence from both of my companions. "Guys," I started after a few moments, "I'm kidding! They can't legally say that." My words were starting to slur a tad. I felt giddy. My head fell back and I smiled wide, my eyes closing in delight.

"Do you like it, John?" Lily asked, amused at my reaction to her drink.

Eyes still closed and thoughts swimming in a pool of elation, I managed to ask, "What is it?"

"The 'what' should be obvious, silly. It's the 'whose' that should interest you," she said with a shark's smile spreading across her beautiful face.

"Whose blood is this?" I asked while trying to shake off the creeping tingle that was spreading up my head and down my body. It was hard to fight because I didn't want it to stop.

"Mine, of course," she said.

I had never drunk from a supernatural before, and now, in one night, I had imbibed from a centuries old werewolf and an ageless Fae.

The blood was like if her pheromone scent had been extracted and magnified. My skin heated, and my mini-me leaped to attention. I wanted her. *Needed* her. I could feel the predator inside my head start to fight for the wheel.

"What's happening to him? What have you done?" I could hear Depweg ask from far away as I lay back on the reclining seat, feeling its comfort envelope me. I was so tired all of a sudden.

"This," I heard Lily say from the other side of a thin wall. Her voice muffled as I relented toward unconsciousness. I knew what was happening, but didn't care. The reclining chair felt so incredibly good against my back. It cradled me and promised well-being and happiness.

I could vaguely hear a gasp from somewhere far away. I struggled with my remaining strength to open my eyes, and I saw Depweg trying to swat at his nose, as if a particularly heinous fart had just been released. He relaxed after a one-sided battle and let his head drop to the passenger window.

"*Bitch,*" was all I could manage with a yawn before sleep enveloped me. The hum of the engine faded as I fell unconscious.

Chapter 33

I awoke inside my own body. Disoriented, I lifted my arm and pinched the bridge of my nose. When I opened my eyes, I could see the back of the driver's seat *through* my hand. Looking down, I noticed the solid flesh of my limb was still resting on the armrest.

Sitting up in the reclining chair of the pink Rolls-Royce, I noticed my hands were made out of mist. I stood straight up and went through the roof of the car, where my hands promptly explored my entire body. I was somewhat relieved to find I was solid to my own touch. I was incorporeal and out of my undead body.

"Neat," I said in a voice that echoed, growing in cadence and quickly dissipating. "*Neat.*" Louder this time, with a more pronounced echo in return.

The background grabbed my attention and refused to let go. The sky was a blood orange that offered inadequate illumination of the scene around me. Trees were still green, but dull, as if I was in a painting of diluted matte colors.

The trees didn't move in the wind. Heck, I couldn't even feel the wind. Then I noticed the car wasn't speeding down the road anymore. I was frozen in time, sticking out of the top of the unmoving, solid car. Rather, *nothing* was moving. Birds hung in the air but appeared to be moving from a shimmer that surrounded everything. It was like looking through a mirage in a color-drained setting. The color was still there, but the once bright-and-popping pink of the Rolls was now a flat shade, as if it had aged a decade in direct sunlight.

"Confused?" a voice echoed beside me.

Startled, I cried out and tried to move back, but only succeeded in tumbling in midair, ass over nose. A hand grabbed my head and prevented a full rotation.

Lily stood, incorporeal as well, though she was upside down. Scratch that, I was upside down.

With all the elegance that only centuries of assimilating every language I came across could afford, I summoned my vast vocabulary to better express my confusion.

"Uh...the fuck?" I said with grace befitting royalty.

"We don't have much time," Lily said uncharacteristically. "I brought us to the in-between." Her cadence had become sharp, bordering on urgency.

"The what now?" I asked, trying to wiggle myself back upright. Lily took her hand, which was still on my head, and swiped sideways, making me tumble again. She grabbed my ankle as I spun and pulled me down to eye level with her.

"The place between planes. Couldn't you have figured that out by the name?" she asked in annoyance. "Now, listen carefully."

I listened as she spoke, darkness creeping up from my gut and my heart sinking to meet it in the middle.

Chapter 34

PRESENT DAY

I crept into consciousness and slowly started to gather that I was on a cold, cement floor. Head swimming, I looked around to see a wide, empty warehouse with swaths of light on the floor from the powerful fluorescent bulbs hanging far above.

Looking straight up, I got dizzy and fell backward. A large, warm mass stopped me, and I realized I was tied to someone, back to back.

"Dep-Depweg," I stammered.

He answered with a moan, like someone waking from a night of excess drinking. A skull-pounding headache greeted us like an old friend.

My wrists ached, like they were submerged in flames. The pain spread in both directions, making my hands and forearms tingle as if electrified.

Straining to turn my head, I saw that both of our hands were cuffed with the chains interlaced, making separation impossible. I noticed there were a number of small crimson circles on the ground. As I watched, a drop of blood fell and created another circle. Puzzled, I looked at my numb hands and saw that there was a trickle of blood coming from my palm, right where the thumb connected.

"I told you to stay the fuck out of this, Jonathan," a familiar voice stated from above.

"It's just John," I said drunkenly. Though the effects were wearing off, I slapped the thickness on for good measure. Best to appear more incapacitated than I really was. I started scratching at the small hole in my palm, using my nail as a guide. I knew I was on the right track when I commanded the finger to move and the nail would sometimes catch on the hole.

With a dramatic *thunk*, the lights above were shut off. To my left, floodlights pointed directly at us and thrust on, blinding me. I heard footsteps descending metal stairs, then padding on concrete. A figure stepped in front of the glaring lights and filled the entire warehouse with a long shadow. Locke's body was unmistakable, with his freakish height and stringy frame.

"Do you cosplay as Slender Man?" I asked with slurred words.

He started walking forward, letting the light slowly swallow his shadow as he approached.

"Sometimes," he said, matter-of-factly. "It is quite popular."

"Plus, you get to wear a mask to hide your fucked-up piehole," I added insolently.

I could see his head drop to his chest as he started chuckling to himself. As if my comment made what he was about to do to us that much sweeter.

My nail found purchase and I ripped a big chunk of my palm open. Blood started to drip more quickly.

Locke stopped just short of where I sat and tilted his head; the gold outline of his mask glinted in the lights. I realized he was hearing the drops hit the concrete, and I moved my hands closer to the ground, pulling Depweg's hands with me. He moaned in protest.

I rubbed my wounded palm against the other, and then grabbed both wrists with bloody hands, making it look like my wrists were bleeding from the restraints. As Locke's eyes fell upon our cuffed wrists, I let my hands drop back down.

Finding nothing of substantial interest, Locke's gaze returned to meet mine.

My fingers found what was hidden; a small piece of iron. I gasped lightly when my fingers touched the metal, sending sparks of electricity up my digits.

From under a mask that left only his mouth exposed, Locke smiled when he saw me wince in pain.

"How are you enjoying your stay with us so far? Anything I can get you? A spare pillow, perhaps? Oh, I know, a mint for that bloody breath of yours." At this, Locke covered his mouth with his fist in an attempt to hide the smile that had crept up on him.

"The important thing is that at least *you* think you're funny," I said. His smile disappeared and he let his hand drop, clearly annoyed that I had taken his self-induced mirth away.

A click caught Locke's attention. Eyes narrowing, he started to walk around to my side.

Quickly, I let my fingers drop from the cuffs again, leaving the key in place. It was facing downward, and Locke was walking on the wrong side to really get a good view.

"Oh dear, you've cut yourself, Jonathan," he said while continuing the walk around his prizes. He stopped when he was in front of Depweg.

"Why don't you use your pixie powers to heal me?" I challenged. This grabbed his full attention, and he was back in front of me in two furious steps.

He crouched down and grabbed my chin with one hand. In his other, he produced a ball of light the size of a grain of rice. It was bright, like looking into a military-grade flashlight. Locke moved it closer to my face, allowing me to feel the warmth emanating from it. I tried to turn my head, which made his grip on my chin tighter. His physical strength surprised me. Either that or I was weaker than I'd thought from the iron cuffs. It must have shown on my face because a shit-eating grin grew on Locke's.

"Feeling weak, are you? You'll be tickled to know that I had the cuffs made especially for you. A little iron, a little silver, and a touch of holy magic," he said, letting the light fade from his palm.

"You can do holy magic too? Whose dick did you suck to learn that?" I asked while removing the key and moving it to the other cuff.

His smile grew, the corners of his mouth disappearing under the black mask. "I stole it from your priest. Now, pray tell, why did your Father Thomes Philseep have a special pair of handcuffs made specifically for you?"

"Did you hurt him?" I asked flatly, feeling my head swirl.

"What? Did I kill your only means of redemption in the eyes of God?" He let my chin drop and stood up, clapping his hands together gleefully. "What would you do if I did?" he said without humor.

I looked up with a scowl that hurt my face. Tears brimmed in my eyes, threatening to blind me. I forcibly shook my head, making them fall away to the ground, and let sorrow be replaced with a building fury. There was no way in Hell I was about to let Locke see me weep.

Locke's smile faded as another click rang out.

"Kill you," I whispered in answer to his question as the cuffs fell from my wrists.

With the blessed metals off my skin, I let my predatory side take full control of the wheel. Everything was in slow motion, but my mind was sharp and overclocked.

In one swift motion, I half stood, half levitated to my feet in front of a shocked Locke. I grabbed him by the throat and pulled him close. My teeth pierced his neck without preamble, and I tried to inhale as much of his blood as I could before I was, presumably, gunned down, set on fire, or whatever horrors he had waiting for me.

In my single-minded focus of relieving Locke of his pesky blood, I failed to notice the palm of his hand creeping up to rest on my chest. With a grimace, Locke uttered a command word, and a massive wave of force crashed into my sternum and threw me back so far that I crashed into the wall of the warehouse. Chunks of cement rained down all around me. As I rebounded and hit the ground face-first, I was kindly made aware that my breastbone had been effectively turned into shards of broken glass and sand. I tried to push myself up, but my pectoral muscles had nothing to attach themselves to anymore. Blood drooled out of my mouth, and I was vaguely aware that it was flowing much more freely than possible, even for having just eaten. My lungs must be punctured, and they were hemorrhaging.

All this took a back seat to the elation I felt coursing through the pipeline of my arterial system. His blood was old and powerful. I didn't even have to focus on my sunken chest for it to start healing. The crimson elixir carried with it such immense energy that I could barely focus.

My sternum popped audibly, filling in again. The muscles knitted themselves back into bone, and my lungs sealed. I moaned with half pain, half pleasure.

Whole once again, I looked up from where I was now able to push myself up, and I immediately locked onto my attacker. He had been thrown back equally from the shock wave and had just regained his footing. Locke's mask had shattered and was falling away from his face, revealing grotesque burn scars that reminded me of the Hound in *Game of Thrones*; or the Phantom in *The Phantom of the Opera*, depending on your taste and sophistication.

He was shuffling away while holding his neck with both hands. His feet barely adhered to his commands to walk, and his knees tried to buckle. My predatory side felt the inescapable urge to chase after my wounded prey.

I pushed myself back onto my haunches and then launched into the air, fracturing the stone floor. My black Frankenstein's monster of a coat billowed from the friction of piercing the air with preternatural speed.

I was about to wrap my hands around Locke's neck and tackle him to the ground when an unseen force smashed into the center of my back like a ten-ton garbage truck being dropped from the Empire State building. I felt claws pierce my flesh as we cratered into the ground.

I turned my head to see a slim demon with skin that smoldered like a dying ember. The black, leather skin glowed with the differing colors of hellfire that roamed over his flesh with perfect symmetry, like a living kaleidoscope. His appendages were too long for his body and were covered in ropey muscle that had a road map of veins tunneling in all directions. At the end of his limbs were birdlike talons with thick, sharp bones sticking out like claws.

My eyes drifted further, and I could see he was devoid of horns or tusks like most demons I had encountered. He had a normal-sized mouth that was curled in a grimace of anger, showing one row of slightly serrated teeth on both his top and lower jaws. There were two slits where a nose would have been with slightly protruding skin flaps that flailed with each breath, akin to a horse's nostrils.

Above that was...nothing. He had no eyes or even indentions where eye sockets would be. It was as if his forehead and nose slits had decided to cut out the middleman and meet in the middle of his face.

Even without having any eyes, I was uncomfortably aware that he was staring right at me. Assessing his prey like a vulture trying to decide if the carrion had marinated in the sun long enough.

I heard the warehouse door burst open and then slam shut as Locke fled. He was weak, and I needed to finish this.

The eyeless demon lifted one of his taloned feet and moved it up toward my neck. I pushed myself in a half circle with my left hand, which threw the beast off center, forcing him to let go.

Knowing one of the best ways to kill a demon was to decapitate it, I threw my blood-whip out and around its neck, forcing razors along its length. As I got to my feet in a swift motion, I pulled with immense force and spun in a circle, losing my balance.

The demon had vanished right before my eyes, leaving my whip in midair, holding nothing.

A flash of white stars erupted in my vision as the beast appeared next to me and swiped at my head with his taloned hands. Warm liquid raced its way down my neck and into my shirt and coat. Instinctively, I lashed out with my arm, where I hit only air.

Claws smashed into my left calf and threw me in a complete 360, forcing me to hit the ground with my ankle and then tumble to the ground. My left leg below the knee was numb. I could feel blood seeping into my other pant leg.

"Shit," I said to myself, knowing things weren't looking good for ol' Johnny boy.

I had to think of something before I was torn apart. My eyes darted around me to try and find something, *anything*. My gaze locked onto Depweg, who had his hands in front of him as he undid the last cuff lock. I had made damn sure to put the key in his hands before I attacked Locke.

Depweg looked at me and nodded. I mirrored the action as a plan came to mind.

Letting myself drop my head, I started crying out, "I give up. Please, no more!"

At this, the demon appeared in front of me as if walking into the light from the shadows.

I laid it on thick. "Please, benevolent one, show me mercy!" I wailed with hands outstretched in a submissive, begging posture.

The beast stood in front of me and cocked his head to the side, confused. A hand wrapped around my throat and lifted me effortlessly. I was hanging, tiptoes grazing the ground. His other hand pulled back at chest level, ready to spring forward and rip my heart—and probably spine—out. As his arm reached back all it would go and was about to launch forward, a silver kukri blade pierced through his chest, severing his heart.

His grasp weakened on my neck and I dropped to the ground, trying to land on my feet. My left leg refused to cooperate and I fell over, breaking my fall with my hands. I looked up to see one of Depweg's lunch-box hands pushing down on the demon's shoulder while his other hand forced the blade upward, cutting through bone and organs with relative ease. Black blood spilled out of the demon's mouth and nose slits as he jerked with quickening, minute shudders. It was like he was being electrocuted.

"Hey, Bennett," Depweg whispered into the demon's earhole. "Let off some steam."

The vulture beast's glowing skin coalesced into a singular mixture of color and enveloped his entire body, like primed charcoal. With a few more spasms, he dissolved into ectoplasm and sloshed to the ground.

Depweg stepped over the puddle where I was lying and extended a hand.

"Did you like that thing I said?" Depweg asked, proud of himself.

I didn't have the heart to tell him the quote had been off by a tad, and that it hadn't really fit the situation.

"Oh yes," I said, emphatically nodding my head while simultaneously wincing from my wounds. I noticed I couldn't heal them. "The bastard infused his claws with hellfire, man. Shit's gonna take some time to heal."

"Why didn't the attacks cauterize the wounds?" Depweg asked, bringing up an excellent point that reddit users would blast me on if I didn't cover that base.

"Asshole knew what he was doing. Locke planned this out and told him vamps are weak to hellfire. He used enough to prevent me from healing, but held back so I would bleed out. Clever girl."

"What should we do?" Depweg asked.

"Locke is hurt. We need to finish him," I said as I started limping to the exit Locke had escaped through.

"You're hurt too, in case you had neglected to notice." Depweg said with more concern in his voice than reproach.

"I ain't got time to bleed," I said with my best Jesse Ventura impression.

"Question: what if you created tissue around the wound. I mean, looks pretty deep, wouldn't that contain the blood?" Depweg asked.

"Why don't you shut up?" I asked while mentally smacking myself in the head. "Hey, what's that over there?" Depweg's gaze followed my finger as I pointed into the darkness. While his attention was diverted, I told my skin to form a temporary cover to keep my precious blood from leaking.

Depweg turned back to face me.

"Must have been a squirrel or somethin'. Anywho, we ready to burst through this door?"

The corner of Depweg's mouth curled up in a smirk as he noticed I wasn't trailing a crimson shadow anymore.

"Go on ahead. I'm going to slip into something more...terrifying," he finished with a fanged smile.

I nodded in agreement before pressing my shoulder against the emergency exit Locke had fled through, where I was met by a fireball the size of a Lilith-damned basketball.

It exploded on the wall just as I passed through the doorway and burned the shit out of the back of my head and left shoulder. I dropped to the ground, cursing about my duster—which hung loosely off my back now—and beanie—which fell to the ground on fire. I quickly scanned the area around me and found Locke, who was conjuring another fireball, though he seemed to be on wobbly legs.

Letting my coat drop to the ground, I crafted a spear from the blood that I willed through my palm, took aim, and lobbed it right at Locke. He was so intent on his creation, with cords sticking out of his neck and teeth bared in a grimace, that he didn't even notice as the spear flew toward him. It pierced his right quad, causing him to drop the ball of fire which exploded at his feet, throwing him backward and setting his pants ablaze.

I dropped to one knee, having just lost the energy from the bloodspear. After a moment, I regained my mental breath and stood again, right as Locke patted the last of the flames out. Leaning forward, I commanded my legs to start running toward where my enemy was attempting to get back to his feet.

Urgency invigorated my body and mind as Locke put his feet under him in a crouch position, almost standing. My feet started moving at preternatural speed, albeit with more faith than motor function in my left leg. I knew if I flexed my thigh at the right time, my knee would straighten and my foot would (hopefully) find purchase on the ground. I crossed the distance between the warehouse and the edge of the parking lot where a demolished landscape was being prepped for another building.

Locke turned his head and saw me coming. Dirt that covered the concrete parking lot whipped up like a train through a snowbank. My fangs were bared, my fingers sprouted bloodclaws, and the purple in my eyes dulled to a blood red. Surprise exploded in his face, which was immediately replaced with focus. Locke rolled to his side, falling belly up, right as I leaped toward him with claws outstretched.

Locke threw his open palms at my torso as I flew over him, my hands raking over his sternum, rending flesh. An unseen wave of energy slammed into me and threw my body toward the full moon overhead. Wind tore at my hair and clothes, threatening to deafen me by whistling into my ears.

At the cusp, I regained my senses enough to realize my insides were on the outside. They hung in the air around me and attempted to flee in all directions after a lifelong prison stint inside my body. As I began to fall, I grabbed my innards and pulled them in hand over hand until a big ball of guts was cradled in my arms, like a defiant extension cord.

As I neared the ground, I pushed the ball-o-intestines back into my chest cavity and concentrated on my stomach knitting itself closed. I landed on my feet right as I finished, the jolt of the sudden stop testing my handiwork. It held, but I knew I was going to have to go back in later and straighten everything up.

A deafening roar that shook the very ground I stood on bellowed from behind me, followed by a pillar of fire that struck my back between the shoulder blades. I was launched forward into the construction site like a flaming meteor. An embankment of dirt and rocks broke my fall, splintering bones and lacerating skin. As if remembering a dream while it fought to escape, I took note that either the fire or my weakness prevented my skin from holding together against the pointed debris of the dirt hill. Oh, the lessons we learn.

The smell of burning flesh invaded my nose, and I became aware that the fire had moved down my back and was threatening to burn my ass off. Panicking, I rolled in the dirt to put the flames out. I was rewarded with the giddy laughter of Locke behind me.

While my back rested on the dirt, I raised my head to see a giant flame dragon pulsating with waves of blue, white, green, orange, and red flames.

Locke was approaching just behind the dragon, balls of light forming on both outstretched hands.

My jaw clenched and my teeth held a protest that they would break if conditions continued. I pushed myself up to a sitting position, palms down in the dirt. As Locke and his pet drew closer, I willed my blood into the mound and spread outward like a giant bowl.

"Knock, knock," I said to Locke.

Puzzlement showed on his face as his scarred head tilted to the side. The dragon mirrored his movements.

"Who's...there?" Locke asked, confounded.

"Shards of rock," I said with a devilish smile.

Locke stopped in his tracks, realization spreading over his face. He pointed his hands toward me, palms out, right as I sent all my focus and sheer willpower into the dirt mound. The blood acted like a catapult, bolting up and over my head and sending debris hurling in the general direction of Locke and his pet, Puff the Magic Dragon.

Locke screamed with as much surprise as anger as the wall flew toward him. His hands clapped together, and a cone of flame shot out in front of him. Dirt was thrown back at me as rocks melted and fell with the force of the flame spout. My tactic worked, however, and Locke was swallowed whole by the sheer mass of the debris.

With the combination of Locke's focus shifting and the rocks and wet dirt hitting the dragon with enough force to collapse a house, Puff went out like a candlewick in a hurricane.

The tidal wave of dirt crested and broke, sending debris tumbling into the warehouse parking lot. A few spinning, bouncing rocks hit the warehouse exterior. Puff was no more, and Locke was crushed and buried.

Exhausted, I let my chin hit my chest and closed my eyes. I was starting to feel every bump, bruise, broken bone, and skin tear. I knew I was going to have to feed to heal all my grievous wounds. The hunger was already growing uncontrollable inside me. I was also super looking forward to letting someone cut me open and rearrange my waterslide. My hands went down to my bulging stomach, and I cradled my protruding guts like a pregnant woman.

"Neat," I let out with a tired sigh.

The ground in front of me exploded. Razor-sharp rocks and bulbous stone smashed into me as I flew, cutting deep gashes and breaking even more bones. I was thrown back and down the other side of the mound I had been perched upon, hitting even more debris as I tumbled tits over feet, like a human slinky. For some reason, the thought of me laughing at YouTube videos of skiers tumbling down a mountain shot through my mind.

I landed in the mulched earth hard enough to create a crater; I was getting really good at that. Dirt flew in all directions in a circle around me. Little pale bugs swam in my blackened vision as my brain tried to reboot.

A pinprick of light appeared in the center of my existence and slowly spread, bringing with it a growing pain that told me I wasn't dead yet. More dead. Deader. I wasn't deader yet.

A long, drawn out moan escaped my mouth as my brain came back online and I tried to move.

The dirt was cool against my face. My fingers pressed into the earth as I tried to push my limp, drained body up, desperately seeking to get any air into my lungs out of pure reflex. After several moments, my diaphragm relaxed, and I inhaled so loudly and ferociously that it sounded like a train had just barreled from my face.

A cloud of blood erupted from my gaping mouth as I propped myself up on unstable, exhausted knees. My crimson life force joined the pools of others that were scattered around. The ashen ground beneath distorted like a kaleidoscope as my head attempted to reboot. There was the smell of my own seared flesh that began at the top of my skull and continued down the back of my broken, and all but useless, body. I couldn't feel the pain of the burn, which I knew was probably not a good thing. Probably.

"Finally, you kneel before me," I heard an exasperated voice proclaim between heavy breaths.

It took everything I had to keep from collapsing onto the inviting ground, like a comfy bed promising that your boss wouldn't mind if you came in late, or tomorrow. I lifted my face to see him standing on the edge of the crater that I had the pleasure of creating with my once sexy body. My eyes shifted in and out of focus, but I could make out a tall figure with arms outstretched.

"Fuck...you..." I managed between coughs of blood.

"What, no witty retort? No clever comeback?" The tall man chortled. "Then I suppose it's game over for you, mosquito," he finished with a booming voice as he raised his outstretched hands. A small light the size of a bead of rice formed. It started growing in volume and brightness as it began rising into the space above him. First a tennis ball of orange, then a basketball of blue. The star of death, not to be confused with the legally different Death Star, kept growing until, lastly, a sphere the size of a house made from blinding white light loomed ominously. I had to shield my eyes from the bright sight. Wisps of smoke rose from the ground around him from the immense heat.

"Goku would be so pissed if he saw this," I said, trying to sound like my old self. The star started to incinerate the ground around the entire crater. The pools of my blood on the ground—which I had been saving for later, damnit—started to boil and evaporate. Stone melted like ice cream in the hot Texas sun, leaving growing pools of, in the words of Dr. Evil, liquid hot magma.

My shielding arms caught fire, and I collapsed to the ground; defeated. As I dropped my arms to my sides, I looked up to watch my death as the ball was thrown upward and toward me. I saw a bright light expand in my vision, followed by a dot of blackness that quickly engulfed everything I saw just before my eyes started to melt in their sockets and drip down my cheeks to evaporate. My face caught fire and started to slide off the bone, as if I had opened the Ark of the Covenant.

Chapter 35

PRESENT DAY

Locke controlled the star-o-death as it descended on me. In his weakened, maddened state, he had failed to notice the massive salivating wolf that was running its way up the mound.

At the last second, Locke heard and turned his head, stopping the star and then letting it wink out of existence as Depweg leaped. Locke held up his hands but nothing happened, as the energy he had used was just returning. In his last moments of existence, Locke looked at his hands in confusion before powerful jaws closed over his face.

Depweg's maw enveloped Locke's jaw all the way to his neck. He bit down like a hydraulic press, and what could be seen of Locke's burned face crumbled like a coke can. Teeth scraped vertebrae. Skin was rent from bone. Depweg readjusted his mouth to Locke's throat for the kill just as Locke sent a focused blast of fire through Depweg's torso. It burst out his back like a lightsaber before billowing into the night.

Depweg reeled in agony as the flames started spreading across his fur like a wildfire. He dropped Locke and started running chaotically with his front paws. His back legs were limp and useless.

I had used their back and forth to climb the embankment to where Locke lay. I couldn't see, but I could hear his heartbeat, and it lit up in my vision like a beacon. Every erratic pump sent a sonar signal to my senses, and I could see his red outline in the blackness. As I crested the top, I could also see Depweg crawling away. His essence was shrinking and growing dim.

Locke's head turned right as I climbed on top of him, his eyes growing wide in terror and realization. The entire front half of my body was burned to muscle and bone. My skin was still burning at the edges, with the hellfire growing over my body like a...well, like a damn wild fire. The flames had a voracious appetite that wouldn't stop until my entire body was consumed. All Locke saw as I mounted his body was a blackened skull interlaced with singed tendons and a fanged, lipless grin.

Through my sonar vision I could see Locke raising his hands to attack. I grabbed both of his wrists with my burning hands and bent them backward. Bones crumbled and ligaments snapped. The skin tore as I continued to push his hands, making his knuckles touch his forearms. Locke tried to scream through his crushed face, but only succeeded in whistling out of his bubbling nose. Mucus and blood shot down from his nostrils into his obliterated mouth.

I continued pulling his hands until only skin held them to his body, then I ripped them off with a satisfying tearing sound. Locke inhaled forcibly through his nose.

With vocal cords that were well-done, and a voice that could have been from a George A. Romero film, I said to Locke, "For my parents, you dick," right as I sank my fangs deep into Locke's neck, like a starving lion on a plump gazelle. Locke squirmed as I let the blood flow, not in any hurry to stop. I had to tilt my head to allow any of the crimson goodness to flow down my throat, as I no longer had lips. Even with the angle, most of it fell to the ground. I was starving, and my predatory side was about to explode trying to get to the precious blood.

I willed a small dagger in my left hand and plunged it into Locke's liver, just above his right hip. I pulled in as much blood as I could, but it wasn't enough. Most spilled out through the torn artery in his neck that I couldn't catch.

When I heard Locke's heart start to flutter, I retracted my blade into my palm, placed my left hand on the top of his head and my right on his shoulder, and I ripped his disfigured skull right the fuck off in pure fury and agitation. I lifted it up into the night sky, proclaiming my vengeance to the universe.

Holding my grisly treasure to the sky, I let the last of his blood drop from his neck into my mouth as his eyes blinked and looked around before slowing, and eventually, glazing over. Once his life force left his body, I laughed into his face with a mix of emotions. Relief that I had avenged my parents. Agony from the hellfire that was still eating my skin. Anger that his pain hadn't lasted longer. Worry about my best friend, Depweg.

I dropped the severed head to the dirt. I was vaguely aware of his nose breaking as it smacked into the packed earth.

As the hellfire sapped me of my life, I fought to remain standing. I looked around with my preternatural senses and found what I was looking for. Depweg was still in wolf form, as far as I could tell, and was still burning. I could smell the burnt fur in the air.

What energy I stole from the now very deceased Locke, I used to extinguish Depweg; I pointed my hand and, with full knowledge of what would happen to me, commanded a torrent of blood where Depweg had collapsed, covering him like a busted fire hydrant. The flames went out, and Depweg lay still, whimpering. As expected, the fire decimated the first wave of my blood energy before being overwhelmed by the pure quantity I commanded forth. Though not even a full second had passed, the flames did their part and stunned me. Unable to will the rest of the energy back in, I let the connection drop at my hand, losing the remaining life force. I was ready for the long sleep.

My legs went numb and gave in. I fell to the ground, exhausted. Nothing was left in the tank. I could hear Depweg whimpering, which was good.

All I could do was laugh through a lipless mouth as the hellfire continued to eat away at my skin, spreading like a California brush fire. As muscle dried and snapped from bone, I inhaled and let out a deep breath, accepting my fate. My parents had been avenged, Depweg was alive, and those things brought a metaphorical smile to my face.

I let the darkness wash over me like the tide coming in. Little by little, my head became lighter and my thoughts slowed. Nothing hurt anymore. My last thought was a question: which eternity would I be met with?

Then my mind went blank, like a subsiding ripple on a glass lake...I floated in a now familiar nothingness. I was seriously debating on decorating, or at least leaving a magazine behind.

My eyes focused on a point in front of me where I expected a beam of light to coalesce. Instead, warmth spread over my back like a blanket.

Struggling to turn my head, I saw a blinding pinprick of colors emanating from the darkness. Light swirled in the color of hellfire. Red and green fought for their chance to shine in my eternal nothingness.

Gravity came into existence at that moment, and I could feel myself being pulled toward the chaos of color.

A bright white light shone in front of me, reaching with its own gravity and effectively halting me in between the lights. The forces pulling me seemed to crawl over my body;

my legs were pulled forward while my arms were sucked backward. Then they switched. It was as if both were vying for the right grip, but they were evenly matched.

There I remained, stuck in an evenly matched game of tug-of-war. I tried sticking my limbs out in front of me to allow the white light more purchase, but to no avail. The rear force latched onto my torso, refusing to relinquish its prize.

A shadow blotted out the light in front of me, allowing the darkness to grab hold and pull me back. I moaned helplessly, understanding what was happening; Hell would have me. Without warning and out of nowhere, a massive armor-clad hand wrapped thick fingers around my neck, holding me in place.

All I could see was the silhouette of a colossal angel complete with outstretched, feather-clad wings and a burning halo saturated with white flames. I was pulled toward its shadowed head where two white flames shone through orbs where the eyes should be. Then he spoke.

"Not yet. Your role on the board has yet to be played, abomination," the angel said in my head. His voice was annoyed, as if through a clenched jaw, like a reluctant employee who had been told by management to issue a refund to the customer who insulted him.

Abruptly, both lights winked out of existence and allowed stars to litter the sky like wisps of dense clouds.

"Aw...shit," I said right as the angel let go and I catapulted through the after-verse. Stars streaked past as if I were the Millennium Falcon fleeing from the Empire. A familiar blue orb appeared at the center of the tunnel and grew larger by the second.

"*Whee!*" I yelled in defiance as the stars slowed and the blue sphere grew, showing details that were the continents and oceans. It wasn't long before I was hurling toward a big city near the gulf coast.

An idea struck me, and I attempted to control my descent by spreading out all my limbs. It seemed silly to me while doing it, as I was incorporeal and air resistance wouldn't play a factor, but the act itself seemed to work and I began to slow. I controlled the speed of my descent and quickly learned I could maneuver on command, though I allowed the general direction to stay true; I didn't want to get lost in my incorporeal form.

It wasn't long before I saw the warehouse and construction zone. A blood-covered Depweg appeared in frame and began to come into focus as I continued to float toward my corpse. He had reverted to his human form and wasn't moving. As I got closer, as if zooming into a picture on a computer, I could see his skin was seared and blackened. He would have come in first place in a Freddie Krueger look-alike contest. There was a cauterized hole the size of an open hand that severed his spine. Closer still, I could see the dirt he was lying on through his brand-new flesh tunnel.

I could see a flickering glimmer of light at his core, fighting to remain.

Motion over my body caught my attention. Lily was there, holding a blood-soaked wrist over my head. The powerful scarlet life flowed freely, and she flicked her hand over my body, sprinkling droplets all over me. I was amazed to see that the blood soaked into my body, providing immediate energy that was used to grow back disintegrated flesh.

I felt my incorporeal self yanked briefly toward its home, like a fish getting hooked. I was off-balance, as if getting caught in a crashing wave. My arms wheeled, and I tried to regain my equilibrium. This no-gravity thing was difficult to get used to.

"You look ridiculous, lover," an amused, silky voice said.

I gained some semblance of control and saw Lily looking at me. She was upside down. Rather, I was upside down...again.

"We have *got* to stop meeting like this!" I said. "How are you healing me?"

"How is not important. *Why*, on the other hand, is so much more interesting," she purred with a devious smile.

I gulped before asking, "Why...?"

"I am saving your life," Lily said as my body tried to inhale my essence, "so you will be indebted to me."

"Always looking out for yourself, Lily," I said while rolling my eyes. Another moment passed and my feet were pulled into my torso.

"Someday, and that day may never come, I will call upon you to do a service for me," she said, her smile a mix of amusement and mischief.

"Did you just Godfather me?!" I cried out while my recently empty shell of a body swallowed my form up to the knees.

"It was apropos, but I am also dead serious. You are bound to me now, Jonathan. A life debt. You will do my biding until the life debt is repaid; and let me tell you, I have eluded death for over a multitude of millennia."

I scowled at this. She was right. I would be compelled to do her bidding until I saved her life. It would hurt my very essence and make me physically ill to disobey. I'd even heard of some supes that had lost their minds from resisting. Thralls could be created this way. Simply locking a willful subject in a dungeon and commanding them to do some mundane task like picking a flower could be all it took to create a mindless minion. It could take years, or even decades depending on how strong your mind was, but no one had ever fully resisted a Fae's commands and kept their wits about them. I would have to make sure to do whatever Lily commanded, as my mind was my favorite part of being me—besides my sweet, sweet biceps.

Muscles reconnected with bones and plumped back to their original size. Organs regrew in their proper place (score!). My eyes began as two specs of dust in the back of my sockets and grew like melons on the vine. I frowned when I noticed my trusty duster was in tatters. I didn't think Da would be able to fix that.

I was fully sucked into my body, and my essence spread out like a hand slipping into a custom-tailored glove.

My eyes fluttered open, and I could see the approach of dawn. The stars became less prominent in the night sky. The black seemed to lighten. I didn't have long before I had to find a place to sleep.

I turned my head to see Lily had moved on. She was cutting pieces of her thigh off with Depweg's own silver kukri and feeding her flesh to Depweg, who was growing stronger with each bite. I could see his hole shrinking and eventually sealing. His bubbling skin shrank, smoothed over, and regained its color, although a little pink. Even his hair grew back on his head, arms, and torso.

"Shit," I managed to breathe out as Lily looked at me with a most devilish smile and eyes that sparkled with delight. She had just gained two henchmen that would have no choice but to do her bidding.

My eyes went from hers back down to her thigh, which was rapidly healing despite the silver. My brow furrowed at the implication that not even the deadliest of supernatural weapons could be more than a mild inconvenience to her. That was going in the ol' floppy disk for later.

As my body regenerated to full capacity, my focus shifted to the red streams that flowed over Lily's alabaster skin with each pass of the blade. Saliva flooded my mouth. The tips of my fingers and nose tingled, my lips joining a moment later. Someone had put my head in a gyro and was slowly making it tumble in all directions.

With bloodlust creeping over my senses, I got to my feet and started making my way to where Lily was feeding Depweg the last scrap of flesh. He was fully healed and lay still, breathing heavily while staring unfocused into the stars above. I could immediately sense he was also in a losing fight against his predatory side.

As I neared, my eyes shifted and teeth elongated. Depweg's hands elongated into boney claws, and his jaw popped as a snout extended out from his face. His eyes were yellow with black slits. He sat up and began reaching for Lily, who took one large step back, a confident smile upon her beautiful face.

She let us get within arm's length before holding one hand up in a universal stop gesture.

It was as if my blood had been replaced by quick-drying cement preventing my muscles from obeying my brain's commands. From my peripheral vision, I could see Depweg frozen in place, a clawed hand outstretched midmorph.

"Now now, boys. Didn't your mothers teach you to keep your hands to yourselves?" she purred with delight, having just confirmed her power over us.

The sun grew beyond the horizon, preparing to crest and greet us with morning light. The distant light shone with chaotic shimmers, like heat waves on black asphalt.

"Oh dear, would you look at the time," Lily said as she manifested large cat-eye sunglasses. "We will continue this another night."

At this she shifted planes, leaving behind a vacuum of air that collapsed with an audible bang.

Both Depweg and I fell to the dirt, free of her command for the time being.

"That...bitch," I said between heaving breaths.

Depweg looked at me with an expression that said *really?*

"Oh, right. That stray cat!"

"You better get out of here, John," Depweg warned, gesturing to the horizon.

As I started walking away to find a hole away from the construction zone that I could sleep in, I turned and asked Depweg, "Hey, in all these years, I've never asked; what's your first name?"

"Jonathan," he called back with a smile evident in his words.

I stopped undead in my tracks, turned around to face him, and said, "No fucking way..."

THE END

Epilogue

PART I

The next night, Depweg and I met up outside my lair. His house was still burned to the ground, and he had nowhere else to stay. I told him to expect a mess, but it would be safe with Locke out of the picture.

We wordlessly stood at the entrance, assessing the damage, before we walked past the fallen door. I noticed where chunks of the stone had been taken out by a crowbar, sledgehammer, or some other device. I assumed Locke hadn't used magic as to not alert Da or me before he had everything in place.

We entered to find my faux coffin had been shattered into pieces. I shrugged and started walking down the stairs, lighting the torches as we went.

"Nice trick," Depweg said.

"It's fun at parties," I replied, pretending to be my old, nonexhausted self.

As we passed through the door and into the first shipping container, I was greeted by Father Thomes, who had a giant black garbage bag in his hands. I froze as we made eye contact.

"Hello, my son," Father T said warmly.

"H-hi, Father," I responded, obviously confused.

"I do hope there are no hard feelings, child. I thought it best to keep you secure until your bloodlust was under control and the supernatural community had stopped looking for you. You understand?" he asked like a parent explaining to a child why spanking them was actually for their own good.

"I suppose you might be right," I relented to Father T, letting my shoulders relax and posture return to normal. Val had warned me that the supes were out to get me, free from all consequence for revealing myself to mortals.

Once I let my focus relax from the father, I looked around to see that the Fortress of Solitaire was mostly empty.

Da floated in from the bedroom and saw me looking around at the places where our furniture used to be.

"The water damage was extensive, I'm afraid. We've already removed the damaged pieces before they started to mold," Da said informatively. I looked at him and nodded. He had forgiven me for my trespasses.

An idea struck me and I ran to my locked cabinet. Undoing the lock, I opened the doors to reveal my intact *Battlefield Earth* collector cups.

"Oh, thank Lilith!" I said, breathing a sigh of relief.

"I told you we should have removed them when we had the chance," Da said to Father Thomes. I wasn't entirely sure he was joking.

"Da," I began unsteadily, "the...boy?" I looked up to see him bow his head and nod it up and down.

"He is well taken care of. I found him a home and provided a stipend from your funds that will provide him for his entire life," Da said with a calm, soothing voice, as if he were explaining a tough situation to a child who couldn't quite grasp the severity.

"Thank you," I said with tears in my eyes. "I am truly blessed to have you all in my unlife." I turned and regarded my three friends, who were smiling and nodding.

"Not just us, John," Da said. "Val is crafting us new furniture as we speak." He regarded Depweg. "Should we suggest one more bedroom set?"

I looked at Depweg who was still smiling, though there was pain behind his eyes. "Yes. It's my fault Depweg lost his home, and his family," I said with emotion building in my voice. "It's the least I can do."

"It wasn't your fault, John," Depweg said, walking over to place a hand on my shoulder. I admired how strong he was as he comforted me. "Let's just make sure they didn't lose their lives in vain, shall we? It's the best honor I could bestow on them."

"You damn right," I exalted, feeling the sadness recede and give way to hope. "But first, I need some time off after all of this excitement."

"Before you take a vacation," Father Thomes said with his index finger raised, "there is still that demon to take care of."

Turning to the group, I threw my frayed and burned duster to Da, who caught it with his little body, and said, "But Daaaaaaddd. Can't I do it tomorrow?"

Epilogue

PART 2

Across the ocean, on a hill just outside of London, a tree had grown miraculously larger than all the others. It was this tree, which sported thick branches, that a black cat sat patiently under. With the sun having retreated for the day, the feline blended with the shadows, creating only an outline that could barely be seen; all except for purple eyes that glowed dimly in the dark like amethysts.

A woman pushing a stroller passed by, heading to the nearby homes, prompting the featureless black cat to meow. The woman glanced over her shoulder as she continued to walk, paying the animal little mind. The cat's eyes squinted in agitation, following the woman as she walked away.

Within a few minutes, a portly man named Jacob—who reeked of ale—stumbled into view. The cat began meowing again, calling out to the plump Jacob. In his inebriated state, the large man looked around, trying to locate the source of the noise. The cat, seeing his chance, called out again, louder this time. Jacob screwed up his face trying to see in the shadows before noticing the amethysts in the dark.

"Oye, 'ello kitty kitty," the man said in a thick, drunk cockney accent as he got closer. "What cha do'n in tha dark, eh?"

Jacob approached, barely able to keep his balance, and fell to his knees to pet the cat. The purple eyed animal did something that made him cock an eyebrow; it smiled a Cheshire grin.

"Wha' tha..." were Jacob's last words as the cat swiped at his throat, opening a geyser that sent a torrent of blood cascading to the hungry dirt below. Fat fingers tried in futile desperation to cover the crimson waterfall; but he might as well have been using a shot glass to try and stop pressurized water from an opened hydrant.

Jacob gurgled with wide eyes the size of dinner plates, blood flowing from his mouth like a statue in a fountain. His head became heavy and he dropped his hands to the dirt to try and stay upright. The ground was now slick with warm mud and Jacob slipped to land face down in the muck. Unbeknownst to Jacob, the very spot he spilled his life's blood was where the vampire that once caused the Great Fire of London had slumbered so many years ago.

As Jacob's vision began shrinking to a small circle, he vaguely noticed the mud was turning back into dirt, as if the liquid was being sucked away.

A blackened, blood-covered skeleton hand, complete with tendons that were growing at an impossible rate, burst from the ground and seized the back of Jacob's neck.

The last thing Jacob saw was a skull emerging from the dirt, as if the Earth was giving birth to a monster.

The black cat meowed before disappearing into the shadows, purring in satisfaction as it went.

Afterword

F inal words from the author

If you enjoyed this Urban Fantasy eulogy for Sir John Cook*, would you consider leaving an **honest review**? Click <u>here</u> to go straight to the Amazon review page.

On the next page I have created links so you can:

- Preview a few pages of the next book in the series right from the Amazon Kindle platform

- Check out the Audible page and listen to samples of Audible Hall of Fame narrator, Luke Daniels, as he brings John to life with his amazing performance!

- I also left a link for Facebook, Goodreads, and BookBub

Thank you for giving John *unlife* after death. The series dedicated to my bromego will be 13 full novels with a handful of novellas and short stories for good measure. So until next time, John On!

*not actually knighted

Click here for a free preview of the next book in the series

Audible: Series page, listen to free samples here

Connect with Me

T-shirts, signed books, and more await at

www.HunterBlain.com

Facebook Author Page

Goodreads Author Page

BookBub Author Page

Also By Hunter Blain

THE PRETERNATURAL CHRONICLES

Deliverance

I'm Glad You're Dead

Dawn and Quartered

Shadow of a Doubt

Moonlight Equilibrium- Book 3.5

Mouth of Madness

What the Hell

Holy Sheoly

Those Wonderful Toys

Crack the Sky

Fall From Grace

THE SOL SAGA

Dawn's Light

Midday's Sun- Q4 release, 2023

Dusk's Night- coming soon

THE CHRONOS PARADOX

Wielding an Hourglass

Sands of Time

Made in the USA
Thornton, CO
10/05/24 14:48:17

d158fdc9-5ec1-4780-8c8d-254983abdde3R01